D0015706

PHOENIX BURNING

PHOENIX BURNING

BRYONY PEARCE

Sky Pony Press
New York

First published in the United Kingdom by Stripes Publishing, an imprint of Little Tiger Press, 2016.

This hardcover edition published by Sky Pony Press, 2018.

Sky Pony Press books may be purchased in bulk at special discounts for sales promotion, corporate gifts, fund-raising, or educational purposes. Special editions can also be created to specifications. For details, contact the Special Sales Department, Sky Pony Press, 307 West 36th Street, 11th Floor, New York, NY 10018 or info@skyhorsepublishing.com.

Visit our website at www.skyponypress.com

www.bryonypearce.co.uk

10 9 8 7 6 5 4 3 2 1

Library of Congress Cataloging-in-Publication Data available on file.

Jacket photo by iStock
Jacket design by Sammy Yuen

Hardcover ISBN: 978-1-5107-1645-2
EBook ISBN: 978-1-5107-1647-6

Printed in the United States of America

This book is dedicated to my in-laws
Pat and Charles Pearce, who live young.
With thanks for everything.

If I had to choose a religion,
the sun as the universal giver of life would be my god.

NAPOLEON BONAPARTE

PROLOGUE

Toby was going blind.

He had long since lost edges. If Toby turned his head against the rope that held his forehead, he could see the blurred outline of the cathedral roof; nothing more than a smudge against a lighter background. Soon the sun would steal even that.

His vision would have been lost already, except that a cloud had built in the sky as they were being tied down and had blotted out most of the sunlight.

He had no idea how much time had passed; the only way to tell was by the prickle of sunburn on his naked chest and legs. That was nothing compared to the itching of his eyes. He would have given anything to blink.

The captain coughed. "How are you doing, son?"

Toby had to swallow before he could answer. "I'm okay."

"We're going to get out of this."

"Sure." Toby didn't even try to look at his father. He was staked out just the same as Toby and the others: his forehead tightly bound, his eyes taped open and his hands and feet stretched out to either side.

They weren't getting out of this.

The tape above Toby's left eye was peeling slightly. Among the pain of sunburn, cramping muscles, biting insects, grit, sand, and the agony of his vision being flayed from him, the peeling tape seemed the worst. He knew that if it would just loosen a little more, just a tiny bit, he'd be able to close his eye.

The skin on his cheeks was tight where his tears had dried. His ducts were empty now; not even the swimming of tears could protect his vision.

"Is Simeon still unconscious?" Toby strained against the ropes again and managed to gain a slight tilt to his chin. A trickle of blood wormed its way down his right temple.

"Must be," Hideaki croaked. "He's lucky. When he wakes up this'll all be over. It won't be long now, and if that cloud cover clears . . ."

"It'll be seconds, I know." Toby ground his teeth. After all he'd been through in the last few weeks, to end up here, like this. "Where do you think Ayla is?" If he had been able to close his eyes he would have pictured her.

There was the sound of a struggle and a shout, then a cool shadow fell over Toby's face. He gasped, relief surging through him.

The captain's roar made him jump. "You! Leave us alone."

ONE

"I thought you said you could read this." Toby leaned over Hiko's translation of the map. Weak afternoon sun shone through the portholes to illuminate the paper. Beside them stood a small brazier loaded with combustibles they had pulled from the sea; in a couple of hours they would need to light it if they wanted to carry on working. There was already a smoke stain on the ceiling of the mess hall above their table.

"I *can* read it." Hiko tugged his new red scarf from his throat, the one that marked him as a true member of the *Phoenix*'s crew, and slammed it on the table in frustration. "That symbol is definitely *spiral*"—he bit his lip—"or possibly *bird*."

"Why in all blazes would any map say spiral *or* bird?" Toby slammed back in his seat and glared at the soot on the ceiling as if it were responsible for their problems. Polly hopped off his chair and squawked crossly.

"Toby's right, Hiko." Dee pushed her own stool back from the metal table and rubbed at the healing stab wound on her chest. "None of this makes sense. It's sounding more like a bunch of crazy instructions for a board game than any map I've ever seen."

Toby lifted Polly on to the table and then turned back to Hiko. "It's been three weeks since we found the map and all we've got out of it so far is bizarre poetry." He turned the translation so he could read from it. "Avoid the fast mist and take three swift turns around the white doom spiral . . . or possibly *bird*." He thumped his chair, making Polly jump again. "What's a white doom spiral?"

"What's a white doom *bird*?" Dee shot back. She pressed the heels of her hands into her eyes and groaned. "And that's just one of the lines—there're a whole bunch of them equally as senseless. If only I could recognize one of the land masses, but nothing matches the Atlas." She kicked the precious book where it lay discarded under the table. "I should burn the blasted thing. It's been near useless since Yellowstone erupted and the tsunamis destroyed the old coastlines. There could be a clue to the nearest mainland hidden in this text, but we don't even know what language it's written in."

"Arnav thinks it could be related to Ryukyuan." Toby's back cracked as he straightened. He winced and automatically tried to brush his hand through his blond hair. It had been three weeks since his head was shaved and old habits remained. He dropped his fingers. "Are you *sure* you're reading this correctly, Hiko?"

Hiko jumped to his feet. His left hand went to the cross-hatched tattoo on his right forearm: eight horizontal lines and eleven vertical. Tony knew it reminded him of his father. "I'm sure I am. My dad taught me before he—"

"You could be mistaken." Dee touched his hand gently. "You were very young when he died and a lot of languages look similar. It's easy to confuse one symbol for another."

"This is getting us nowhere," Toby said. "We need a break."

"Fine." Hiko slammed his pencil on to the table so hard that it broke in two. Half rolled across his paper and stopped on a water-damaged section of the map featuring a series of smudged pictograms.

Toby sighed and retrieved the stub. "At least we know one thing."

"What's that?" Hiko snapped.

"If we can't translate our copy, the *Banshee* certainly can't translate theirs."

"That's if they survived the St. George attack." Dee tried to catch Toby's eye, but he refused to look at her. "Toby, you know the *Banshee* could be at the bottom of the salt."

"It's not," Toby said firmly. "We'd have heard."

The door to the mess slammed open and the captain swept in, his compass swinging on his chest. "How are you getting on with this?"

Instinctively, Hiko ducked behind Toby.

"It's no good, Captain," Dee said. "The map is useless without a key or some coordinates. We don't have either. There's just no starting point."

"What about Hiko's translation?"

Toby pushed the paper toward his father.

"What's this?" The captain's face darkened. "Is this a haiku? A joke?"

Toby shook his head. "It's the translation. At least we think it is."

"It is," Hiko muttered.

The captain ran a hand through his beard. "If you're sure, Hiko, then I believe you. But this is no good to us." He tossed the page onto the table. "Toby, you haven't been on deck for two days. If you're willing, I need your sharp eyes and nimble fingers on the bridge. Hiko, you can keep trying to translate this gibberish if you want to, but you'd be more useful on deck right now."

"Why, what's going on?" Toby settled Polly on his shoulder, where she dug her claws into his collarbone.

"The solar array is ready. It's time to lift it into place, connect the wiring and set sail."

Toby caught his breath. The *Phoenix* was going to be solar powered. The old boiler—her burning heart—would soon be redundant. Then he frowned. "Hang on—sail where? We can't use the map."

"You've tried long enough. It's time to return to our original plan. Theo and Simeon are back from Bergen, they used the barter we got for the spare panels and so now we have everything the *Phoenix* needs for a long voyage. We're going to sail where the weather takes us—farther and deeper into the salt than ever before. We'll find that island." He pressed a hand on Hiko's shoulder. "So we don't have a map we can use? We didn't have one before. It would have been nice to have a shortcut, but nothing worth having ever came easy. We'll do this the hard way."

Toby squinted as he followed Dee and Hiko on to the deck, the bright sunshine in stark contrast to the gloomy mess hall. It took a moment for his eyes to adjust then the changes that the pirates had made to the *Phoenix* came into focus.

"Toby, good to see you out in the fresh air." Marcus swung down from the rigging.

"You've done so much in two days!" Toby looked up. "You've already finished the retractable weather shield we designed."

A tall pole rose over his head. Around it, a series of curved metal panels made from hammered-out car hoods hung like a skirt.

"How does it work?" Gingerly, Hiko touched one of the panels.

"Like an umbrella." Toby patted the metal and made it clatter. "If the weather's bad, we'll open it over the solar panels to protect them."

"Bad weather will damage the panels?" Hiko looked alarmed.

Polly spoke up from Toby's shoulder. "A severe hailstorm could crack the surface glazing of the panels." She hopped on to Hiko's shoulder and tilted her head, so she was looking him in the eye. "The connections will also deteriorate over time, allowing water to penetrate into the solar cells."

Marcus smiled. "Don't worry. They look fragile, but they can withstand fairly extreme conditions."

The array of photovoltaic cells shined like oil in the bright light, reflecting the clouds that slid across the sun.

"Our own slice of sky," Dee breathed.

"It's perfect." Toby hurried to where D'von and five of the crew were polishing the cells with their scarves. The mirror sheen of them attracted him like treasure. He reached out a hand and D'von blocked him.

"I already polished that piece, Toby-who-knows-things. You keep your hands to yourself."

Toby's smile widened. "How're you doing, D'von?"

"Better than slaving on the dock, that's for sure." D'von stretched. "I get breaks. It's easy work."

"Not for me." Nisha sat on her heels and rested her hands on her pregnant belly. "My back's killing me."

"Won't be so easy once we set sail, neither." Peel was sitting bolt upright, plucking a gull. Every time he bent, Toby saw the pain caused by the healing wounds in his shoulder and stomach. A cloud of feathers covered his feet, and every so often one drifted across the panels, sticking like static to the glass covering the silicon. Naked bird carcasses were piled in a bowl in front of him.

"Gull pie for dinner again?" Toby guessed.

"Shut yer face, Toby," Peel snapped. "You're lucky you're gettin' anything at all, what with all the trouble you caused me."

"I thought Theo had brought in a load of supplies." Dee looked disappointed.

"They're for when we need 'em, not for when we're so close to land we can slingshot birds from the masts."

Toby swallowed. Callum was the one who had always done the hunting—catching gulls and fish when there seemed nothing to be caught. But Callum was gone now, lost in Tarifa along with Harry, Carson, and Dobbs.

"You're thinking about Tarifa." Polly hopped from Hiko's shoulder and crawled up Toby's arm.

"We all miss them, Tobes," Dee added.

"Big Pad should be here, too. He'd have loved this."

"You're right, he would." The captain appeared at Toby's side and wrapped an arm around him. "Give Polly to Hiko and come with me."

They walked together into the shelter of the empty steerage. "Time was I could rest my arm on your shoulder quite comfortably," Barnaby grumbled. "Now you're almost as tall as I am. When did that happen?" He released Toby and brushed his beard with his fingertips. "About Paddy—you can't feel guilty. The minute he realized he was paralyzed, he knew he'd have to return to land."

"But we just left him in Cobh." Toby looked up at the furled sails. "After he saved my life."

"With his brother. With money and supplies: a darn good pension."

"It's not the same."

"I know." The captain laid an arm on the gunwale. "Some sailors have left us and others we've had to leave behind along the way. You can't dwell on each and every one. Just look where we are now. We're going to *find that island*."

Toby tried to bring to mind some of the pirates who had left the *Phoenix*. Some had gone due to injury or pregnancy, others had tired of the sea and found safe ports. He expected their faces to turn in his thoughts, but instead his traitorous memory fed him an image of Ayla in her salt-sodden boots and Peel's old shirt.

"It isn't just *friends* we've left behind." Toby touched Nix, the short sword that hung at his hip. "Do *you* think the *Banshee* was sunk?" Toby couldn't meet his father's eyes. Instead, he focused on the giant sunburst stenciled on to the central cells of the solar panels.

The captain paused, then said, "I think we'd have heard in Bergen or Cobh if the *Banshee* had been defeated by Graymen, don't you?"

It was true. The *Banshee* was the terror of the seas; if the Graymen had defeated her, every harbormaster would have posted the news.

There was no way Ayla could go with them to the island, no world in which the *Banshee* and *Phoenix* could work together.

But he couldn't stop thinking about her.

He had offered Ayla a place on the *Phoenix*, and she had rejected it. She had taken the precious map and then, when Toby followed, had knocked him unconscious and had him locked in the *Banshee*'s brig. Although she eventually changed her mind and released him, he had almost been killed. And after all that, they had found out the history both of their captains had been keeping from them. Toby had no illusions. He had no future with Ayla; she was *Banshee* through and through.

Toby knew he should hate her, but it was the memory of her kiss that really burned. That she had left the *Phoenix* only hours afterward: *that* was the knife that twisted in his gut. He had trusted her completely and she had turned her back without even saying goodbye.

He clenched his fists.

The captain pointed Toby to a bollard and sat down on the one beside it.

"So you do think the *Banshee*'s still out there." Toby flattened his hands on his thighs. "I understand why you didn't tell me about your friendship with Nell before, but—"

"You have questions about the past." It was a statement, not a question.

"I'm not a child anymore." Toby's voice was level, matter of fact. "I want you to be straight with me. No more secrets."

Barnaby sighed. "What do you want to know?"

"When you escaped St. George, you left without my mother. You didn't wait for her. Why not?"

Barnaby exhaled slowly. "I went to get you from school and Nell agreed to go and warn Judy, who was working a security detail. I didn't think about the fact that Nell would have to wait for Judy to leave her post before she could speak privately to her. All I knew was that when we reached the dock, she wasn't there. My team got the *Phoenix* ready to sail"—his eyes were distant, staring down the past—"then we waited. I wouldn't have just abandoned my own wife. Zeke—one of my engineers—kept watch for us in the harbormaster's office. When he called to say the Graymen were coming, we were forced to fire up the engines. I stayed in the crow's nest till the very last second, hoping I'd see her running for the gangplank. She never appeared."

"I don't remember any Zeke." Toby frowned.

Barnaby shook his head. "He never made it on board."

"He was killed?" Toby swallowed.

"Yes. Hopewell used him to try and make us turn back. He gave us two minutes; when we didn't reverse into dock, he shot him right in front of us. I had a team of ten working on the *Phoenix*. Of those, eight sailed with me. Oats and Dee are the only ones left."

Toby gripped Nix. "Why don't I remember anything from back then? I should have *some* memories."

Barnaby's fingers drummed on the bollard. "Not necessarily."

"I think I remember a classroom—the pictures painted on the walls." Toby hung his head. "I can't remember *her* at all."

"Your mother."

"Not her face, her smell—not even the sound of her. I don't know, maybe that's a good thing." Toby looked up, his face drawn tight. "After hearing what she did, I'm not sure I want to remember."

Barnaby closed his eyes, then opened them again. "You did spend a lot of time in that classroom—I'm not surprised you remember it. Judy adored you, but she loved her work, too. And you know me. Once I got into an invention, I could be gone for days."

"Did I know Ayla when I was a kid? Were *we* friends?"

"Nell and I worked in the same lab, but her husband stayed at home with the children. He was a better dad than—"

"Than you?" Toby grabbed his father's hand. "Never."

Barnaby's smile sagged around the edges. "No matter what else Judy or I have done, you're the best of us both. Wherever she is, if she's still alive, she loves you, maybe even as much as I do."

Toby squeezed his father's rough hand. Their fingers were both zigzagged with old scars and ingrained with soot.

Barnaby patted Toby's shoulder and stood, captain of the *Phoenix* once more. "Come and help me get the wiring sorted out." He pulled Toby to his feet and stamped back toward the panels. "Hiko, grab a cloth and help D'von polish. Dee, what're you doing just standing there?"

Dee huffed. "Don't worry, I'll have a course plotted by the time you're ready to move the panels into position."

Toby took a final moment in the fresh air and looked around. Faroe Rocks were behind them, a low cluster of caves and ridges that sheltered the *Phoenix* from prying eyes. Ahead, it was open sea almost all the way to Eire.

Toby strained to see as far as the horizon, his heart thumping. He had been born before the sun's return: his eyes saw better at dawn and dusk and he always kept a piece of light material to cover his face when the light dazzled.

As always, he was looking for any sign of the *Banshee.* Nell would never give up her vow to seek revenge on the *Phoenix*. And now that Ayla knew about her murdered sisters, she wouldn't try to stop her mother.

The *Banshee* was coming and one day there would be a reckoning.

Toby turned from the railing and headed toward the bridge. He waved at Hiko as he passed. His serious little protégé crouched next to D'von, whose face was as open and sunny as the sky. The two were as different as the *Banshee* and *Phoenix*, yet had more in common than almost anyone else on the ship—both had lost their families and been sold as slaves.

Yes, Toby's mother was gone, but at least he had his father.

Inside the bridge, Toby chose a pair of wire strippers and looked at the captain. "You've made all the changes to the engines, like we planned?"

The captain nodded. "They should work fine with the solar power, but we'll know for sure soon enough." He rolled his shoulders.

"She'll be able to reach ten, maybe fifteen knots with her engines running," Toby said with a grin.

"We'll burn up the salt, all right! Get the rest of these small wires stripped and ready to connect and I'll check the inverter. It'll be in the final crate—there's only one we haven't unpacked." He raised his voice: "Rahul, I'm ready for the last box." He forged out of the bridge and on to the main deck as the wind caught in the furled sails with the sound of a flock of birds.

Toby twisted a wire between his fingers, then carefully he stripped the plastic and laid the wire down. The sun shined through the holes drilled in the bridge roof, ready for the cables from the solar array to snake through. All Toby had to do was attach each to the panel via the inverter and the *Phoenix* would be powered by electricity.

Electricity. All he'd ever seen of it was a bulb swinging in a

Tarifan dungeon, but he knew its power. Thrilled, he rubbed his hands together. The *Phoenix* and her crew were already wanted by several governments; now, with engines running at full capacity, she would be the most sought-after ship on the salt.

Toby shuffled Polly onto the table. "Sit here and tell me if I'm missing anything." He worked his way through all of the wires his father had left him, following each back to its source and ordering them.

As he worked, he realized that the deck had gone quiet.

He raised his head just as the captain's voice boomed across the ship. "Well *find it*."

Toby raced into a scene of panic. In the center stood the captain, hands on his hips, an empty crate at his feet.

"What is it?" Toby slid to a stop.

Marcus looked up from beneath the gunwale. "Toby, help us look. The inverter's missing."

Toby stared at his father. "But we can't use the panels without the inverter! Isn't it in the box?"

"Yeah, have you checked the box, Cap'n?" Crocker sneered from the other side of the second mast. "Wish we'd a thought a that, hey, Peel?"

Peel was crawling around the solar array, eyes glued to the deck. "Good job Toby's here, ain't it?"

"Did anyone see it before we started work?" Toby was growing cold.

The captain shook his head and glowered at Rahul.

Rahul pointed at the plastic crate. "All that was inside were wires and more silicon sheets."

Toby exhaled. "Okay. So let's search the wreck room in case it fell out in there."

The captain nodded. "Marcus, take Hiko. Theo, Simeon, if it isn't found, take *Birdie* back to Cobh and find Dorah—make sure you didn't sell her our inverter." He turned to Rahul. "You and Nisha inventoried. I want a list of everything that came out of that storage container."

Toby straightened. "What can I do?"

"Keep working. We're going to find that inverter and when we do, we'll need to be ready for the installation."

"And if we don't find it?"

The captain clenched his fists. "Then all we have here are some very expensive ornaments."

TWO

As the sun began to sink lower in the sky, Toby checked the cables again.

Polly nudged him with her cold head. "You've done all you can." He ignored her. "Toby?"

His knuckles turned white on the handle of his pliers. "If we hadn't had the coordinates of the panels, the *Banshee* would never have attacked. We wouldn't have needed to dock in Tarifa." He continued to coil and uncoil wires. "Our friends died for those panels, and now they're worthless?"

"Toby, please stop."

Carefully, he placed the last wire. "We're ready to go." He cleared his throat. "I suppose we'd better go and tell the captain."

As Toby stepped on deck, the *Phoenix* rolled against her anchorage. He automatically adjusted his balance and wiped the stinging spray that splashed his face. Once, he had been told, the salt had been clean, but seven billion people had filled it with trash. Then the super-volcano had poisoned the sea with gases and the tsunamis had broken up the great garbage patches. Fifty years ago, people had swum in the sea; now it was the salt, and he had to wipe it from his face in case it burned his skin.

Under a swaying canopy, Uma was repairing a net. She looked up as he dried his hand on his pants. "How are you doing, Toby?"

Toby shook his head, unable to answer. "When will Theo and Simeon be back with news?"

Uma looked up. "A week? Sailing day and night, it'll be at least two days each way."

Toby groaned. "Any word from Rahul?"

"He and Nisha are still going through the inventory with the captain. If there's a box or piece missing, we'll know about it. Here, hold this." Toby caught hold of the needle she offered while she examined the netting she had just sewn.

Toby took a moment to check the sky; they were anchored a day out of Reykjavik and he worried about hail. He and the captain had weighed the danger that bad weather posed to the solar panels against the fact that the oil war between Reykjavik, Scotland, and St. George, which had started over the North Sea oil reserves, would keep St. George ships away from Faroe Rocks. They had decided the anchorage was worth the risk.

At the moment, the clouds seemed to be racing away from them. Toby squinted up at the crow's nest where Arnav was keeping watch, then over the swinging plastic shades to the bow where Peel had set up a barbecue and was cooking gull stew for dinner.

As he watched Peel stir the broth, Toby thought of how the awful cook had tried to save him from the *Banshee.* That led his mind down familiar pathways back to Ayla. The last time Toby had seen the *Banshee*, she had been facing a St. George naval vessel and fighting for her life. Even with one arm broken, she had whirled like a tornado.

"You're thinking of her again." Uma touched his arm.

Toby flushed. "How do you know?"

Uma smiled. "I remember how you looked when you brought her to me, injured."

Toby shook his head. "It doesn't matter. Even if the *Banshee* escaped St. George, we'll never be together again."

Uma tied off a knot. "Because the *Phoenix* left the *Banshee* to the Graymen?"

"Because my mother betrayed Nell and had her family killed." Toby sat at her side and adjusted Nix so that the sword wouldn't dig into his thigh. "Nell blames the captain."

"If the captain hadn't fled, Judy would never have been in Nell's home—it would never have happened."

"I know." Toby leaped to his feet as the deck hatch that led ultimately to the wreck room was flung open and the captain appeared. He climbed up the ladder and stood with his shoulders bowed.

Toby froze. "Bad news?"

"We've been through that inventory three times." Rahul climbed on to the deck behind the captain. "We never pulled any inverter out of the salt."

The captain growled. "It must have been in a separate shipment."

"All of this for nothing?" It was Oats. He was standing with Marcus by the winch and his hook glinted as he raised it over the panels. Toby couldn't tell if he meant the work they'd done getting the solar array fixed up, or the loss of his hand.

The other pirates started to mutter and Polly hopped quickly across the deck, her metal wings clattering as she spread them for balance. Toby lifted her on to his shoulder.

"You'd a known we needed that inverter from the start," Crocker snapped. "You shoulda made sure it was there before we worked our butts off gettin' those panels all fixed up."

"Watch it, Crocker." Dee stalked forward. "That's your captain you're speaking to."

"Crocker's right," Rita called. "Why wasn't this checked before we started?"

"The box was there—" Rahul began.

Toby raised his voice. "There's no use arguing about it. What's done is done. Your work hasn't been for nothing. All we need is an inverter. Fix the panels in place, then I'll fire up the boiler, and we'll find one."

"There's a problem with that." Marcus tugged at the scarf that covered the scar on his throat. "The solar panels on land were all destroyed in the riots—that's why our salvage was so precious. And if the panels were all destroyed, their inverters likely were, too."

"Marcus is right," the captain said roughly. "There might not be any inverters left to find."

Toby swallowed. "But you can make anything out of anything, right? Make an inverter."

The captain spread his palms. "I can try, but I'll need components compatible with the Solaris array. I just don't know . . ."

"So, we're stuffed," Oats spat. "That's just great."

"Well, *there's* a surprise. Looks like the *Phoenix* needs me again."

Toby's brain stuttered. It was the voice he had been hearing in his mind for weeks. Polly jerked upright, digging her claws through his shirt.

As the rest of the *Phoenix* erupted in furious cries, Toby slowly turned. He could barely believe it, but his ears hadn't lied. Ayla was climbing over the side of the *Phoenix*, the beads in her hair clattering on the railing.

"Ayla!" D'von's face was bright as midday. "You came back." He grabbed her arm and helped her over the gunwale.

"Let go of me." Ayla swung her legs over the side of the *Phoenix* and brushed rust from her hands.

"Arnav, what the blazes?" the captain yelled up at the crow's nest as he pulled his blunderbuss from his belt. Dee grabbed a hook.

Arnav waved frantically. "I were distracted—listenin'. Sorry."

"Are there more of them?" Marcus shouted.

Arnav pressed the binoculars to his eyes. "Only the girl." He called eventually. "She's come alone . . . again."

"Well, now," Crocker sneered. "Weren't that stupid!"

THREE

"How'd she get on board?" Dee ignored Ayla and spoke to Rita, who ran to peer over the side.

Rita gasped. "There's a lifeboat tied to the anchor cable. It looks like she climbed it . . ."

"And from there, I caught the pulley for the winch." Ayla strutted forward with a swing in her hips.

"Amit, Ajay, we need razor wire around the top of the hawsepipe. Get on that," the captain shouted as he marched to intercept Ayla. "How did you find us?" he growled, blocking her view of the solar array. "Rahul, check her for weapons."

Ayla held out her arms so that Rahul could frisk her. "Once we found out where you'd off-loaded your spare panels—and thanks for those, by the way—all I had to do was work out where you'd go to install yours. Faroe Rocks are the nearest safe cove."

"Where's the *Banshee*?" The captain scanned the horizon.

"Reykjavik," Ayla said. "We wanted more supplies and there're none in this barren place." She still hadn't looked at Toby. "Don't worry, Captain, we've got a lot of repairs to do—we're in no position to take you on right now."

"So you escaped the St. George warship. I'm glad."

"Sure you are." Her almond eyes roved over the ship's crew and finally came to rest. "You're looking well, Toby."

Toby forced ice into his voice. "You, too. Your arm?"

"Getting better." Ayla opened and closed her fist to show him. She was wearing a new long jacket over her old leather jerkin. Her hair remained lopsided where the explosion had taken it off—on her left side it formed spikes around her ear, on the right it swung down to her elbow, mixed with the braids that kept it off her face.

"You took your cast off early." Uma pushed her way forward. "It's only been three weeks. That break won't heal right."

"Nell wanted it off. A cast on her second-in-command? It shows weakness." Ayla's eyes flickered.

"I'll take a look at it, assuming . . . ?" Uma looked at the captain.

"We'll see. What are you doing here, Ayla?"

"Yeah, your invitation was rescinded." Crocker hopped on to the steerage to glower down at their visitor. "We offered you a berth on our ship and you shoved it in our faces, got Toby jailed on the *Banshee.* Got Peel stabbed an' me almost keelhauled by yer crazy mother. You ain't welcome on the *Phoenix* anymore. No way, no how."

The sun caught in Ayla's hair, sparkling among the beads and creating a slick of color in the black. She was thinner than when Toby had last seen her, her eyes shadowed with dark circles. Toby could see she was in pain even as she straightened her back against the crew's jeers.

Something inside her had been broken by Nell. She had said she never wanted to see him again, yet here she was. Toby was drawn to her as if she had a fishing line and he was hooked on the end of it.

Ayla sneered at the shouting crew. "You know, we saw the *Phoenix* leave us to the St. George Graymen. Saw you sail past, with your paddles churning as fast as they could go—you couldn't get out of there fast enough. Cowards."

"We offered Nell the chance to work together against the Graymen, dint we?" Peel's fingers traced his stab wound. "She turned us down flat. Your captain can't complain when she gets what she wants."

"Oh, she's not complaining," Ayla retorted. "In fact it worked out well for us. Slimmed down the crew, of course, but we picked up some decent salvage from that ship before we sank her. And we got the panels anyway. That Dorah was a friend of yours, wasn't she? Very helpful."

"What did you do to Dorah?" The captain's voice was low, dangerous.

Ayla turned her smile to him. "We traded honestly. More or less."

"Less, I'm guessing," Uma spat, and the crew surged forward.

"I'll show you cowardice," Crocker yelled.

"That's enough." Toby moved to Ayla's side. "She's no threat—we know she's alone."

"We've only got her word the *Banshee*'s in Reykjavik," Oats yelled. "And we know what *her* word is worth. They could be preparing an ambush."

"Then why would I be here, warning you?" Ayla shook her head. "You really aren't that bright, are you, Oats?"

"You're the one being a fool." He lifted his hook. "Coming here after what you did."

The captain raised his fist. "*Enough!* I'm going to get to the bottom of this. The best way to find out what the cursed *Banshee* wants this time is to talk to its second-in-command. Take her below, Toby."

Toby turned to Ayla. "I'll take you to the mess."

"Not the mess—the galley," the captain snapped.

Toby realized instantly that Ayla could not be allowed to see their map and Hiko's translated text.

"I'll join you in a few minutes," the captain added. "There are a few issues left to deal with up here."

Toby gestured toward the nearest hatch and Ayla marched across the deck, the eyes of the crew boring into her as she passed.

"Be careful." Dee touched Toby's shoulder. "Don't get drawn into her scheming."

Toby only nodded as he followed Ayla into the bowels of the ship.

"You said you wanted nothing more to do with the *Phoenix*. Why are you here?" Toby sat on Peel's butcher's block, Ayla on the work surface beside the oven. He frowned as Polly shuffled on his shoulder. "You said you got our spare panels from Dorah. Did you install them?"

Ayla gave him a measuring look. "Yes, just like you did. And just like you, we found out a key component was missing."

"You were coming to steal our inverter." Toby's eyes narrowed.

"It crossed my mind." Ayla shook her head. "But as you don't have one either, we have to go straight to plan B."

"Plan B?" Toby's breath caught. "You have a way to get an inverter?"

Ayla pushed the long side of her hair back over her shoulder. "Obviously."

"Tell me."

Ayla's eyes flashed. "I'd say stop ordering me around, Ship's Engineer, but as I wanted to talk to you without your captain anyway . . ."

"I won't hide things from him."

"You don't have to. I just want to tell *you* my plan first. Then we can talk your captain into it together."

Toby frowned. "You mean he won't like it."

"I mean that whatever I suggest, he's likely to shoot it down without thinking it through. You're more . . . visionary."

"You mean gullible."

"No, that's not what I—"

"Fine," Toby growled. "Tell me."

Ayla folded her arms. "You've heard of the sun worshippers?"

"Of course—the Solar Order." Toby thought of Morris and Javier, the two crew members who, long ago, had been so entranced by the sight of the sun returning to the sky, they had gone blind staring at it. "The captain dropped off some crew at their sanctuary near Malta a few years ago. They were a friendly port."

"They're less friendly now." Ayla licked her lips. "We have a sailor who used to live on Gozo. He got out when the Order gained complete control of the island. It's theirs now and they're strict. The islanders either agree to worship the sun, or are exiled."

"From their homes?"

"Most stayed," Ayla said.

"So they were all blinded!"

"Not all." Ayla shook her head. "The sun worshippers consider those who've gone sunblind the most holy in the order, but they allow others to worship the sun and keep their vision. They need workers: traders, gardeners, fishermen, cooks, cleaners, same as any other place. The point is, Sebastiane told me that even when he lived there, anything dredged from the sea or traded that was remotely related to the sun had to go to the sanctuary. They were particularly keen on collecting items showing the Solaris logo."

Toby gasped. "There might be inverters inside."

Ayla nodded. "Almost certainly. The sun worshippers believe the old-world reliance on solar power was an affront to the sun. They say that's why Yellowstone erupted and blocked it out for so long—a punishment and a warning of worse to come. By collecting everything related to the sun, they think they're protecting us from another cataclysm." She laughed. "Idiots."

Toby's mind was racing. "Even back then, the sanctuary was like a fortress. We can't do a straight raid."

"No." Ayla grinned. "But I've got a plan."

Toby leaned closer, caught on her hook. "What sort of plan?"

"On the longest day of the year, the sun worshippers have a festival."

"That's in a month," Polly mumbled.

Ayla ignored her. "At the festival, a specially chosen couple, representative of the Sun and Moon, will hand out gifts to the pilgrims. For the weeks beforehand this couple will live in the sanctuary to prepare for their big day."

"So?" Toby frowned.

"In one week, the Order will choose that couple."

"You're suggesting we send someone in for this choosing," Toby said. "Whoever gets picked will have a couple of weeks in the sanctuary to find the inverters and smuggle them out."

"We can't just *send someone in*." Ayla air-quoted his words back at him. "The couple have to fit the criteria in order to be selected. There are rules."

Toby raised his eyebrows.

"The couple has to be male and female—to represent the different energies of the Sun and Moon."

"Easy enough."

"For the same reason, one must be blond and one dark-haired."

"And?" Toby pressed Ayla.

"The couple also have to represent the New Year, which they measure from the longest day: youth, innocence, rebirth, and so on." Ayla mocked the idea with a curled lip. "So only those between the ages of thirteen and sixteen are considered."

"*That's* why you need us," Polly squawked matter of factly. "You and Toby make the perfect couple for this festival."

Ayla smiled winningly at Toby. "We're the right age, your hair is growing back, and if anything you're even blonder than when I last saw you."

"That's because he hasn't been blowing soot out of the boiler room," Polly muttered. "He still isn't going though. Right, Toby?"

"I don't—"

"Listen," Ayla said. "On the longest day, the crew of the *Phoenix* visit the sanctuary as pilgrims—all we need to do is hide the inverters among the gifts and hand them over. It'll be easy." She bent closer, the long side of her hair dangling to her knees. "We go in, we get chosen." Here she lifted strands of her own black hair and let them fall through her fingers. "We spend a couple of weeks living in the lap of luxury while we look for the inverters. Where's the problem?"

"I—"

The doorway darkened and Toby looked up. The captain and Dee stood in the passageway.

"So," the captain began, "why are you here?"

Ayla looked at Toby, silently demanding his support. Then she turned to the captain. "I've got a plan to get us both an inverter, if you'll hear me out."

The captain paced the room, stroking his beard. "If these zealots find out we're fitting our ships with solar panels . . ."

"We'll have the sun worshippers after us as well as the world's navies." Ayla laughed. "They're blind prayer-mongers, we're pirates. I'm not worried."

The captain thumped the counter beside Toby. "And what does Nell think of this? I can't believe she'd ask anything of the *Phoenix*."

Ayla bit her lip.

"Ayla?" Toby frowned. "What are you hiding?"

Dee leaned on the doorjamb with her arms folded.

"Nell already tried her way." Ayla refused to look Toby in the eye. "She sent a crew member into the sanctuary disguised as a medic. We never heard from him again." Ayla sighed. "I liked Hideaki."

"You think he was caught stealing?"

"Must have been." Ayla still did not look up. "It's been over a week. He'd have been out by now."

"That still doesn't explain . . ."

Ayla raised her head, her eyes blazing. "Nell doesn't know I'm here, okay. She wants nothing from the *Phoenix*. Last I heard, she was planning on sending a full raiding party into Gozo. Stupid." Ayla leaped up and pressed her forehead onto the cloudy Plexiglas porthole, as if her mother watched through her own reflection. "The crew's still recovering from the battle and, like you said, that sanctuary's a fortress."

Dee spoke without moving from her position by the door. "You expect us to believe you're here without Nell's say-so?"

Ayla's shoulder's sagged. "Nell kicked me off the *Banshee.* I said it was stupid to send in a raiding party. I told her my plan, and when she refused, I tried to sell it to the crew. Most were on my side. No one really wants to be in that raiding party, not when the *Banshee* is so torn up. Nell found out I'd gone behind her back."

"You bloody mutinied!" Dee breathed.

"Not exactly." Ayla's reply was so quiet Toby could barely hear her. "I never wanted to take over from Nell; I just thought she might listen to me if I had the crew on my side. I—"

"That's mutiny." The captain frowned. "I'm sorry, Ayla, but you expect us to believe, after you showed us how loyal you are to your mother, that you have since betrayed her?"

"It wasn't *betrayal,*" Ayla snapped as she spun to face the captain. "Nell's not thinking straight. She's going to get the whole crew killed—me along with them. I'm not suggesting the *Banshee* and *Phoenix* team up. I just need to work with one of you. Then, when the con's over, we share the inverters."

"You want Toby," Dee said.

Ayla nodded and glanced at him, seeking support.

Toby did not meet her eyes. Was this something he wanted to do—go on a mission with Ayla again? His heart thudded. It couldn't possibly work, there was too much between them. Ayla had imprisoned him on the *Banshee*, she hated his family, *and* she had watched the *Phoenix* abandon her to die. He'd be a fool to trust her.

But if they didn't get the inverters they would have to give up on the island. Without solar power, the *Phoenix* had to sail close to shore—no venturing into the deep salt. Things would go back to the way they were, and suddenly that didn't seem like any kind of life: living from hand to mouth, fighting for survival, knowing the Graymen or the *Banshee* would catch up with them eventually.

Only the hope of finding the island had kept the crew going. If they gave up that hope . . .

"Your pulse is accelerating." Polly nipped his ear. "Don't even think about it."

"We *need* those inverters," Toby said eventually. "Ayla's plan makes sense."

"We have other blond crew." Dee scowled. "We could send Rita with Rahul, Amit, Ajay . . . any of them."

"They're all too old," Toby explained.

"So Ayla says." Dee narrowed her eyes.

"It'll be easy enough to confirm the rules when we get there," Toby said.

"*When*?" Dee marched up to Toby. "You've already decided!"

From the corner of his eye, Toby saw Ayla's wild grin.

The captain held up a hand. "I can't allow it, not after last time. You imprisoned Toby on the *Banshee* and he was almost killed."

Ayla ignored the captain and leaned towards Toby. "It's not nearly as dangerous as rescuing you from Tarifa. Between us, we have two ships, both with unusable solar panels. I don't know about your crew, but ours isn't too happy about that. Nell needs an inverter, or she *will* be facing a mutiny. From what I heard when I climbed on board, I reckon you're in the same position." A sly look entered her eyes. "Did you translate the map?"

"So that's what you're after." Dee narrowed her eyes. "You want our map translation!"

Ayla shook her head. "Honestly, no. I just wondered, is all. Our map is useless, our panels are useless, our ship is damaged, and our crew is injured. We need these inverters and my plan will get them for us. Sebastiane told me all about the sanctuary, how it works. I know how we can get in and out."

The captain's eyes slid to Dee's.

"I don't trust her," Dee snapped. "There's no way she's here without Nell's permission. They're after Hiko."

Toby tensed.

"Keep Hiko locked up below if you like," Ayla replied. "I won't even look in his direction, let alone go near him." She spread her hands. "It's an inverter we need right now. If I can go back to Nell with the piece of equipment she's after, she'll have to let me back on board." She swallowed. "She'll have to forgive me." Her hair fell over her face. "I made a mistake, Captain, can't I atone for it?"

"Are you referring to your mutiny on the *Banshee*, or your betrayal of the *Phoenix*?" the captain asked.

"Either. Both." She widened her eyes and Toby had to bite his cheek to stop himself from laughing.

"All right." The captain looked at Ayla's rust-covered palms. "You've made your point. Toby, take Ayla to clean up. Once Rahul clears the mess we'll have a meeting with the rest of the crew. If we're going to consider this, we need a solid plan. That means I want input from everyone who has ever had a dealing with Gozo."

As Toby closed the door behind him, the captain turned to Dee and started to speak in a low and urgent voice.

FOUR

"So, the traitor's gonna tell us how to pick up an inverter," Crocker sneered.

Peel turned to the captain. "Put her off the *Phoenix* now, before it's too late."

"Too late for what?" Arnav hawked and spat. "We ain't going anywhere and nor's she."

"We need that piece of equipment." Nisha sat close to Rahul, his arm closed around her. "If we put Ayla off ship without listening to her, where will we get one?"

Rahul tightened his arm. "No reason we can't take her idea and do the job without her."

Toby watched Ayla smile slightly as Rahul spoke. She knew that only she and Toby could complete the heist. She wasn't worried.

Marcus stood beside his partner; he had been silent for the whole meeting. Now he spoke. "Dee doesn't like it, I can tell."

Toby whirled to look at Dee, who hadn't said a word. "Dee?"

She rubbed her healing wound and said nothing.

"You're my second, if you've got something to say . . ." the captain prompted.

Dee sighed. "You know my thoughts, Captain. I don't trust her."

"If Dee says she can't be trusted, then we shouldn't," Marcus said.

"I hear you, Dee," Rita called out. "But without Ayla, I'd be hanging from the ramparts in Tarifa, alongside Rahul, Theo, Oats, and you, yourself, Captain. We owe her. We should at least hear what she has to say."

"Rita . . ." Dee said, her voice low in warning. "She's *Banshee*."

The crew growled at that and the atmosphere thickened.

"We don't know why she's really here!" Oats shouted. "Could be the *Banshee*'s more badly damaged than she says. Could be they want the *Phoenix*. Could be a trick."

D'von started to sidle closer to Ayla. Toby caught his friend's shoulder and shook his head. "They're being mean to Ayla," D'von grumbled.

"She can look after herself," Toby murmured as Ayla vaulted on to a tabletop and raised her voice.

"We don't want your bucket of a ship. I'm here because we both need inverters and my plan to get them requires the *Phoenix*'s crew."

"Why not use your own crew?" Rita shouted.

Ayla snorted. "For a start, I need a partner in crime and *Banshee* pirates are all easily identified."

"She's right," Toby said.

"Well maybe her captain should stop tattooing her crew!" Dee snapped.

"Basically you need one of us to help you because we haven't mutilated ourselves," Uma grunted. "Nice."

Ayla glared at her. "I don't need 'one of you.' I need *Toby*."

Uma leaped to her feet. "Not a chance."

"Uma!" Toby frowned. "This isn't your decision."

She spun to face him. "Have you forgotten already? She'll get you killed. Maybe she wants you to go with her because you're expendable. That'll be the real reason she won't use *Banshee* pirates—because she cares what happens to her own crew."

Toby caught his breath.

The crew began to call out. "Get off the table . . . we don't need you . . . get off our ship!"

The voices grew louder and uglier but Ayla shouted over them all. "There are inverters in the sanctuary of the sun worshippers in Gozo."

The crew went quiet.

"How do you know?" Nisha finally demanded.

"Intelligence gathered." Ayla narrowed her eyes. "Toby and I can get into the sanctuary disguised as devotees, in advance of the solstice festival. We go as representatives of the Sun and Moon, who must be under sixteen. Once we've found the inverters, you arrive disguised as pilgrims and we hand them over to you."

Marcus stood shoulder to shoulder with Dee. "You're asking Toby to infilitrate the sun worshippers' sanctuary with *you* at his side. It wouldn't be safe for him to go into that sanctuary with a trusted companion, let alone with you."

"There's no downside here," Ayla replied. "Toby and I get dropped off at the sanctuary where we live in comfort for a couple of weeks. We find the inverters, we pass them to you. We get out."

The crew shuffled and muttered, then Arnav cleared his throat. His wrinkled face was thoughtful. "Heard of this festival, I 'ave," he said. "An' there's one thing you 'aven't mentioned, girlie."

Ayla fidgeted shiftily.

"Thought as much." Arnav nodded. "Yeah. You 'aven't mentioned what 'appens to those Sun and Moon kids when the festival's over."

"What happens?" Toby spoke slowly.

"It's not a problem." Ayla opened her hands.

"What happens, Arnav?" he insisted.

"The Sun an' Moon are special, ain't they? So the ones who are chosen get the proper trainin' to become high-ups in the Order."

Marcus's chin shot up. "Hang on! Doesn't that mean they have to be sunblind, like Morris and Javier?"

"Yep." Arnav nodded. "After the pilgrims get their gifts, the Sun and Moon get staked out with their eyes taped open. Blindness takes a minute or two, or the rest of the afternoon—dependin'."

"On what?" Nisha whispered.

"On how cloudy it is." Arnav directed his attention to Ayla. "Wasn't goin' to mention that, were ya, girlie?"

Ayla appealed directly to Toby. "We'll be out before then."

Toby scowled. "If we're the focus of attention during this festival, how the hell do we get out again before we get blinded?"

Ayla hissed. "I *have* thought this through. We have a chemist on the *Banshee*. He's been working with an old sleeping tablet: Tuinal. It's a respiratory depressor. He's given me pills that fake the effects of death. If we can't get out the easy way, we can each take Tuinal. They'll think we've died. There's no way they'll stake out a couple of dead bodies."

"They might cremate them," Amit spoke up.

"Or bury them," Ajay added.

Toby caught his breath. He could all too easily imagine being buried alive. It would be like the aftermath of the explosion in Tarifa, only with no light, no friends, and no hope. He exhaled shakily.

Ayla rolled her eyes. "I already thought of that. Sebastiane told me what the order does with their dead. They're known for it. They don't cremate—they believe it's too close to worship of the eruption. They don't bury, because they don't have a cemetery. They entrust their dead to the salt."

"To the salt," Rita said slowly. "Like we do?"

"There's a low cliff behind the sanctuary. The dead get wrapped up and thrown over the edge. They land on the beach and the next tide takes them. The order thinks of it like going over the horizon, toward the sun. Really, they just get eaten by acid and buried in junk."

"So what happens when you get dumped over this cliff?"

"Easy." Ayla grinned. "*Birdie* picks us up."

"This plan depends on far too many things we don't know." The captain gestured for Ayla to get down from the table. "I agree, if there're inverters anywhere they're most likely to be on Gozo, but you don't have any actual proof. There may not be any, or there may be only one. If that's the case who gets it, the *Phoenix* or the *Banshee*?"

Marcus stepped forward. "You don't know if you'll be able to find the inverters, let alone steal them without being caught."

"That's right," Peel growled. "I already saved the boy once. Me an' Crocker ain't going to get 'im outta Gozo for no good reason."

Crocker hawked and spat. "You could be so closely guarded in there, you won't get to do nothin' but pray."

"Or we could be left completely alone." Ayla folded her arms. "They're *blind* remember!"

The captain glowered at her. "They're not *all* blind, Ayla, in fact I'm sure most of them aren't. The best way to fail a con is to underestimate your mark. You should know that."

"And then there's your exit." It was Uma's turn to fold her arms. "What if you can't escape and have to rely on that suicide pill? I haven't tested this 'Tuinal' you're talking about. What if it doesn't work? What if the order realizes you aren't dead? You'll be completely helpless—asleep probably—when they deal with you."

Toby shuddered.

"And all of *that* depends on the pair of you being chosen as the Sun and Moon, among a number of others." Uma nodded, satisfied that her case had been made. "It's not worth the risk."

Ayla opened her mouth and the captain raised his hand to silence her, but she ignored his gesture. "It's the best plan we've got," she snapped.

Rita stood. "Not worth the risk? Without the inverter we might as well toss the solar panels back in the salt where we found them."

"We ain't tossin' nothing back in no salt," Crocker shrieked.

"Without the inverters, they're good for nothing but cluttering up the deck." Rita frowned. "If the sun worshippers have the only inverters, then we have to at least *try* and steal them, otherwise we're back where we began."

"Would that be so bad?" Ajay asked and his brother nodded agreement.

Oats slammed his hook on the tabletop and the sound of metal on metal rang through the room. "Of course it would," he shouted. "If we hadn't been going for those solar panels, the *Banshee* would never have attacked; we'd have outrun that storm and never needed to be in Tarifa seeking repairs." He dragged the point of his hook along the surface. "We lost more than just my hand in Tarifa. What would Carson say if he knew we'd got nothing out of it? No panels, no chance to find the island. He'd bloody turn in his grave. If he had one. Which he doesn't. We're bloody pirates! Our whole lives are a risk, or have you forgotten that?"

"There's taking risks and then there's sending Toby in on a con," Uma retorted.

"Why's Toby so special?" Crocker sneered, squaring up to her. "Would we be 'avin' this discussion if we were talkin' about sendin' someone else in? How about Delgado or Alvarez?" He pointed to the group of Spaniards standing at the back of the mess hall.

"So you're saying we should send Toby into the sanctuary with the traitor?" Uma asked. "With only some of the information we need."

"And a half-baked exit strategy," Marcus supplied.

"It's a sound enough plan." Oats was defensive. "Send 'em in. If Toby and the girl don't get picked as the couple, it's no skin off our noses, they just come back. If they get in and can't find the inverters, they sneak out, come back, we've still lost nothing. But if they find the inverters and get them to us, we've gained everything. They don't have to wait till the festival—get in, get the inverters, get out."

"The *Banshee* sent someone in already." Dee looked up. "He never came out."

Oats fell silent.

"Maybe he was a fool an' got caught doin' something stupid," Crocker rasped. "Maybe he decided life in the sanctuary was better than on that stinking tub they call a ship. Our Toby's bright, he might not get caught." Crocker turned, sharp as a ferret. "I don't know about you lot, but I want to find that island. Fink about it—our own place, all shiny an' new, away from Graymen and their laws and taxes. We're so close, I can smell it. I ain't givin' up on that. What d'you fink, boy? Can you do this?"

The eyes of the whole crew turned to Toby, but he only saw Ayla. Her head was cocked to one side and her eyes sparkled with challenge.

"Is there no other way in?" Toby asked finally.

Ayla shook her head. "Not according to Sebastiane."

"Nonsense." Dee slashed her hand across her body. "They must get deliveries. We could pretend to bring supplies or we could bring them some of the solar panels, say we found them and wanted to hand them over. That would get us in."

"To the inner sanctum?" Ayla sneered. "Did you get in when you dropped off your crew?"

Uma groaned and shook her head. "We left them at the outer wall."

"They're even more paranoid now. They send missionaries out into the world, into communities to make converts, but the only time their worshippers get to see inside the actual sanctuary is at the summer solstice. The only other way in would be as an attendant—a sister or brother-in-training, but the *Banshee* already tried that. It has to be more than one person working together. People they'll trust."

"They won't suspect kids of trying to steal equipment," Rita said thoughtfully.

"And if we get caught where we shouldn't be, we can say we got lost, or were playing a game, or looking for some privacy."

Ayla twitched her eyebrows. "Toby—we'll be fine."

As she looked his way, Toby's stomach flipped. "I don't want to go back to where we started." He turned to the captain. "We can't ask the crew to give up on the island. If we don't go for the inverters, that's what we're doing." He wiped his forehead. "All right. I'm in."

FIVE

Immediately, the crew started to push and shove, yelling over one another to be heard. Toby winced and glanced at Ayla as Crocker threw a punch at Marcus. Ayla leaned on a table away from the melee, with her right arm tightly folded over her broken one.

"Stop this!" the captain roared.

A table crashed to the floor. Hiko hid behind Toby and D'von moved to his side.

Rahul hauled Nisha to safety and Rita burst from the pack to stand with them. "If you want to do this, Captain, it doesn't have to be Toby!" she panted, "D'von's the right age and I've passed for sixteen—remember Kabul?"

D'von's face lit up and Ayla looked away from the fight, offering what seemed to Toby to be a genuine, gentle expression. "It's a good offer, D'von, but there's too much risk of you being rejected by the order if they realize that Rita's not a teenager. Toby and I stand a better chance of being accepted as the Sun and Moon."

The captain sucked air through his teeth. "Rita, could you work with D'von?"

Rita nodded swiftly.

"All right then," he roared. "This isn't a democracy. Settle down or you'll all be on a charge."

The battling crew fell silent.

"I've made my decision. Rita and D'von are going to Gozo. Ayla—you'll give them the pills and *if* we retrieve two inverters, well . . . I'll make sure you get one."

Fury darkened Ayla's green eyes. "You can't cut me out of my own plan!" She poked him in the chest, looking as if she wished she were using a knife and not her fingernail. "She's too old. It won't work!"

When the captain ignored her, Ayla appealed to Toby. "They won't get picked. If they're turned away, we'll have to wait another year for a second chance. And by then we'll be too old to try ourselves. You may *as well* throw those panels away."

Toby looked at D'von. Yes, there was a chance he'd be picked by the order and get inside the sanctuary. But would he be able to sneak around and steal the inverters without being caught? D'von was not as slow as he looked; there was a deeper well of cunning inside him that had surprised both Toby and Ayla in Tarifa, but he was honest, open and did as he was told.

Hiko gripped Toby's hand. "You can't let him go," Hiko whispered. "He'll be caught."

Polly glared down at him. "Be quiet, you," she squawked.

Toby turned to the captain. "So . . . are you planning to keep Ayla prisoner on the *Phoenix* until the heist is over?"

Ayla's eyes widened. "I'd like to see you *try*."

Toby put his hands on his hips. "If she gets away, she'll go to Gozo and tell the order that Rita isn't sixteen."

The captain frowned and Toby carried on.

"Or she'll get herself another partner and go in without the *Phoenix*." He turned to the crew. "If that happens, Ayla will get an inverter for the *Banshee* and the *Phoenix* will get nothing. Nell has the map, same as us. You want the *Banshee* getting to the island first? Even if we *could* translate our map, we can't do a long sea voyage without those inverters. It may as well point us to the moon."

Polly swayed from side to side. "I don't like where this is going," she murmured.

"If we don't join Ayla, there's no way to stop her cutting us out."

"There is one way." Peel ran his finger along the knife he kept at his belt.

"Peel!" Toby snapped. "We're not murderers."

"We're *pirates*," Crocker spat.

The captain rubbed his eyes. "We may be pirates, but we don't murder little girls because it's convenient."

"Little girls!" Ayla bristled.

"Shut up, Ayla." Toby spun round. "If we could trust you, we wouldn't be having this problem."

As Ayla smirked, Dee shoved her into a chair. "We should never have heard her out. You think she's not planning a double-cross?"

"Toby's right," the captain groaned. "I don't like it, but he is." He twisted his compass. "I don't trust the girl and nor should he, but he's bright enough to keep an eye on her and make sure he gets an inverter for the *Phoenix* despite any hidden agendas."

"I don't have—" Ayla interjected.

"Enough," the captain growled. "Toby is going. But Rita and D'von are going, too, as insurance. If they're the ones to get picked, all the better."

"They won't," Ayla stated confidently.

Dee slid her blade free and Ayla closed her mouth.

The captain sighed. "It's not ideal, but I can't think of any other way that doesn't put a stain on our souls."

"The stain doesn't have to be yours." With a terrifying suddenness Dee raised her knife.

Ayla was still seated. As she tried to get up, to protect herself, her foot caught on the chair leg.

"No!" Toby screamed.

Fast as a snake, the captain grabbed Dee's wrist. The knife hovered above Ayla's chest. She kicked backward and the chair toppled, taking her away from the blade. She rolled from the seat and in one smooth movement moved into a crouch, flicking her long coat away from her face.

As it settled, Toby realized that she, too, had drawn a knife.

"Where'd she get that?" Crocker called into the shocked silence.

"That's one a my kitchen knives. Get if offa her," Peel roared.

Ayla lunged toward Dee and the captain swung his second-in-command behind him. Ayla froze as she came face to face with the captain. Her knife hand trembled.

"Drop it!" Marcus ran to disarm her and the captain raised a hand.

Toby could hear the harsh rasp of Dee's breath even over the pirate's muttering.

"No one is to harm our visitor." The captain spun to Dee, putting his back to Ayla and her knife. "Do you understand?"

"It's the only way." Her face was pale, her scarf a livid slash of color around her dark hair.

"It's not *our* way." The captain opened his hand and released her. "Toby's right—if we let her go, she'll sabotage our own attempt on the inverters, and if we try and keep her prisoner she'll do all she can to escape."

"So you'll allow your son to go with her on this crazy mission, to risk his life, just so you don't have to take hers?"

"Careful, Dee," the captain warned.

"I'm your second-in-command, why won't you *listen* to me?" She spun to face Toby. "You're a pirate, stop being a hero."

Toby sighed. "It's not heroism, Dee; it's good sense. Rita's too old. Yes, she and D'von might get into the sanctuary, but they might not. I *have* to go: it's the best thing for the *Phoenix*."

As Dee moved to object, the captain spoke first. "Toby, take Hiko and get the boiler running. It's almost a week's straight sailing to Gozo. We leave at first light."

"No!" Dee shook her head.

The captain caught her arm and lowered his voice. "You know better than to undermine me in front of my crew."

Dee pulled free of the captain's hold. "I've been on this ship as long as you have. I've supported every decision you've made, but not this one." She shook her head.

"You *will* support me, or at least remain quiet—"

"Or?" Dee's eyes blazed.

The captain sagged. "Stop forcing my hand."

"I can't stand here and watch you—"

"Then don't!" the captain groaned. "Theo and Simeon will be back in a few days. If we leave at first light, they won't know where we've gone. Someone needs to stay behind and tell them where the *Phoenix* is. I was going to ask Arnav, but . . ."

Dee's mouth flattened into a line. "You're ordering me off ship."

"We both need to cool down."

"You need me to make you see sense. And I'm not just your second—I'm navigator, too."

"Rita can navigate, she's spent enough time on Steerage. Toby can be Second."

Toby paled. "What?"

"It's about time, Toby." The captain raised his voice. "Any of my crew disagree with the fact that Toby should be second-in-command while Dee's off ship?"

There were a few mutterings, but the crew said nothing. Even Peel and Crocker kept their voices down.

"So, you don't need me any more, is that it?" Dee slammed her knife back in her belt. "If you order me, I'll go, but I won't come back."

Toby jolted forward. "Don't say that."

"Of course you will," the captain said.

"No. You don't respect me or my opinion. You don't need me any more so I'll get another berth." She looked at Ayla. "I hear the *Banshee* needs new crew members."

Toby caught his breath. "You wouldn't!"

"Well, Captain?" Dee's eyes were hard and dark as steel.

"I'm ordering you off ship." The captain's voice almost trembled.

Dee swung round and stalked toward the mess door. She paused at Marcus's side. "Marcus?"

“I’m with you,” Marcus said quietly. His freckles stood out against the paleness of his cheeks and sweat stuck his red curls to his forehead like bloody smears. He looked at Toby. “Toby, I—”

“I know,” Toby murmured.

“Take care. And don’t trust *her*.” Marcus tilted his head toward Ayla.

Dee, too, looked at Toby. “Keep Nix close.” She called Marcus to her side. “Start packing our things, we have to be off the *Phoenix* by nightfall.”

SIX

It was cold on deck. The sun's meager heat had vanished when it dipped below the horizon; now only the residual red glow of its light remained. Peel had lit his barbecue but wasn't cooking. Despite the chill, the whole crew remained on deck. Toby, D'von, and Hiko were clustered around the salvage hooks. Toby was running a cloth up and down the length of Nix while Polly hunched on his shoulder. Other crew members pretended to swab the deck, repair rigging or coiled ropes. In an unspoken pact, they were waiting for Dee and Marcus to emerge.

The captain was below deck watching Ayla. Uma had checked her arm and announced it was healing well. Ayla had then, showing unusual sensitivity, retired to the sleeping quarters.

Finally the hatch leading to the storage area opened and Dee stepped on to the main deck with a bulging canvas bag over one shoulder. Her long curls were tied back into her red scarf and there was a smudge of soot on one cheek. Marcus followed behind her. The crew immediately stopped what they were pretending to do.

Toby clenched his fists as Dee walked among her friends, touching hands and faces, pounding shoulders, murmuring farewells. Tears pricked his eyes, but he refused to allow them to fall. He had known Dee his whole life.

"Toby?" Polly squawked low, so no one else could hear. He shook his head and passed her to Hiko.

Dee reached Nisha and put her arms around the other woman. Rahul pressed her upper arm, his own face drawn and miserable.

When Dee indicated that she would speak to him next, Toby felt something inside of him shatter. He ran toward the galley hatch, grabbed the wheel, turned it and dragged open the door.

"Toby . . ." Dee called.

"Just go." He turned and found himself face to face with her.

"Tobes." She held out a hand, but Toby jammed his arms straight down at his sides, his fists pressed against his thighs.

"Why are you doing this?" He forced the words out.

"You know why." Dee sighed. "It's the right time for me to move on. You're Second now." She gave a grim smirk. "Ayla's given me a note of recommendation for Nell. I might try the *Banshee* after all."

Toby choked.

"You don't think it's a good idea?" Dee raised her eyebrows. He shook his head and Dee held out her arms. "Say goodbye properly. You'll regret it if you don't."

Toby stood still. His arms felt as if anchors were weighing them to the deck. Slowly, he raised them.

"Thank you."

His chin rested on Dee's shoulder and her hair tickled his nose. He tightened his fists on her back. "It'll be all right, Toby. We'll see each other again."

"Not if we find the island," Toby croaked. "Isn't that the whole point of this?"

"I suppose. Though I will see you again, I promise."

Toby nodded, no longer trusting his voice.

"We've got to go." Dee turned and walked to the gangplank. At the top she tugged at her scarf—the red bandanna that every crew member wore. Slowly she unwound it from her hair. Taking his cue, Marcus uncoiled his from his throat and handed both to Uma.

Then, together, Marcus and Dee left the *Phoenix* and jumped on to Ayla's lifeboat, which had been prepared to take them from the ship to Faroe Rocks.

Toby ran to the gunwale in time to see the small boat vanish into the darkness.

"Will they be all right?" Toby asked Uma.

Uma closed her fist around the discarded scarves. "Marcus has a tent, fuel and flint in his kit. Peel slipped supplies into the boat. And there're caves. With all the combustibles that wash up with the tide, they'll be fine till Theo and Simeon get back."

Toby stared after them.

The boiler room was empty. Toby slipped through the door and checked the gauges. The water levels were good. The soot needed cleaning out of the blowers, but otherwise, she would be ready to push the paddles in the morning.

Gozo. Toby looked out of the porthole where a tiny glow sputtered, a fire had been lit among the rocks.

Everything was changing.

Toby fetched the brushes and began to clean, taking comfort in the familiar routine. Polly's weight was missing from his shoulder and for a moment he wished she was grumbling about the soot in her feathers. But she no longer had feathers and she was with Hiko now.

For a little while, Toby wanted to pretend that everything was as it had been before the *Phoenix* had heard of the sunken solar panels. He imagined a blue and scarlet Polly up on her perch above the attemperator, Dee on the bridge with the captain, Marcus playing Perudo with Crocker and Harry napping in the storage area when he should have been working.

As his muscles burned, he kept his mind's eye on the memory he created and refused to think of anything other than the job he'd done a hundred times before. When he finished, he stored the brushes, arms shaking with exhaustion. Then he fed more fuel to the compressor and topped up the combustion chamber.

At the door, he hesitated and shook his head. If he went to the sleeping quarters, he'd find Ayla. Toby remembered the last time they had sat together on his bunk, the trembling pressure of her lips. It wouldn't be like that ever again. She needed him to complete her plan, but their bond was broken. His ears rang with the memory of their conversation on the *Banshee.*

"It's over then?"

"How can it be anything else? After what your family has done to mine."

Ayla had been right, there could be nothing more between them than the plan to get the inverters. He leaned his forehead on the hull and listened to the chug and grind of his resting ship. He wanted to go to Ayla, but she had betrayed him.

He turned back to the boiler room and unrolled a blanket from beneath his 'useful one day' pile. He kept it there for the nights he had to nurse the boiler. It had been a while since he had slept in the heart of the *Phoenix*. Curling up beneath the control panel, Toby allowed the whistle of superheated steam to soothe him to sleep.

The North Sea was rough and junk rose and fell on either side of the *Phoenix*, banging into her paddle cages despite the ice-breaker hull pushing it to each side.

Toby stood on top of the bridge and braced himself on the main mast as he shaded his eyes to watch Faroe Rocks turn into a distant smudge. The sails above him snapped in the brisk wind, pulling the *Phoenix* onward, and he shivered.

"You can't avoid me forever." Ayla climbed the ladder toward him then crouched on top of the bridge. The *Phoenix* tipped into a thrashing wave that carried salt spray and a tumble of cans over the gunwale. As she rubbed the poisonous spray from her face, Toby saw that today she had braided her long hair, but left the short half sticking wildly up. The stinging salt had reddened her cheeks but she had her collar turned up against the wind, covering the burn mark on her shoulder. The glitter in her green eyes added to the savagery of her appearance. As the ship tilted, Ayla rolled into the rigging and came up grinning.

"I waited for you last night." She greeted him with a tilt of her pointed chin. "I thought we should talk. Where did you sleep?"

"Somewhere else." Toby tightened his grip on the mast.

Ayla wrapped one hand around the mast, just beneath Toby's. "Remember the last night we spent in your sleeping quarters?"

"Of course." Toby shivered. "I spent the next morning in the brig of the *Banshee*."

"You'd have done no different." Ayla refused to look down. There was no shame on her face. "I was in an impossible position. Can't you understand?"

"I suppose." This was her way of apologizing. His little finger slipped down the mast, as if to touch her thumb but he pulled it back. "There's still our parents, our history hasn't changed."

"I know." Now she dropped her gaze.

"I never got a chance to say I'm sorry." Toby shuffled awkwardly. "For what my parents did to yours . . . to your sisters."

"I don't remember them." Ayla looked out over the salt as though she could see her family in the distance. "I'd turned Astrid into an imaginary friend—I thought I'd just created a reflection of myself to play with."

"But she was your twin." Toby hugged himself. "And what about your big sister, Freya?"

Ayla shrugged. "Nell won't talk about her—I've asked."

"The captain won't tell me about Judy, either—" At the look on Ayla's face Toby bit off the sentence.

"Why would you want to know about *her*?" Ayla flinched back from him.

"She *was* my mother." Toby sighed. "I just wanted to know *how* she could have done what she did. How could anyone?"

"Right." Ayla settled back down.

"And your father, will Nell speak about him?"

Ayla shook her head. "I get it. It hurts her too much. Those scars won't ever heal."

"And that's why the *Banshee* will never work with the *Phoenix*. You know that better than anyone." Toby frowned. "So I don't understand why you came up with a plan that involved me."

Ayla sat and patted the bridge roof. The *Phoenix* rolled and knocked Toby into her. Swiftly he moved away, leaving space between them. Their legs dangled above the bridge door. D'von looked up from his cleaning job and waved. Ayla returned the gesture, her face relaxing.

"You like D'von," Toby said.

Ayla nodded. "He doesn't overthink. He's a good guy, isn't he? Not like us."

Toby inhaled sharply.

"You know what I mean. You and I, we're born pirates. D'von—he'll be a pirate to please you, and a great one. But he'd have been just as happy on land, in a smithy, or a bakery or something. You or I would go insane in a job like that."

"So you think you'd have set sail in the end? Even if your family hadn't . . ."

Ayla shook her head. "Perhaps not. But I'd have always been unsettled and a little miserable and never known why."

"You think the salt's in our blood?" Toby covered his bare face as the *Phoenix* pitched and spray hit them again. Above them gulls wheeled as the Irish coast blurred on the horizon.

Ayla nodded. "You and me, we're alike. You said it once before, we make a good team. I thought about other partners for the plan, but I kept coming back to you. I know you can fight, I know what you'll do in a tight spot and I can trust you."

He stared at his hands for a long time. "You can trust me," he said. "But can I trust you?" He leaned farther from her. "You expect me to go into this sanctuary and work with you to find the inverters. How do I know that you won't just take them and leave me behind?"

Ayla pressed her lips together. For the first time she looked uncomfortable. "I won't," she muttered.

"You did before," Toby insisted. "You took the map, snuck out and left."

"That was different. I almost died saving your captain and crew, doesn't that count for anything? I promised I'd rescue Captain Ford and I did. Make me promise, if that's what it takes. Ask me not to betray you when we're inside the sanctuary."

Toby stared.

"How about if I swear on Astrid's grave?" Ayla hopped down, and thudded on to the deck. She looked up at Toby and lifted one hand to her heart. "I swear that while we're in the sanctuary I'll have your back. I won't betray you." She dropped her hand. "Is that enough?"

"I don't know." Toby exhaled. "It should be."

As the *Phoenix* passed what was left of the Balearics, Toby left Hiko filling the compressor in the boiler room, pulled his eye-gauze low over his eyes and climbed on deck to bask in the warmth.

"You'd better take that off, Toby." It was Uma. Her own gauze was tight over her face. The crew had been wearing it since they had passed the meridian and the sun's brightness had become unbearable to their unaccustomed eyes.

He didn't move. "Why?"

"True sun worshippers don't use it. I believe it's considered blasphemous to hide from the sun's rays."

Toby glanced at Ayla. She had long ago removed her jacket and now wore a light shirt for work on deck. The captain had her cleaning out the bilge pumps, but she made no complaint. In fact she had thrown herself into life on the *Phoenix* and did every job tossed her way with good humor. She had even earned a reluctant grunt of approval when she returned Peel's fish to him gutted, boned, and dressed for the crew's dinner. Her own eyes were naked to the brightness.

Reluctantly, Toby unwound the light material.

"You need to get used to going without." Uma smiled. "Start off with short periods of time, then go longer."

Toby put the gauze in his pocket. "I feel exposed."

The captain appeared behind him and huffed. "You'll be all right." His fingers vanished inside his jacket. "Here, I've drawn this for you." He pulled a piece of slate from his pocket. There was a chalked image on it. "This is what an inverter is likely to look like—it'll be small enough to fit in the palm of your hand. It should have a Solaris logo, but most importantly there'll be holes with pins inside that will fit these." He opened his other hand to show Toby cables with connectors. "Got it?"

Toby nodded and the captain handed him the slate and wires. "Show Ayla later, make sure you both have it memorized."

Ayla looked up at the sound of her name.

"What's going on over there?" Toby slipped the wires into his tool belt and pointed to the solar panels, where Rahul, Nisha, Amit, and Ajay were pulling tarpaulins tight and pinning them down.

"We're covering the panels," the captain replied. "We'll be in sight of the island in a day or so and we don't know how far their scopes can see. We won't take the *Phoenix* all the way in, but we don't want to risk them seeing what we've got here. They might attack us, or suspect you of foul play."

Toby nodded. "I'll help." As Ayla went back to her own job he caught a rope and helped Nisha pull it tight. His eyes already felt sore and watery, but he would work for at least an hour before he put his gauze back on. Uma was right, if the con was going to work, he had to look like a true sun worshipper.

SEVEN

Toby eyed the heat haze that hung over the tiny island like fog. Polly hunched on his shoulder, her weight a comfort, even as the sun glinted from her body.

"Have you been to Gozo before?" Ayla leaned over the gunwale, as if to urge the *Phoenix* to break through the junk faster.

Toby shook his head. "Last time we were here we brought Javier and Morris and I wasn't allowed off ship." He picked at some rust on the railing. "The *Phoenix* anchored in Malta, above the castle—you can see its remains under the salt when the tide shifts the junk—and the captain took them in. The Maltese hate St. George because they refused to help with the evacuation when the tsunamis hit. There are hardly any survivors on Malta, so not much to trade, but they're a safe anchorage for the *Phoenix*."

Ayla rose to her toes and pointed. "Look, I can see the sanctuary."

Toby jumped as Rita thumped into the rail beside him. Her blonde hair tickled his cheek. "It's bigger than I remember," she whispered.

Ayla nodded. "Sebastiane told me they're always building. It started off as a Catholic cathedral."

"Now look at it," Rita added. "Doesn't it remind you of . . ."

Toby's stomach lurched. Rita was right; there was a feel of Castle Guzman about the thick blocky walls, gray concrete paving and massive slabs that now surrounded the delicate stonework of the original structure. He closed his eyes, blinded, as the sun caught the massive bronze circle that adorned the bell tower.

"Wow," Ayla muttered. "I guess we're in the right place."

With the sanctuary hidden by the glow of the bronze dial, Toby shifted his attention to the houses that clustered around its base like rats around a supply crate.

"They all work for the Order?" Rita murmured.

Ayla nodded. "The original islanders had to become sun worshippers, or move to Malta. They provide the sanctuary with most of its food and supplies."

"What if they *couldn't* leave?" Rita didn't take her eyes from the houses.

Ayla said nothing. At one side of the building, the island had cracked. A huge chunk had slid downward to create a cliff leading to a narrow bay that backed right up against the rear wall. As Toby watched, surf crashed into jagged rocks and salt splashed the sanctuary, spraying white foam into the heat haze.

"Is that where they leave their dead?" Rita's eyes widened. "We'll be killed."

Ayla rolled her eyes. "They put the dead out when the tide is low. *We'll* be long gone by the time the salt's this angry, if it comes to it."

D'von came running up to them. "We're here?"

Toby nodded. "Are you sure you want to do this, D'von? It isn't too late to back out."

D'von frowned. "If you're going, Toby, I'm going, too, don't worry."

Toby glanced at Ayla.

"He won't get in," she whispered.

He jumped as Arnav began to blow the *Phoenix*'s whistle; although the *Phoenix* wasn't going to dock, they still had to get through the dam keeping the debris from Gozo's waters and that meant announcing their arrival.

Although the Azure Window had long been destroyed, the sun worshippers had used the cliff to make one side of their dam, which stretched across the harbor. It was a rusting wall of trucks and old ships hammered and welded together to form a sieve that allowed fish and smaller garbage past, but kept the more dangerous pieces away from the main dock. The rest of the island was kept clear by currents or jagged rocks. There was only one way into Gozo and that was through the dam.

As the *Phoenix* approached, a system of pulleys and winches allowed attendants to lift the top of the outer barrier, like a swing bridge.

Amit and Ajay swarmed up the rigging and furled the sails, wrapping them tightly to banish the wind and hold the *Phoenix* back.

Slowly, using only her paddle power, the *Phoenix* passed the raised junk. Toby turned to watch as the shadow of the barrier fell over his face. His heart raced as the paddles propelled them forward. Even Ayla had gone completely still. Toby barely breathed as the *Phoenix* chugged into the gap between the two walls. The junk that had been jostling at the dam wall flowed in alongside their ship. Rotting sofas, tumble driers, and truck beds capered in the waves.

As the wall closed behind them Toby felt even more confined, as though the *Phoenix* had been imprisoned. They were surrounded by a dark well that seemed to be pressing closer with every pitch of the ship. In front of Toby, the cab of a truck peered into the ship, the windshield a cobweb of shattered glass.

The *Phoenix*'s paddles still ran, trying to push her through the dam, but she couldn't move and her frustrated churning rattled around them.

Ayla's hand closed on Toby's.

"What if the *Phoenix* needs to leave quickly?" D'von murmured.

"The *Phoenix* isn't staying." Ayla squeezed his fingers. "She'll anchor close enough to the beach so we can go ashore then she'll leave again, to meet *Birdie*. She'll be waiting for us off the coast of Malta."

"What's your business in Gozo?" The voice from the top of the dam reverberated from the metal walls and echoed over the *Phoenix*.

Toby jumped as the captain replied through his bull-horn.

"This is the *Phoenix*. We're bringing Sun and Moon candidates for the festival. Two pairs."

There was no reply and the *Phoenix* remained locked in suspension, tilting from side to side with the waves, her paddles pushing her nowhere.

"There's something wrong," Rita whispered.

Then there was a rushing sound as the sluice gates opened. The *Phoenix* banged against the inner gate as the tide pulled her forward. Toby gasped as the deck jerked beneath him. He leaned over and watched the last of the junk, a plastic shopping basket, and a black garbage bag that sucked and slid in the waves, slide through the gates, then the sluices closed.

Toby tightened his fingers around Ayla's as the wall in front of them began to ascend. The rusting truck lifted until its jagged windshield stared down at Toby from above.

A sliver of light appeared at the bottom of the *Phoenix* and worked its way up her rusting sides, highlighting the faded bird painted on her, the hawsepipe from which the anchor emerged and, finally, the little skiff, *Wren*, the small boat Ayla had arrived in, which was now hanging from *Birdie*'s winches, the gunwale and the crew. Toby stared ahead.

In front of them was the harbor. Trash floated on the waves but nothing like they had sailed through. A line of lobster baskets bobbed ahead of them, and on the pier he could see children lifting crab lines and mussel nets from brackish water.

"We're here," he murmured.

"It's time to go below." Polly nudged his cheek. "We need to anchor, so you'll have to put the paddles into reverse."

Toby patted her with his free hand, his fingers still hesitant over her metal body.

"You know you can't bring Polly into the sanctuary." Ayla tilted her head at him.

Polly squawked angrily and Toby stroked her head. "She's right, Pol. The sun worshippers might decide to keep you, or worse, destroy you."

Polly bobbed up and down. "I thought I was going. You'll need me in there."

The captain's heavy tread made them all jump. His hand descended on to Toby's left shoulder.

"This is the point when we have to trust that we've taught Toby enough to survive without us. Do you think we've taught him enough, Polly?"

"Yes, but—"

"Then that's that." The captain lifted Polly from her perch and placed the parrot on his own shoulder. "Go below, Toby. There's work to do before we dock."

In the boiler room, Toby found Hiko filling the compressor with combustibles.

"I wondered where you were. Didn't you want to watch us sail through the dam?" Toby approached the control panel, pulling his goggles over his eyes.

"This needed doing." Hiko kept his head down, his back to Toby.

"It could have waited." Toby pressed the lever that diverted steam from one delivery line to another. He felt the *Phoenix* judder, stop, then, slowly, begin to reverse. On deck he knew the captain was directing Rita to steer the *Phoenix* to a safe anchorage, close to the shore.

He rubbed away the sweat that threatened to drip into his eyes. Hiko was determinedly shovelling, still refusing to look up. The light from the porthole showed his shoulders hunched and tension in the lines of his arms and back.

"Are you all right?" Toby stepped closer.

"I'm fine." Hiko's shovel jammed against the hull with a clang and he shook the vibration out of his fingers before he returned to his work.

Toby moved closer. "Stop for a minute."

Hiko shook his head. "I'm your assistant, so I'll be engineer while you're gone. I'm getting started, making sure everything works right . . ."

"Everything here is shipshape." Toby caught Hiko's shoulder and he jumped.

"Just talk to me. I'll be leaving soon."

"I know." Hiko threw the spade down and it clattered across the floor.

"You're angry?" Toby blinked.

"You're going without me," Hiko blurted, finally turning. His eyes were rimmed with red. "Remember last time you were on land. You can't even *walk* straight."

"I'll have Ayla to watch my back." Even as Toby said it, he realized that his words were probably no comfort to the boy who had been caged on the *Banshee*.

Hiko's fists clenched at his side. "You don't know everything, Toby," he snapped. "You know the sea, but I know land better'n you. I should be going." He pulled away and pointed to his own thick mop. "I have black hair. *I* could be your partner." His voice dropped. "I'd have your back *and* I'm small. What if you need someone to crawl through a vent to get the inverters? Ayla can't do that."

Toby cleared his throat. "You're right, you'd be a better partner." He pulled Hiko to the floor and sat beside him, one arm around his shoulder. "But Ayla said it had to be a boy and girl."

"Why? Two boys can be partners, so can two girls. I saw it in the slave market."

"True." Toby nodded. "But I think it's a contrasts thing: sun, moon; light, dark; boy, girl. See?"

Hiko squirmed free. "I get it." He kicked at a dried chunk of MDF. "What if you don't come home?"

"I'll be back," Toby promised. "And knowing you're here, doing my job for me, means I'll have one less thing to worry about."

"Huh." Hiko looked toward the porthole. "I won't know if you need help. Polly won't even be watching."

"I'll have to rely on Ayla." Hiko sneered at that. Toby touched his arm. "She was great in Tarifa, wasn't she?"

Hiko sighed. "I'm going to keep translating that map. Maybe I'll have it done by the time you get back."

"That would be great." Toby grinned.

"Don't tell Ayla," Hiko begged suddenly.

Toby shook his head. "I'm telling her you can't do it. Just in case."

"So you *don't* trust her . . ." Hiko's eyes glittered in the dim light.

Toby sighed. "She's promised not to betray me while we're inside the sanctuary."

"Do you trust her to bring you home?" Hiko leaned close, looking for a lie in Toby's face.

Toby shook his head. "I'll bring myself home."

For the first time in his life, Toby placed his foot on the gangplank of the *Phoenix*.

"What are you waiting for?" The plank shook as Ayla loped past.

The captain waited until Ayla had left the ship. "It's not too late to change your mind."

Toby shook his head. "I'm doing this." He took a step. The *Phoenix* tilted beneath him.

"Another adventure for us," D'von lisped; then he put his arm through Toby's and they walked down the plank together. The captain followed, but his face was grim.

As soon as his toes touched rock, Toby stumbled, feeling disoriented as the land failed to move beneath him. He took his time to get his land-legs, stepping across the rocks and using D'von to help him balance. Ayla was already striding smoothly onto a short stone pier, her hair shining in the glow of the bronze sun that hung above the cathedral.

Rahul jumped on to the shore behind the captain. "I'm coming with you," he called. "At least to the gates. Uma insisted."

As the captain nodded his agreement, Toby followed Ayla onto the pier and looked around.

To his left, another two teenagers were clambering over the rocks; a girl with shoulder-length blonde waves and a boy whose hair was almost exactly the same length and texture, but black. At the same moment, the pair looked up and Toby blinked at the matching blue stares. Their chins were tilted at the exact same angle, their narrow forearms raised to protect their eyes from the sun.

"A matching pair," Ayla lowered her voice as she scoped them out. A small row boat rocked behind them, tied up against the jetty. Inside, a woman with eyes like chips of blue topaz was waving at the twins.

Toby caught up with Ayla. "How can we compete with twins? They've got to be who the sun worshippers are looking for. What could be more perfect?"

A shadow passed over Ayla's eyes.

The captain caught up with them. "We knew there would be

other candidates arriving today. They look good, but you and Ayla look good, too. And if they choose based on hair color alone, Rita's blonde is brighter than the girl's. Don't second-guess."

"And if we're not picked?" Toby clenched his fists. Until now, he hadn't entertained the thought that they might not even get past the first hurdle.

"We think of something else," the captain replied.

Rahul put an arm around Toby's shoulder. "Let's find out where you have to go." He nodded upward. Ahead of them, standing at the end of the pier, a single brother stood. The light bounced from his bowed head and a pendant showing what looked like the Solaris logo dangled in front of long gray robes. He looked up as they approached.

"*Benvenuto.* Welcome." He raised one hand as if to prevent them from coming nearer. "You are here for the festival?" He looked particularly at Rita and Toby and offered a thin smile. "You are quite late. The choosing begins in two hours—when the sun is at its highest."

Ayla stepped to Toby's side. "That's why we're here." The beads in her hair clattered and the brother blinked.

"Two couples then." The brother glanced at D'von who was standing next to Rita, obviously unsure whether or not to take her arm.

"Trois." As one, the twins marched in front of Toby and Ayla.

"Three," the girl corrected her brother. "English, Adrien."

"Yes, Adele." He looked sideways at Toby. "We are here to be chosen." He nodded at the man's pendant. "Praise *Soleil.*"

The man's head dipped in acknowledgment and Ayla stiffened.

The captain's deep voice replied, "Of course. Praise the Sun." He slid swiftly between Ayla and the twins. "Where is it our couples need to go?"

The brother gestured in the direction of a narrow path that led up the cliff edge that bisected the island.

"Let's go then." The captain hustled them toward the path, Rahul dropped back to shadow them. Once more the brother raised his hand.

"The applicants go alone."

The captain looked back at the French mother sitting in her boat. His lips pressed together. She had already known.

Adele and Adrien marched on with their eyes fixed on the sunlit belfry.

"It's all right," Toby said as the captain pulled him to one side.

"I thought I'd be saying goodbye up there." Barnaby tilted his head to indicate the main entrance.

"Either way it's the same," Ayla said.

The captain ignored her. "Be careful, Toby." He gave him a swift, tight hug. Then he looked at Rita and D'von. "You, too." He stared at Ayla for a long moment. "You remember your cover stories?"

"Of course." Ayla looked insulted.

"Then look after each other," he said.

Rahul shook Toby's hand. "Good luck." He clapped D'von on the shoulder.

"We won't set sail until tomorrow," the captain started back toward the ship. "Just in case."

"You mean in case we don't get in," Rita muttered.

The captain nodded. "Assuming you *do* get in I'll send Rahul with the little boat, *Wren*, to watch the northernmost point of the island—just in case you get out early. We'll have to anchor the *Phoenix* off Malta first, and Rahul has to sneak into position without being spotted, so it'll be a day or two before he's looking for you. Until then, you're on your own. If Rahul doesn't pick you up, the *Phoenix* will be back for the festival."

Toby smiled. "We'll be fine." He moved to Ayla's side. "We'll be eating good food, relaxing in the sun, and looking for the inverters when everyone else is asleep. There's nothing to worry about."

"I'm going to enjoy the break." Rita stretched. "Come on, D'von." She shoved the big teen ahead of her toward the pathway.

Toby squeezed his father's hand. "See you in three weeks."

The captain pounded up the gangplank and Toby looked one last time at the *Phoenix*. The giant ship rose and fell on the tide, her rusting orange hull like a piece of evening sunlight that rested on the sea.

He turned back to the pathway; Rita and D'von were racing ahead. He fell into step with Ayla and together they followed their crewmates, only swaying slightly now with the stillness of the land.

EIGHT

The path they climbed wound along the jagged cliff. At first, Toby's bare toes kicked up sand as he walked, but the sand gradually turned to dust. When he looked over the cliff edge, he could see houses, like teeth, submerged beneath the waves. Gaping roofs and landslides of tile and brick were revealed and then hidden by salt spray and clumps of rubbish that had passed through the dam. Through one unbroken window he could see a drowned living room: children's toys floating against the pane—a doll with her arm outstretched, as if pleading for rescue.

He shuddered and turned to Ayla; she faced the sanctuary. Now that he was closer, Toby could see patterns cut into the gray concrete wall. Sunbursts covered the stone; some of them carved deeply, others mere scratches. Some of the images glittered with shining stones, had glass embedded in the center, or long rays made from chains of beads. Directly ahead the path forked; one way—their way—headed into a low archway that bisected the wall, the other led into a formation of houses.

The properties were squat, with no chimneys; what would be the point in a world where combustibles had all but vanished?

The walls were whitewashed and there were no trees planted in the wide streets. Everything was designed to reflect the sun.

The streets remained silent as they passed the fork; no voices greeted them, no eyes followed their path.

"Where is everybody?" Toby whispered.

"When you get past the ports and go inland, this is what most land is like," Ayla replied. "Almost everyone died from wars, disease, or starvation. You think there're a lot of people on land because you've only seen the docks, but that's just where most people ended up. Inland it's like this almost everywhere."

"But there must be people here somewhere, you said—"

"They're all sun worshippers and today's a big day. They'll be up there." Ayla pointed. "Waiting for us."

Toby exhaled. "Do you think we're the last to arrive? How many couples do you think are up there?"

Ayla smiled. "At least *trois*." She pointed as Adele and Adrien passed through the arch, D'von and Rita close behind them. "Are you ready for this?" She adjusted the collar of her jacket. "How do I look?"

Toby cleared his throat. "You look fine." He stared at his filthy feet. "Me?"

Ayla used her palm to brush a rain of grit from his hair. "You look fine, too."

"Okay." Toby held out his hand. "Let's go."

Ayla closed her fingers around his arm. "It'll be like catching lobsters in a pot," she said.

Inside the archway, Toby found himself facing another wall. As his eyes adjusted, he saw a solid gate.

"This must be where deliveries are left." Ayla indicated a hatch with a nod of her head. Toby nodded and she knocked.

The hatch creaked open and a second brother stared out at them. This one had blond hair, paler and shorter even than Toby's. "State your business with the Solar Order," he said in a Gozoan accent.

"We're here for the festival." Ayla gestured at Toby. "He's the Sun."

The brother cracked a lopsided smile. "Of course he is." He vanished from the hatch and Toby heard the creak of bolts being drawn. Then the gate opened and Toby gasped. Ignoring the brother altogether, he stepped into a square as big as the deck of the *Phoenix*, drawn by the building that faced him.

The stone of the old Catholic cathedral was pale; golden in the noon sun and Toby could see watermarks halfway up each pillar where the building had stood against the battering of the sea.

A larger-than-life-size statue of the Virgin Mary raised her arms in an alcove above a vast vaulted door that would once have been made of wood, but was now a mishmash of sun-burned metal. The iconic statue now sported a bright copper sunburst on her head. Covering half-seen coats of arms, more images of the sun surrounded the doors.

On the top of the building was the giant circle of bronze that they had seen from the *Phoenix*. Toby shaded his eyes with his free arm.

"There're the people." Ayla pulled Toby past a crowd of native Gozitans. Gathered behind a cordon, they leaned close to watch them pass; hollow-eyed and hungry-looking. When their murmuring rose, Toby edged farther away and looked for Rita and D'von.

Rita's bright hair stood out even in the crowd of younger teens gathered around her.

“Did you expect so many?” Toby muttered under his breath.

Ayla swallowed. “Of course.” But she didn’t meet his eyes.

They walked over to the large group. Toby was taken aback by the differences in the shades of blond and dark that faced him. The variations ranged from a girl with dark blonde, almost brown hair that was cut into a short mohawk, to a true white-haired albino boy whose pink eyes followed Toby as he came to a stop.

The youngest of their competitors, a delicate-looking doll of a girl, seemed no older than thirteen.

Toby looked at Rita, trying to view her with a critical eye. Was her age noticeable to the others? She was eight years older than Toby, but seemed younger than that. Toby wasn’t sure if she could pass for an old-looking sixteen, but she and D’von did make a good pair. Toby waited for a twinge of jealousy, but felt none. He was completely over his youthful crush. He looked sideways at Ayla, who stood next to him. “Now what?”

“We wait,” she replied. “They make their selection at midday, remember? There’s a sundial if you want to track it.”

Toby couldn’t take his eyes from the line of the sundial. He was not the only one. The crowd behind the cordon tracked the moving shadow, with pointing fingers and restless eyes. And as it drew nearer to the center of the square, the murmuring of the other pairs quietened, enough for him to be able to make out individual conversations.

“Praise the Sun.” His chin jerked up at the almost defiantly angry tone. A boy with dark hair so fine that it stuck to his head in sweaty streaks stood before a swarthy teen whose crater-marked face told Toby he had suffered a pox and ignored anyone who had told him not to scratch.

The younger boy had clenched fists and, even though his words were prayerful, he spoke through gritted teeth.

"You're such a dupe," the older boy sneered. "You believe all this sun crap."

"Why are *you* here?" the younger boy raged. "This is a festival for worshippers of the Sun. Non-believers shouldn't be here."

"Ha!" The swarthy boy cracked his knuckles.

His companion, a wispy-looking blonde, narrowed her eyes. "Obviously, we're here for the money." She rubbed her hands together.

"What money?" Toby looked at Ayla.

She looked mystified. "Sebastiane didn't say anything about money."

"You should be here for the glory of the Sun," the younger boy insisted. "Not for your own gain."

Toby realized that the watchers nearest them had fallen silent and were listening as intently as he.

"You have to admit the money helps." Another girl, whose hair was a dark brown mass of straw, spoke with a thick Hungarian accent. "We're here for the glory of the Sun." She looked at the younger combatant. "But would we be here if it weren't for the promise of the stipend for our family?" She shrugged. "Maybe not."

"If they offer us money, we will turn it down," the boy spat. "Is that not right, Lenka?"

"Yes, Matus. Those of us left in Croatia know the meaning of true devotion." The girl's fine blonde hair looked as if she had poked a finger in a socket. It stuck up around her head in a flyaway mass that matched her wide, shocked-looking eyes and the two permanent worry lines that sat between her eyebrows.

The crowd murmured its approval and the small group realized they had been overheard. The straw-headed Hungarian tossed her hair and swaggered closer. Toby saw with a jolt that her nails were possibly the longest he had ever seen, like claws. How did she do any work?

"We understand devotion," she snapped, raising her voice for the benefit of the audience. "But we also know how to survive. The more of us who live to worship the Sun, the greater the glory of the Orb."

"Ha! The Order will see through your contempt for the Sun's glory."

"A bunch of idiots who went blind staring at the sky—I don't think so." The crater-faced young man laughed and his companion joined in. The Hungarian couple looked nervous and backed away, swiftly disassociating themselves as the crowd's quiet developed a hostile edge.

"A bunch of idiots?" The voice that hissed out over the square ended in a sibilance that sent chills down Toby's spine. When Toby turned, he saw a man with the milky eyes of the sunblind, facing the mocking speaker as though he could see him.

"I am Father Dahon. Come to face me," the man whispered.

The young man and his wispy companion looked at one another.

"I will not repeat myself." Although he didn't move, the father's anger seemed to make him grow in size. Toby stared at him. He had a low widow's peak and his black hair was oiled back from his brow. His face and hands were deeply tanned, but the arms that protruded from his long sleeves were as pale as his eyes.

The swarthy boy with the terrible skin finally recovered his bluster. He dragged his companion to the front of the group.

"We didn't mean—" she began.

"Silence." The father turned to someone behind them. "Are these good candidates?"

From deep in the shadows behind the father a woman appeared. Her eyes were so deeply overhung by her sockets that Toby couldn't tell what color they were. Her cheekbones protruded almost as far as her forehead and her lips were so thin and colorless that Toby could barely see them move when she answered.

"The blond is average in coloration; she would make a middling Sun."

The girl gasped and her partner kicked her into quiet.

"Neither would the boy be any loss."

The crowd jeered its approval and the couple flinched as their disdain rolled over them.

The father turned back to the couple. "Leave."

"W-what?" the young man protested. "You can't do that. We have no way off the island."

"Then we will allow you to remain on Gozo until the pilgrimage, when you should be able to find passage. You had better hope that you are a better fisher than a devotee. And, as all who live on the island must abide by our rules, we will expect to receive three-quarters of all you catch and mandatory prayers at sunrise, noon, and sunset in at the island's center. You will be watched."

The father raised his head as if to look past them, dismissing the couple from his world as effectively as though he had erased them altogether. The crowd clapped as they stumbled out of the area reserved for the candidates.

Toby leaned close to Ayla, hoping that she had learned the same lesson he had. "Praise the Sun," he said, pointedly.

Ayla nodded. "Praise the Sun."

"I am Mother Hesper." The woman spoke almost reluctantly, as though her name was precious knowledge that she was squandering by saying it out loud. "Before we enter the sanctuary"—she raised her right hand and spread her skeletal fingers and Toby realized she was making an approximation of the sun's rays—"we require you to allow attendants to wash your hair." She gestured and a line of fully sighted men and women appeared, each carrying a sloshing bucket of water. Each wore identical knee-length robes and sandals made from tire rubber. "If you must address an attendant, you can do so as Brother or Sister."

"Is she serious?" Toby blinked.

"I suspect she's always serious." The boy who answered him was as large as D'von. His dark curls formed a line along his forehead. "I'm Arthur." His voice was deep. He held out his hand.

"Toby." Toby shook and smiled. "We don't know much about this ritual."

"Your missionary didn't tell you?"

Ayla spoke before Toby could answer. "He died before he gave us all the details. But from the little he told us, we knew it was something we both very much wanted. Praise the Sun."

"Well, Summer knows everything it's possible to know. She studied and studied under our minister." Arthur shifted and Toby saw the tiny blonde doll he had noticed before. "We're from Cornwall. I heard your accent, you're St. George?"

Swiftly Ayla shook her head. "We're from Saunders," she said coldly.

"Where's that?" Even the girl's voice was tiny; a squeak, like that of a squeezable toy.

"The Falklands," Toby added, confident in this part of the backstory they had planned. "It's basically a big sheep farm."

"And that's why you sound Georgian." Arthur nodded. "No offense but we seceded from St. George a few years ago and there's still a lot of resentment."

"Too right. Who doesnae hate th' Georgians?"

Toby spun, alarmed, and came face to face with the lanky freckled girl he had seen earlier, whose dirty-blonde hair rose above her head in sharpened spikes. She was eyeing him with deep suspicion. "You sure ye arenae Georgian? Ye sound like it."

"We hate the Georgians as much as you do," Ayla snapped. "Believe me."

The girl must have seen something in Ayla's face because she sniffed, mollified. "All right. Our dads died in th' North Brine wars, see—mine and Brody's. They were brothers." She gestured to an equally freckly, stocky boy. Brody's hair was as darkly brown as the girl's was blonde. "I'm Moira."

Ayla nodded. "My family was killed by Georgians. You won't get an argument from me." She looked at Summer. "So we have to wash our hair; then what?"

"Then we go inside," Summer said. "No one knows much about

what happens then, no one has ever told. I just know there are competitions . . . tests of devotion."

"We're good at competitions." Brody grinned, revealing teeth almost as brown as his hair.

"So are we," Toby added.

"What sort of competitions?" Rita leaned close. "What'll we have to do?"

Summer turned to Rita. Her long pale hair reached the waist of her baggy cream dress and it rippled as she shrugged. "No one knows—it's a big secret."

Rita tutted and looked at the buckets of water. "Well, we'd better get started."

Ahead of them a line was forming. Each candidate had to kneel down and face the crowd, then an attendant poured a bucket of water over their hair and scrubbed.

"Is that soap caustic?" Rita was horrified. "That's not touching my hair."

"They're checking for dye," Summer explained, anxiously touching her own gleaming and perfectly brushed golden waves.

One girl at the front of the line was resisting as the sister behind her tried to force her to kneel. "It isn't necessary. My hair is fine. Look at it, dark as night."

"It's natural, I can vouch for her." Her partner's platinum curls glinted as he moved to her side.

"Quiet." Father Dahon spoke once more. "Either you submit to the washing or you leave without it."

Toby strained to see as the girl grimaced and, slowly, kneeled.

As the attendant behind her sloshed water over her head, she clenched her fists. Then the woman scrubbed her scalp. When she was finished she pulled the girl's head up. Dark streaks covered her face from her hairline to her chin.

"Dyed," she spat, pushing her to the ground. The girl landed in the dirt, her mousey tresses flopping in front of her.

"You can't treat her like that." Her partner dropped to the ground beside her. "We believe more strongly than anyone else here. Who would be a better Sun and Moon?"

"You were not meant to be in the festival." Mother Hesper stared down. "If you truly believe, submit yourselves to the sanctuary to become attendants, as these have done, or sunblind yourselves as an act of worship. Leave."

The sobbing girl rose to her feet, helped by her companion. They plodded slowly after the couple who had already left. This time the crowd was quiet, simply watching them as they departed.

"Two couples down," Rita whispered.

Toby nodded. "Eight to go."

The candidates stood in a line. Toby's knees ached where he had been held down and his head tingled from being scrubbed, hard. His shoulders were wet and he was grateful for the cool, but the sun was fast drying him out. All along the line, blonds were brighter and water had turned dark hair black. No one else had been sent home.

He squinted sideways to see Ayla untangling her braids. One of the brothers had tried to remove her beads and received a vicious pinch for his troubles.

Summer stood to his left, the doll-like girl looking like a tiny mermaid with her wet hair stuck to her face and arms. Arthur hovered beside her, looking like he wanted to put his arm around her, but didn't dare. Toby caught his eye and offered a slight smile—allies were valuable in every situation. His smile was returned.

Father Dahon walked the line, inspecting them. When he reached the center he stopped and turned to the crowd. "True believers of Gozo, our candidates will speak to you for the last time until you meet the true Sun and Moon from among them."

He gestured and the girl at the far end blinked water out of her eyes. "Me?"

"Yes. Who are you, where in this world are you from and declare yourself—Sun or Moon?"

The girl caught the hand of the boy next to her. Her dark hair was so thick that, even wet, it overpowered the delicate features of her face. "I'm Celeste and this is Aldo."

The boy's blond hair was so fine that Toby could see his scalp. His nose was large, but there was something indefinably handsome about his face. He squeezed Celeste's hand and gave her a smile. "I'm hoping to be the Sun and Celeste the Moon. We have been sent by the priest of the community near Pompeii, in Italy. Praise the Sun."

Father Dahon inclined his head. "I have heard good things about your community. You have your own colony of the sunblinded, do you not?"

Celeste nodded, then realized that Father Dahon would not be able to see her. "We spent a year tending to their needs, Your Worship."

"Good, good." The father moved on to the next couple in line as the crowd murmured its approval.

Toby leaned forward, fascinated. The next to speak was the albino boy that he had seen earlier. He was standing next to a girl with even darker skin than Theo's from the *Phoenix*. Her hair was cut close to her head and her tight curls were glossy in the sun. To Toby, it seemed almost as if she had been polished.

"My name is Uzuri," the girl said, folding her arms over her chest.

"And I, Zahir," said the boy. He kept his eyes cast down, squinting every time he tried to look up.

Their accents were strange to Toby's ears, clipped yet somehow smooth, like a river flowing over stones.

"Our village is a day's walk from Cape Town. We were born on the same day, at the same time to two different mothers." The boy smiled shyly. "Most men in my country would have killed me for the magical powers of my skin, but the moment we were presented to our Solar missionary, he pronounced our destiny—to become the Sun and Moon. Since that moment, we have been preparing for today."

"And now we are here." Uzuri held her head proudly, like a queen. "I am to be the Moon and Zahir the Sun." She looked down the line as if to say "and the rest of you may leave."

Ayla twitched as the Scottish girl, Moira, curled her lip. Again, the crowd seemed to radiate admiration for the pair.

"Ah'm Moira and this is ma cousin, Brody. We're from Glasgow. We don't have parents—we were raised mostly by the Solar Mission near the docks. That's why we're here. Father Zee said this was the place fer us."

Brody grinned, his freckles glimmering in the sun. "I'm the Moon an' Moira's the Sun. You cannae see it, Yer Worship, with her hair wet, but her Mohawk"—he tilted his head toward his cousin—"that represents the sun's rays. Praise the Sun."

"Nice," Ayla whispered.

"They've all got perfect stories." Toby clenched his fists.

She leaned into his ear. "So do we," she whispered.

The big lad, Arthur, introduced himself next. "We're from Cornwall, the survivors of the shattered coastline gathered in the old Eden project. Summer's been obsessed with the sun since she was born; she knows everything there is to know about the Orb and its worship. She's read every book, taken every lesson. She's the best Sun you'll ever get."

"And you?" The priest cocked his head and Arthur swallowed at the minute gesture.

"I'm with Summer. I'll be the Moon to her Sun and you'll never have a better."

This divided the watching crowd, some cheered and others frowned. "Never have a better?" Toby heard insulted muttering.

"I see." Father Dahon stroked his chin and took the final step that brought him in front of Toby. He was silent for a moment; then he gestured, sharply. "You?"

"My name's Toby." Suddenly their cover story seemed flimsy. What if the father knew the Saunders colony or the missionary stationed there? What if one of the other couples was from the Falklands?

Ayla sensed his hesitation and took over. "I'm Ayla." Her beads clattered as she glared at the priest. "We're from Saunders, in the Falklands. Not many survivors there, but those left are true worshippers. Your Solar missionary died not long after he arrived at the island, from a disease he caught in the Argentinian mainland." She shook her head sadly. "He told us of the Sun Festival." She pressed her hand to her heart and sniffed, feigning deep grief. "Toby and I were with him when he died. His very last words to us were that we should make him proud. All he wanted was to know that he had been the one to find the couple who would lead the festival." She wiped away a tear and Toby's eyes widened.

"I, of course, will be the Moon." Ayla lifted one of her braids. "Toby is the Sun."

Father Dahon bowed his own head. "What was the name of this missionary priest, so I can remember him in my prayers?"

Toby caught his breath, but Ayla was prepared. "He told us only to call him Father, Your Worship." She gave a small sob and Father Dahon pressed his lips together. Then he folded his hands and moved on. Toby's racing heart almost drowned out the crowd's sounds of sympathy and support. They had been believed.

Rita and D'von were next. D'von's eyes were red-rimmed where his attendant had been too industrious with the soap, but he seemed unconcerned. Rita, the consummate con artist, was to tell their story.

"This is D'von." Rita smiled. "He was a dock rat in Tarifa."

"I was," D'von hastened to add to the one part of their story he was comfortable with. "I was a dock rat and it was hard, hard work."

Rita rolled her eyes. "He heard the Solar Mission preach one day and knew he wanted to come to the festival. He stowed away on the ship I was working on. When I heard his story, I was moved. I realized that we were meant to meet. We worked our way from ship to ship till we found one that was heading to the festival." Rita patted D'von's hand. "I am the Sun"—she tossed her bright golden hair—"D'von is the Moon."

Toby held his breath, but again the crowd seemed to like Rita and her story.

The Croatians were next. The girl didn't wait for Father Dahon to ask her to speak. She stepped out of the line and fluffed at her drying hair, which was already reassuming its flyaway appearance, sticking out all over her head. "I am Lenka," she said clearly, "and this is Matus. I am the Sun and he is the Moon. Praise the Sun." She raised her hand, fingers splayed and Matus did the same. "We are from Zagreb, where we worship the Sun day and night, night and day. We want no money, no glory, we simply wish to worship the Sun in the best way we can. This is our way. We are not here to make friends, we are here to win." She stepped back into the line, ignoring the stunned crowd, who appeared torn between cheering and staring, wide-eyed, settling instead on awed silence. Her heel caught the French girl's foot and Adele narrowed her eyes and hissed at her, before linking arms with her twin.

There was no mistaking their relationship. They were perfectly in sync as they moved, their mannerisms identical, their heads held at the same angle, the expression in their sapphire eyes the same.

Toby heard gasps of appreciation as the Gozitans took in the sight.

"I am Adele," the girl said. "And this is Adrien. We are twins. Our only differences are to make us a more perfect Sun and Moon. I am blonde and he is dark," she said for the benefit of the blind Father Dahon. "We are from Brittany. There are not many survivors in our village, but we who are left are strong and firm in faith." They stepped back together, blending back into the line and Father Dahon smiled.

"I-I'm Leila," the next girl said, when beckoned. She had a yellow-blonde fluff of hair, like the head of a dandelion, but her eyes were brown.

"Is that an *American* accent?" Rita murmured.

"I'm not sure." Toby nudged her to keep listening.

The boy overheard. "I'm Noah. Our family live in Agadir now." He adjusted a pair of battered glasses, then, after a hesitation, "But our parents were born in Maine, in America. They evacuated after the eruption of Yellowstone. We have more reason than anyone to want to avert a second cataclysm; we want to do the Sun's work. I am the Moon and my sister is the Sun."

Ayla whistled under her breath. "Real Americans! Thought they were extinct. Didn't the Russians bomb the states that weren't wiped out by the volcano?"

"They said Maine." Toby thought of Dee's atlas. "It was up by Canada, Maybe some got out." He turned to the final couple and stared. The girl was opening and closing her hands as she awaited her turn, displaying those long nails he had noticed earlier. The boy was nervous, fidgeting in his place.

The girl spoke first. "I am Bianca and I will be your Moon. My friend, Cezar, will be your Sun." She looked at her nails, turning them one way and then the other. "We are from Budapest. Our city selected us to come to the festival. We have been preparing in many ways." She held up her hands. "This is to prove that I have not worked. I have been only purifying and praising the Sun."

"They look like claws." Toby shuddered.

"They'd break the moment she touched something." Rita showed him her own short nails. "Don't worry about those."

Father Dahon had reached the end of the row. Now he turned to face the crowd of islanders. "These are exceptional candidates. As they compete to determine who will be the Sun and Moon, their trials will bring light to our island."

"Trials?" Toby met Ayla's eye and she spread her hands, pleading ignorance.

"With candidates as strong as these, this year will be a most successful festival. Pilgrims are already making their way here from all over the world, bringing relics and other trade. Make sure to take advantage of this—greet and house them. Make sure all relics are turned over to the sanctuary and remember the percentage you owe the church from each transaction. Attendants will be on hand to help you calculate."

Ayla snorted under her breath and Toby wondered exactly how the brothers and sisters enforced cooperation.

"You will not see these candidates again until the festival, but you have heard their names, now remember your favorites in your prayers."

The people cheered and Toby groaned. Rita and D'von were being let through.

Ayla put her mouth to his ear. "I thought someone would notice Rita."

"Me, too." He closed his eyes.

"We can't let D'von try to steal from the sanctuary. He'll be caught. He's too honest."

"I *know.*"

"I'm going to say something. If I don't, we'll lose the inverters and . . . we don't know what they'll do to him if they . . ."

"All right." Toby looked at his friend. D'von had a big smile on his face as he waved to the crowd. Slowly, miserably, he raised one hand and pointed to Rita. "Exactly how old *are* you?" he asked.

NINE

The look on D'von's face followed him up the steps of the old Catholic cathedral. Toby barely looked up as his pockets were emptied, although he felt relieved that he had left his tool belt on the *Phoenix.* He heard Ayla grunt crossly when her own clothes were rifled through. He had done the right thing, but he felt no better than Ayla: a traitor to his friends.

Rita had barely restrained herself from outing Toby in return, but she knew that he and Ayla were the *Phoenix*'s only chance to reach the inverters and she left in furious silence.

Miserable, Toby hardly looked at the stunning carvings that arched above him to cast twisted shadows on the sun-bleached steps.

"You should have let me do it," Ayla hissed.

"I can do my own dirty work." But Toby's shoulders remained stooped until he entered the cathedral and raised his head.

Then everything else was forgotten.

Although Father Dahon and Mother Hesper were already walking toward the nave, the group of teenagers had stalled.

"Praise Soleil . . . it's incredible." Adele grabbed Adrien's hand, all arrogance stunned out of her.

"It's all right, ah suppose," Moira said, absently, but her gaze was fixed on the domed ceiling that rose above them, where a tiny gecko climbed along a carved windowsill.

"Wait a minute." Ayla frowned. "There wasn't a dome on the outside, just that big bronze circle."

Mother Hesper turned. "Very observant. No, there is no dome—it is trickery of the eye. We allowed the design to remain, because it is"—the angles of her face softened momentarily—"quite beautiful."

She turned again, expecting the teens to follow her, but the group remained crowding the aisles. Beams of light speared downward from cross-shaped windows set high in the walls and dust motes played in the glow. Farther back a golden mosaic showed two figures. Toby shuddered when he realized that one held a severed head.

There were gaps where curtains had been torn from little chapels to side of him, and in each there hung an ornate chandelier, dust clinging to each glittering crystal.

Everything was gold: gold edging on every pillar, golden flowers across the vaulted ceiling, a filigreed suit of arms below the fake dome.

The floor was made of tombstone slabs from multi-colored marble. Emblazoned armorial shields, prancing animals, and twisting garlands commemorated the long-distant dead. With each hesitant step, Toby thought of the souls beneath him, whose house of worship had been so altered.

"This way," Mother Hesper said.

As the candidates stood gaping at the opulence surrounding them, a bell rang, then another and another, until five had been struck.

“That was a major chord in G natural,” Summer whispered with her eyes closed. “Glorious.”

“Yes.” Arthur’s deep voice resonated with the bass of the bell and Toby realized that, despite the wonders around them, Arthur had barely taken his eyes from Summer. Arthur cleared his throat and looked at Toby. “Summer’s a musician. She plays the flute. We’re going to get it sent over, just as soon as we’re crowned.”

“You mean when *we’re* crowned, doncha?” Moira sneered. “If there’re competitions to be done, you don’t stand a chance against me an’ Brody.”

“Ha.” Adele straightened. “Adrien and I will be crowned.”

“Not if we can help it,” Ayla hissed.

Before Toby could suggest that she focus on making allies rather than enemies, the hair on his neck stood on end. He turned.

From doors that had been hidden in the depths of the chapel, two lines of men and woman appeared. All wore floor-length robes, some gray and some brown, and their eyes, milky with swimming cataracts, stared at nothing. Walking as though they could see every step, their bodies swung in time to invisible music and their hands dangled at their sides, fingers twitching.

Slowly, they lined up along the aisles. There were no pews—they had long been burned—but cushions permitted them to kneel in surreally straight lines.

Toby rubbed his hands together, suddenly chilled. At the end of the right-hand line stood a familiar figure. Morris was there, thin as an oar, wearing a black robe, his head hanging, blind as the day he’d left the *Phoenix*.

“Praise the Sun.”

"Hail Soleil."

The teens who now clustered around Toby were whispering to themselves, using the familiar mantras for comfort. Automatically, Toby reached for Polly, but Ayla caught his fingers. "They're creepy," she whispered in his ear. "Not dangerous."

"I know." Toby looked around again. The robed sunblind appeared to be waiting for something.

"Midday prayers," Mother Hesper said, "are a little late today due to the opening of the festival. As you can see, our holiest sunblind brothers and sisters pray in the cathedral proper. Those in black went blind before they knew of us, through devotion to the new Sun. Those wearing gray robes blinded themselves as an act of worship since joining the Order. They are to be especially revered—some of them are previous Suns and Moons."

Toby gaped. This was the future that awaited the winner. Mother Hesper continued.

"Whenever you are not taking part in a challenge, you will pray at dawn, dusk, and midday precisely. The bells will be your call to midday prayer. Dawn and dusk you will be expected to recognize yourself."

"Where do we pray?" Lenka called.

The mother nodded. "For today, you will have the privilege of joining your sunblind brothers and sisters in prayers led by Father Dahon. On all other days you will pray in the rear courtyard, under the light of the Sun and the eyes of the attendants. The most devout of our brothers and sisters are also permitted to pray within the Reliquary, but at this time, you are not. Please kneel before the altar."

Toby found himself leading the suddenly nervous teens between the lines of blind brothers and sisters. He stopped by a row of empty cushions, lit by the sun that spilled through the open cathedral door. Lenka and Matus were the first to push past and drop to their knees.

Mother Hesper moved to the side of the altar and knelt, leaving Father Dahon standing before them, haloed in a shaft of sunlight.

"Praise the Sun." He raised his arms.

"Praise the Sun!" The reply echoed through the cathedral, multiplying the devotion until it filled the hall. Each made a sun sign against his or her chest. Toby and Ayla quickly copied them.

"On this day, as on every day, we praise the Sun, bringer of life. We give thanks for the gifts of warmth and light. We think of the years of darkness and give thanks for the lessons we have learned." Father Dahon bowed his head. "Pray with me."

Toby realized that every teen in the line was speaking along with the priest. Not only that but he could hear the words echoing from the square outside as the Gozitans, too, joined in. The sound was a tide rising and falling with the cadence of words. His heart raced: surely he and Ayla would be caught out by their quiet.

But then he realized that what Father Dahon was saying was an approximation of the Apostles' Creed. He had heard the Spaniards on board the *Phoenix* repeating it since he was small. By the second line, he was able to join in. Beside him he heard Ayla doing the same, keeping her chin low and quietly fudging a few words.

"We believe in one Sun, The Father, the Almighty, Heater of heaven and earth, Revealer of all that is seen and unseen.

We believe in one true Sun, The only Sun of earth, Eternally begotten of the stars.

Heat from heat, light from light, True Sun from true Sun, Begotten, not made, One in being with the universe.

Through Him all things are made, For humanity and our salvation, He moves through the heavens.

We believe in the Sun, The Lord, the giver of Life, Who proceeds from the East to the West.

With the Moon in the heavens, He is worshipped and glorified.

He has spoken through his absence.

We believe in one holy Order, We acknowledge one way to the forgiveness of our sins, We look for the Sunblind to lead us to new life in the world to come.

Amen."

Toby echoed the final word and relaxed his hand.

Rustling behind him caught his attention and he realized that the blind brothers and sisters were rising and filing out once more.

Ayla pulled at his sleeve. "Look at the stone," she whispered and Toby followed her eyes. The altar was a giant slab of granite, carved with deep-cut straight lines, dark in their depths.

"They look like . . ."

"Drainage," Ayla murmured. "Why would the altar need drainage?"

Toby glanced around them; the other teens remained kneeling, heads bowed.

Father Dahon retreated from the altar and Mother Hesper took his place.

"Stand," she said. The teens rose unsteadily to their feet.

Behind them, the vast cathedral door began to swing closed on hinges that squealed as they moved.

"This is your final chance to leave." Mother Hesper pointed to the narrowing portal. "Once the door is shut, you will be locked inside the sanctuary. You will be able to go into the rear courtyard and take part in trials, but you will not see the front square until the very end. You will be committed to us." She cast a glance at the altar so brief that Toby barely caught it. "Those of you who do not receive the honor of being crowned at the festival will nevertheless remain in the sanctuary as attendants to the Mysteries. This is its own reward."

The door was almost closed now; the gap in it only as wide as the passageways of the *Phoenix*.

Toby looked at the teens around him. Zahir was watching the sunlight disappear as though he might never see it again; his companion, Uzuri, made the sign of the Sun, while Moira and Brody shuddered as their view of the square and the Gozitan people vanished. Only Lenka and Matus seemed genuinely unmoved, facing the altar.

Now the gap was as thin as the vents Toby had once crawled through on the ship. "As if they could stop us leaving if we wanted to," Ayla snorted and, like Lenka, she turned deliberately away from her last view of the sunlit courtyard.

Although Toby wanted to mirror her, he was compelled to watch as the gap narrowed to a slim line.

There was a hollow slam as the doors came together and then a loud clicking.

"Automatic locks," said Cezar, the boy from Budapest. "Magnetic?" He frowned, and looked up at his companion as she poked him in the ribs with one of her long nails. "Sorry, Bianca."

Mother Hesper offered a more genuine, if thinner, smile. "As none of you have chosen to leave, let me tell you about your new home." She pointed to the door the blind priests had used. "The sunblind have quarters through there. At present, we have eighty-nine sunblind devotees who worship with us. They have dormitories, prayer rooms, bathing rooms, and a dining hall—these all remain private. Only they and their silent attendants are permitted inside. They are the holiest of the holy."

Toby thought of Morris, the Englishman who had been one of his father's original crew. His laugh had been loud and he knew more dirty jokes than Peel and Crocker. Now he was the holiest of the holy?

"The silent attendants are those who are privy to the deepest secrets of the sanctuary. They are the most trusted." Mother Hesper smiled at this. "Only candidates who enter the cathedral as Sun and Moon candidates, but fail the trials, may become silent attendants. If you meet a silent attendant, please show the utmost respect, but remember they will not speak to you, no matter what you say." She pointed to a recess beside them, where two armed attendants glowered in the shadows. "Behind that wall is the Reliquary, which used to be the crypt of the worshippers of the crucified god." She smirked. "During the first trial, you will be taken on a tour, at which time you will be permitted to worship before the relics and will learn which items are important to us in the unlikely event you should encounter them during the pilgrimage." She gestured to the opposite side, where a small archway led to a plain staircase that curved downward. "Through there are the attendants' quarters. At the moment, we have two hundred brothers and sisters in total. Anyone can ask to join our Order as an attendant, but only the most devout are accepted. Others join the community of worshippers on the island, or return home. The attendants are split into a hierarchy. The least important do the manual work in the sanctuary: cooking, cleaning, laundry, gardening, and so on. These you know as brothers and sisters. Then we have those who are guards, enforcers of the faith." She indicated the attendants standing outside the Reliquary. "Among their duties is to keep the islanders in line. If it is necessary for you to speak to a warrior, you will refer to him as Uncle."

"What of the female guards?" Ayla stood defiantly straight, as Toby glared at her.

Mother Hesper smiled. "There are none. Among the qualifications for guardianship are a strength and power to which women are unsuited."

Toby grabbed Ayla's arm, but she smiled coldly. "Of course."

"Finally, there are those who have completed their attendancy and have become mothers and fathers. Like myself. Most mothers and fathers work as missionaries or ministers to the faithful. At the moment, there are only five of us on the island: myself, Father Dahon and three others, who you are unlikely to meet."

"And through there?" There were two more doorways leading to the back of the cathedral. Adele and Adrien pointed together to the left one.

"This goes to the quarters of the mothers and fathers."

"And the other?" Adele demanded.

Mother Hesper smiled. "That leads to your own quarters, the bathing area, the dining room, and rear courtyard. When you are not being tested for the festival, you may move about this area quite freely and use the facilities as you see fit. As long as you remember your prayer times and, of course, that the Sun is always watching."

She made another sun sign and bowed her head. "I will show you this area, and then your meal will be served."

She turned and Toby caught Ayla's wrist to draw her attention. "It's enormous."

"I know," she hissed. "But we know where they'll be." She tilted her head at the crypt where the two uncles had subtly shifted their stance, closing their hands around their long clubs and emphasizing the muscles in their necks.

Toby's gaze skittered after Mother Hesper, who was holding open the door, her eyes glittering in the shadows.

"Come," she said.

Once the teens had gathered, Mother Hesper directed them along a short corridor and from there, into a large mess hall. Despite the pressure of Father Dahon's presence like invisible fingers on his spine, Toby's shoulders relaxed at the sight of long corrugated iron tabletops and lopsided stools made from old tires. His nostrils flared at the aroma of bread and stew.

Adele inhaled. "See, Adrien, I told you we would be looked after."

"You're assuming it's for us. Fools." Ayla marched after Mother Hesper, her long braids swinging, beads clacking together, as though the fragrance that had wound a spell around every other supplicant had hit a vacuum when it reached her. There seemed no sign that she had any interest in the stew she smelled. Then Toby saw her hands close into fists. Ayla craved all right, but had long ago learned not to show it.

He caught up to her. "Must you be so antagonistic?"

"Must you be so friendly?" She shot back. "This is a *competition*."

"I will show you to your cells and then you can come back here for your meal," Mother Hesper said. "This way."

"Praise Soleil . . . Hail the Sun . . . Always bright."

As the others demonstrated their gratitude, Toby gripped Ayla's arm. "Cells?" he said.

There were dozens of cells lined up. The gloom was only lightened by holes in the ceiling stopped up by transparent plastic bottles that let the sunlight through.

Each cell had a dirt floor, gray brick walls, and space for a small camp bed and a single tire stool.

"I don't understand." Summer looked around, her blonde hair shining in the kaleidoscope of light cast by the water bottle above her head. "It's so dark. I thought . . . the sun?"

"How can you appreciate the light of the sun if you do not begin your journey in darkness?" Mother Hesper pointed to a cell. "We all have lives of austerity in Solar Order, my own cell is not much bigger."

"Ave Soleil," Adele whispered, stepping closer to her twin.

"Choose your places." Father Dahon had followed them down the stairs and now he blocked what little light glimmered from above.

"Here then." Swiftly Ayla stepped into the cell nearest the stairs. Toby ducked into the doorway next to hers, marking it as his own.

Once Toby and Ayla had taken their places, there was a rush to choose: Arthur ended up next to Toby, Summer after, then Moira and Brody, Bianca and Cezar. Opposite, Zahir and Uzuri, Adele and Adrien, Lenka and Matus, and the two final pairs who Toby had not yet spoken to: the American couple and the Italians, Celeste and Aldo, whose fingers were still twined.

As he was memorizing who was in which spot, Ayla hissed at him under her breath and gestured to her door.

Toby frowned and looked. The doors were made from toughened plastic, not transparent, but not quite opaque, either. Each had a cluster of small holes cut into the front and sported a thick bolt.

Once they were closed, there would be no getting out of them. Toby and Ayla would have to steal their inverters in the light of day.

"Ashes," he whispered.

When the couples tried to sit next to one another in the mess hall, Mother Hesper held up her hand. "For meals and, of course, bathing, boys and girls will be separated." She pointed to a separate long table. "Boys over there." Then she sat at the head of the girls' table.

Toby saw that Father Dahon waited in front of the boys' and he forced his disappointment down; this was not the place to talk to Ayla about their mission anyway. Instead, he nodded and forced out a respectful, "Praise the Sun," as he moved into the group of boys and walked away.

Celeste and Aldo looked regretfully at one another and their fingers touched for as long as they could before they were separated. Ayla rolled her eyes and sat, with a flick of her braids, between Bianca, the girl from Budapest with the claws for fingernails, and Leila, the American with the hair of dandelion fluff. None of them spoke.

Toby had paid little attention to who had sat next to him. Now he checked. On his right was the albino, Zahir, and to his left Cezar, the boy with the limp. Arthur sat two places down on his left and

Brody on his right. Toby nodded to them and turned his own eyes to the kitchen, joining the others who were all tense with anticipation.

As the door opened, Father Dahon raised his hands to the sky, fingers spread. "For what we are about to receive, we are truly thankful to the Sun. Praise the Orb."

"Praise the Orb." Each of his companions raised their hands and eyes.

"Praise the Orb," Toby muttered, spreading his fingers.

Father Dahon turned his head, bird-quick, catching the slight delay in Toby's prayer, as if it was a note out of tune in an orchestra.

Toby ducked, even though there was no way for the father to see him. Then he shook his head and straightened. "What's the worst that can happen?" He gripped the fork that had been waiting for him on the corrugated table.

"Huh?" Cezar looked at him.

"I just . . ." Toby swallowed. "Nothing, I just wondered, what's the worst that can happen? What happens if we lose?"

Cezar blinked. "We'll be trained as silent attendants. Mother Hesper said so." He was turning his fork as though it contained a mystery of its own. Toby could almost see Cezar's brain ticking behind his eyes and he recognized a fellow inventor, one who wanted to know how things worked, to see how things fitted together.

Thoughtfully, Toby lifted his own fork. If he could twist off a tine, he might have something that he could use on the hinges or bolt of his door. Something in him rebelled utterly against allowing himself to be locked up with no tools on his side of the cell.

"Food's coming," Zahir said.

Toby looked up as attendants walked toward them, then leaned back as a bowl and bread roll were placed in front of him. The smell of stew filled Toby's senses and his eyes glazed over: spicy warmth, with a hint of onions on the back of his throat, garlic and the meaty flavor of the herbs. Peel was good, but he was a ship's cook and there was only so much you could do with seagull and herring.

"You think we'll eat like this every day?" Cezar grinned.

Beside him Zahir was leaning close to his own bowl, simply inhaling. Toby glanced across at Ayla. She remained unmoved, only the slightest flare of her nostrils indicating that she knew the food was in front of her. Did she think it was poisoned? Then he realized that she was challenging herself. He could tell Ayla planned to be the last to eat.

Without taking his eyes from her, Toby closed his fingers around the bread that lay on the tabletop. He smiled as he felt the warm dough give beneath the pressure. Once he had lifted his bread, Ayla gave a satisfied nod and picked up her own.

Zahir was licking his bowl clean. Toby watched him with quiet fascination. He himself had considered doing so, but somehow it seemed as though it was giving away too much of himself; exposing a vulnerability. Ayla, too, had left smears in her own bowl, like a badge of honor.

Even Adele, Toby saw, was delicately licking her fingers, her eyes closed with pleasure.

Finally, Zahir put his bowl down with a deep sigh and saw all the teens rubbing their stomachs, drowsily.

"Do you think we'll be given time to sleep?" Adrien stretched. "It's been a long day."

"That would be nice." Zahir nodded. "The journey from Africa was difficult."

"You arrived today? I didn't see another ship." Toby frowned, wondering if there was a second jetty somewhere, perhaps on the other side of the island.

"This morning. The crew dropped us off and left straight away. The captain was superstitious. Didn't want me on board any longer than necessary." Zahir's voice remained soft, but his eyes hardened.

"Why not?" Toby frowned.

He gestured to his face. "Red eyes, white hair—unnatural, is it not?"

Toby frowned. "Rare, but not unnatural, I don't think."

Zahir smiled slightly. "Well, our elders agreed with the Solar Order, that Uzuri and I could have only one destiny. Born in the same hour, at opposite ends of the village and looking like this"—he gestured toward his partner—"the elders will share the money once we are crowned."

"You do make a perfect pair," Toby agreed, thinking that he already had another potential ally in the group.

"This is about more than what we look like," Cezar interjected.

"How do you know?" Toby looked at him.

"It's obvious, isn't it?" This time Arthur leaned in. "If it was a beauty contest they would have just picked out a couple in the courtyard. Instead, we were brought in here. Mother Hesper mentioned trials. There'll be other challenges to face."

"I wonder what." Toby rubbed the left tine of his fork between his fingers, warming the junction where the prong met the handle. Then he wiggled it until he felt it twist. When it broke free with a snap, he placed the fork back on the table, slid the tine between two of his fingers, and closed his hand around it.

He looked up as a mug was placed in front of him.

Celeste's voice rang across her table. "Wine?"

Toby tilted his cup and sniffed. He'd had alcohol before—Crocker's rotgut hooch was a favorite of the other pirates on the ship. He didn't like it.

As Mother Hesper raised her cup, her robe slid back to reveal arms as thin as her face. "To the beginning of our journey together," she said. "Praise the Sun."

Around him, the other boys were raising their drinks.

Toby pushed his away, scraping the table as he did so.

"Drink, boy," Father Dahon's voice snapped out and Toby caught his breath. Those milky eyes were pinned on him. With a shudder he lifted his mug and took a sip. The wine was sour, too warm, and almost vinegar in flavor.

"Drain your mugs." Father Dahon drew out the last word until he hissed like a broken delivery line in the boiler room.

"What if we don't like it?" It was Summer. She had taken some of hers and was now regarding it with a curl of her coral lips.

"Knock it back." Mother Hesper wiped a smear of wine from her mouth.

Toby looked at Ayla. She raised her mug. How much was she used to drinking?

Toby took another sip and Ayla smirked. Without taking her eyes from his, she threw back her head and drained her mug in one go. Then she slammed it down on the table. As though her actions presented a challenge, Uzuri did the same thing, slamming her mug on to the table when she had finished.

"Looks like she's started the competition already." Arthur copied and soon all of the others had slammed their drinks. Only Toby and Summer continued to sip. Refusing to be rushed, Toby forced the liquor past numb lips and a tingling tongue.

Summer finished before him. When the girl had put down her mug with a grimace, Mother Hesper looked at Toby. "We're waiting."

Toby looked in his mug, he had a third left. Could he leave it?

Father Dahon spoke once more, as if Toby had asked the question aloud. "Drain it."

Toby made himself look into the father's empty eyes as he choked down the last of the gritty drink, then he tossed his mug on to the corrugated tabletop with a hollow clang. The mug rolled on its side, spilling a few final drops.

"Good." Mother Hesper nodded. "You are all competitors for the place of Sun and Moon, and so will have to undergo certain challenges, or trials."

The teens grew serious and still; the atmosphere chilled.

"The couples who lose each challenge will be removed from the group and will begin their roles as silent attendants. This will happen until there is only one couple left: the Sun and Moon."

Toby caught Ayla's eye. Maybe they should throw the competition. Perhaps it would be easier to search for the relics if they were not spending time doing these mysterious challenges. Attendants might have more freedom. As if she could sense his thoughts, Ayla shook her head. Determination flashed in her green eyes. She wanted to win.

"Now to the first challenge." Mother Hesper smiled. "The Sun rises and falls each day and night, but one who truly loves the Orb will sit up, waiting; desiring nothing but its return. And so the first challenge is to remain awake *until midday tomorrow*. The first couple to fall asleep before the next ringing of the bells will be disqualified from the competition. If no couple sleeps, then the first individual to have slept will have doomed his or her pair to failure."

"Wait." Summer's head snapped up. "But . . . you gave us alcohol."

"Yes." It was Father Dahon's turn to smile. "Yes, we did."

TEN

Now that Toby was unable to fall asleep, it was all he could think about. The combination of rich food and strong wine made his eyelids feel like slamming porthole covers. Warmth spread through his body from his stomach and, as he looked around the tables, he saw that he was not the only one struggling to keep his head up.

"Toby!" Ayla's voice snapped him out of it. "Get it together."

Around him, the other teens were straightening up in response to Ayla's warning.

Toby felt the fork tine still between his fingers. He jabbed his thigh with it and the sharp pain cleared the fog from behind his eyes.

Mother Hesper glowered at Ayla and stood. "Before you return to your cells, there is time for a tour of the Reliquary."

Every one of the teens stood, relieved that they were not being sent straight into the soporific darkness. Ayla nodded at Toby and he took a breath. They were about to find out if the inverters really were on the island.

Half staggering with the impact of the alcohol, Toby followed Mother Hesper and Father Dahon back into the main cathedral. Summer giggled suddenly from behind him and Arthur had to catch her when she stumbled on a step. Ayla closed her hand around Toby's elbow. "Focus. This is a competition."

"I'm not used to alcohol."

"You only had one cup and you drank it slowly. It'll wear off in a bit. In the meantime, just keep moving."

"Lightweights," Brody and Moira snorted as they shoved their way to the front through the giggling swaying crowd.

"I suppose you drink all the time." Adele tossed her head, but Adrien had to catch her as the movement caused her to lose her balance.

"Aye," Moira grinned. "Kills the bugs."

"I feel sick," Summer whispered as Toby stepped warily back into the main part of the cathedral.

"Line up." Mother Hesper stood in front of the uncles, who remained silent and unmoving, their hands resting on their weapons. Toby and Ayla pushed past Brody to reach the front of the line.

"Behind this door is the Reliquary." Mother Hesper gestured, but all Toby could see were the massive attendants, whose eyes seemed to see everything.

"You will touch nothing unless I give you permission. You are to look at each relic only long enough so that you would recognize another if you were to see it. If there are any brothers or sisters inside praying, you are not to disturb them. Understand?"

Toby nodded and Ayla's grip tightened. He turned to see that her face was flushed and her breath shortened. She was not as unaffected by the drink as she had made out. He could actually tell she was excited.

Mother Hesper said something under her breath to the uncles and they stepped to one side revealing the door to the Reliquary, which was heavy and thick.

"It's wood," Ayla whispered.

"Wood so old it's almost turned to stone." Cezar limped forward and touched it. "Look, it's black, like iron."

Ayla nodded. "It wouldn't have burned well. Maybe that's why it was left."

"It was left because of superstition." Father Dahon's voice wound between them and Toby flinched: his hearing was incredibly sharp. "Behind this door was the crypt. The Gozitans thought that if they removed the door, it would release the souls of all those interred below."

Lenka backed into Matus while Ayla just rolled her eyes. Toby found himself staring at the uncle on his left who glared at them from under thick, frowning brows.

Suddenly the uncle jerked toward Toby and opened his mouth, as if to say "boo." Only a grunt emerged. Toby stumbled into Ayla, his heart hammering. Inside the uncle's blackened mouth there had been no tongue.

Ayla pushed him off. "What're you doing?" she hissed.

Toby shook his head. Maybe he was imagining things. This was what happened when you got drunk. He remembered Peel sobbing after a long night's drinking and yelling at someone named Carla who wasn't even there.

Toby's head had started to thump. The sunlight spearing through the windows high above and glinting from all the gold was hurting his eyes. He wasn't the only one. To his right, Zahir had one arm over his face, while Leila had her head buried in the shoulder of her partner.

"It will be less bright inside. May we go in?" Uzuri was looking at Zahir with concern. "Zahir has an extreme sensitivity to light. His eyes are not like ours."

Mother Hesper smiled as she regarded the albino boy. Then she took a large key from a pocket of her robe and unlocked the door. "Come then." She waved them through.

It was dimmer inside, but not completely dark—small cross-shaped windows high up in the walls let light shine in.

Ayla pursed her lips as she looked up, but Toby dismissed the openings with a shake of his head. They were no good as a route into the Reliquary—even Summer wouldn't fit through them.

Dirt-packed shelves lined the walls on either side of them. Although many of the skulls from the original crypt had been removed, leaving indents behind, several remained, grinning at Toby.

Summer squeaked as she found herself facing the sockets of a skull with clumps of hair still stuck to the bone.

"In here, please," Mother Hesper said as she ducked under a lintel.

Toby was pushed from behind as the teens hurried to escape the chamber of skulls.

Inside the next room, to Summer's obvious relief, the shelves had been cleaned. Each displayed different items.

"That's a solar panel!" Cezar shook off Bianca's hand and limped forward. "I never saw one of those before. I thought they were all smashed!"

"Cezar!" Bianca was mortified.

Toby stared at his feet, terrified that one look at his face would give away his knowledge.

Mother Hesper nodded. "We have collected a few but, yes, most were smashed."

Uzuri raised one hand as if to touch the black silicon, then dropped it quickly when Mother Hesper glared at him.

There was no dust on the panel. Toby's heart rose. "Someone must clean," he whispered to Ayla.

"You're right."

Toby's idea about becoming an attendant seemed more attractive to him by the minute. He brought his attention back to what Mother Hesper was saying.

"It is items like this that caused the apocalypse. Using the Sun's gifts in such blasphemous ways, trapping its rays inside man-made machinery, treating it like a slave rather than the god that it is. No wonder it took its powers from us."

"Ave Soleil," Adele whispered.

"Praise the Sun," Uzuri echoed and Bianca raised her hand to make the sun sign, her nails glinting in the half-light.

Toby mirrored her. Lenka and Matus glowered at them all.

"And now, here." Mother Hesper stopped in front of a set of shelves that glittered with jewelery inside glass cases. Every item depicted the sun: small sunburst earrings, torques in sunbeam shapes, tiaras that looked like rays, crystal suns inside silver pendants, a silver ring with a smiling sun's face on it. Beside this display was another, of jewelery designed with both the sun and moon. Usually the sun was gold, the moon silver, but some were brightly colored, almost cartoonish, and in one pendant set apart from the others, the moon was asleep. Toby leaned close. Something about the moon's slumbering face made Toby think that it was crying. He looked up to find Mother Hesper staring at him and quickly stepped sideways to peer at a bangle with a little dancing sun dangling from it.

"These must be worth a fortune." Bianca's nails ticked on the glass case as she lifted her hands to touch.

Mother Hesper sneered. "We do not care. Once placed inside the Reliquary, an item never leaves."

Ayla's hand closed around Toby's forearm and he could feel the sweat on her palm. "Are those *real* diamonds?" She pointed to a ring in the center.

Mother Hesper narrowed her eyes. "I believe so. As I said, the value does not matter, if it depicts the Sun, it belongs to the sanctuary."

Ayla's thoughtful hum gave Toby a shiver of concern.

"It will be easy enough for you to identify similar items as important." Mother Hesper waved them onward and Toby frowned at the next display. This, too, was in a glass box, but it contained little statues, some with the head of a falcon, some little beetles.

The teens stared solemnly.

"Ah don't get it," Moira said eventually.

"These are Egyptian." Mother Hesper pointed to a statue of a male figure. "The Sun god, Ra. The scarab beetle." If you see anything like this, it too depicts the Sun."

She moved along slightly to a statue of a woman wearing an elaborate headdress. "This is Hindu—another solar deity, Surya.

Many items come to us from the old museums. Just because they do not show a picture of the Sun, does not mean that they do not belong to the Solar Order. Be ever vigilant. Now this . . ." She left the display case and pointed to the next shelf.

"What is it?" Leila leaned close to a thin box covered in numbered buttons.

"I've seen one." Ayla spoke up, surprising Toby. "It's a calculator—for working out sums."

Cezar shoved his way to the front of the group. "I've heard of these." His fingers hovered over them and the Sister slapped his hand away with horror on her face.

"Don't touch. These are some of our most dangerous items. See the gray bar at the top of the plastic casing?"

Cezar nodded.

"Tiny solar panels. This item is solar powered."

With a gasp, Bianca pulled Cezar back.

"But it's so small." Zahir tilted his head.

Mother Hesper nodded. "There were many of these once, but they were thrown into landfills once the Sun vanished—useless. Now they are usable once more and when people find them, they are tempted to take the first step toward the second cataclysm. If a pilgrim brings in anything like this, you must immediately hand it over to me." She glowered at Ayla. "If only you had known to destroy the one you saw. Too late now." She sighed regretfully and Ayla nodded as if in agreement.

The next area looked to Toby just like the jumble of spare clothing in the storeroom on the *Phoenix*.

"Each item blasphemously depicts the Sun." Between two fingers

Mother Hesper picked up a T-shirt with *Little Miss Sunshine* capering on the front. Then she dropped it. "You may touch these—look through so that you can see what I am talking about."

Summer was first to reach in. She picked up a T-shirt that said *Sun's out, guns out.* "What does that mean?"

Ayla picked up another that said *Sun, where rock and roll began.*

Cezar's said *Sun Gym*. Uzuri picked up a T-shirt that said *Blue sun* and stared at it.

Lenka gasped as she held up a bright red T-shirt that said *Hotter than the sun*. "Blasphemy." She threw it to one side.

"You get the idea." Mother Hesper drew them onward and Toby's eyes widened.

"You have books—paper. How?" He thought of Dee's precious atlas, the only real book he had ever seen. "Paper's flammable. The books were burned in the Darkness."

"Not all." Mother Hesper sneered at the covers in front of her. *Eternal Sunshine of the Spotless Mind, Empire of the Sun, Half of a Yellow Sun, The Sun Also Rises.* The bent covers seemed to strain with the force of wasted words bursting to escape.

Mother Hesper turned back to the teens. "If a pilgrim brings a book to you, do not attempt to read it."

Brody shrugged, Moira with her. "Can't read anyhow."

Mother Hesper hummed. "Who among you *can* read?"

Toby glanced at Ayla and she gave the slightest shake of her head, silently warning him to remain quiet about any possible advantage. Finally Summer raised a hand. "I can and so can Arthur."

Cezar, too, raised his. "I can read. Bianca only a little."

Lenka nodded her head. "I read."

"Adrien reads French." Adele looked at her brother. "He learned from the gravestones."

"I read," Leila said eventually. "Noah doesn't."

"Is that everyone?" Mother Hesper looked suspiciously at Toby, but he spread his hands.

"What's next?" Ayla asked.

Next was a display of what looked like junk—items with no apparent purpose, but which showed a sun logo. "Sun . . . Sys-tems," Lenka read out loud.

"These are . . . a mixture of 'things'," Mother Hesper said. "Parts of the most blasphemous machinery ever to be made."

Ayla nudged Toby sharply enough to make him flinch, but he had already seen what she was trying to draw his attention to—a pile of components stamped with the Solaris logo.

"Can we touch?" Toby looked at Mother Hesper for permission.

She sucked in her breath.

"It's hard to tell what they are, is all." Toby pretended disinterest.

"You may touch." Mother Hesper ducked her head, so that her eyes vanished beneath her lowered brows. "I will be watching."

Toby reached out for something that looked like the picture his father had shown him, but Ayla pushed his hand sideways, forcing him to pick up another object that held no interest.

He glared at her, but she too had lifted what looked like a round disc, nothing like the inverter they needed. Soon the others had all picked up one of the strange items and were turning it in their hands. Then Ayla passed her disc to Arthur, swapping with the object he held and soon they were all exchanging items.

Suddenly, Toby held it in his hand: an inverter. It had to be. It had holes that would fit the wires he had been sorting and was small enough to fit in his palm. How hard would it be to slip it into his pocket right now, surrounded by the whole group?

He swallowed and the hand holding the inverter slid towards his trousers.

Ayla slipped between Toby and Mother Hesper, briefly blocking him from the sister's view.

"Toby, are you ready to swap?" It was Cezar.

"I . . ." Toby froze with his hand trembling over his pocket. He swallowed and lifted it once more. "Here."

With a sinking heart he handed the inverter to Cezar and took an old AA battery pack in return.

Ayla's face twisted and Toby had a moment of fear for Cezar's safety as the boy held up the inverter with a wondering gaze. "What are these holes for, do you think? What do you imagine it does?" Cezar squinted closely and Bianca shoved him.

"Put it back, Cezar. Whatever it is, it's dangerous."

"I have a matching one." Matus held his up.

Lenka glared at him. "Stop talking to the competition!"

Matus nodded and his face hardened.

"Now put them all back." Mother Hesper straightened. She counted each item back onto the shelf and Toby shuddered, relieved now that he had not managed to pocket an inverter then and there.

Mother Hesper led them deeper into the Reliquary to a final shelf filled with crockery, mugs, and plates with logos on them. Before it, a single brother kneeled, muttering prayers under his breath.

Mother Hesper held a finger to her lips, asking for silence.

Toby leaned nearer to the display. *BP, Sun Life, Sun Systems*: the mugs declared cheerily that their employees had enjoyed company-sponsored tea and coffee breaks.

Suddenly, Leila swayed. "I don't feel so good." She closed her hands around her stomach, bent forward and, as Mother Hesper shrieked and the brother leaped to his feet, she filled a Kellogg's cereal bowl with vomit.

ELEVEN

"So, we didn't get the inverters, but it was hilarious when the American threw up." Ayla dropped to a crouch next to Toby who was leaning against a wall in the rear courtyard, taking advantage of its shade. Around them, a few of the other couples walked around, trying to keep themselves awake, while others sat and talked together in low voices. The excitement of the day was wearing off and tiredness setting in.

Toby was staring at the wall. "What's on the other side, do you think?" He pointed.

"It's the cliff." Ayla stretched her legs out in front of her with a sigh. "Can't you tell from where we are?"

"I was just thinking that we could get over it if we needed to."

Ayla shook her head and lowered her voice. "Even if there wasn't a long drop on the other side, we couldn't. Look."

Toby blinked into the sun and struggled to see what she was pointing at. "I can't . . ." Then his eyes adjusted to something that glimmered on top of the brickwork. "Is that broken glass?"

"All along the top. And over there"—Ayla pointed—"a guard hut."

"Watching the wall. I don't get it—who would want to escape?"

Ayla lowered her voice. "I'm beginning to understand why Hideaki never made it back to the *Banshee*. It's like a prison here."

"Look at Lenka." Toby pointed. The girl's head had sagged onto her knees. As Toby said her name, she jerked up. "She almost fell asleep."

"This trial business is easy." Ayla put her hands behind her head. "How many overnight watches have you pulled?"

"A few." Toby smiled. "Particularly when the boiler needed work—I can stay awake all night if I need to."

"Me, too, no problem." Ayla stretched happily. "We'll win this for sure."

"But do you think we should?" Toby whispered. "If we became silent attendants, we might be allowed into the Reliquary to clean."

Ayla scowled, considering. "How would we get the inverters out again?" she murmured eventually. She shook her head. "No, we stick to the original plan, at least for now."

"Careful." Toby stiffened and pointed. A brother and sister descended the steps and began to pace around the courtyard, within earshot of the teens. They seemed to be paying no attention to them, but Toby wasn't deceived. They were being monitored.

"Do you think we'll be fed again?" Arthur slid to the ground next to Toby, making him jump. "Summer's hungry."

"I'm used to eating two meals a day." Adele sniffed as she and Adrien joined them.

"We'll find out in a moment." Toby looked up. "There's Mother Hesper."

She was standing in a shadowy corner, her eyes fixed on the teens.

When she saw Lenka drooping once more she smiled. Finally, she stepped into the light. "Time for your evening meal."

Evening meal was corn cakes, rice, and potatoes.

Toby was reaching for a crisp potato when Arthur caught his arm. "You seem like a good guy, I'd like to keep you around a bit longer."

Toby tilted his head, glad that he had taken the time to be friendly. "What do you mean?"

"Carbs," Arthur said under his breath. "It'll make you sleepy. Don't eat it."

Toby's eyes widened. Arthur was right: it was a trap, a bit like the wine at the previous meal.

Around Toby, the others were filling their plates.

Ayla reached for a corn cake, saw the slight shake of Toby's head, and pulled her hand back. On his word, she would go hungry.

After the meal, the teens were taken to their cells. It was still light outside, but the sun was no longer shining on the plastic bottles that let light in through the ceiling and so, underground, darkness reigned.

Ayla marched into her cell.

Moira passed her. "How'll they know if we fall asleep in here?"

Summer hesitated at her own doorway. "She's right—are they watching us?"

"They must be." Toby rubbed his eyes, then realized what he was doing and dropped his hand.

"Where from?" Cezar walked into Toby's cell behind him and started running his hands over the walls.

"Get in your own cells." Mother Hesper stopped outside Toby's room. "You. Out."

Cezar ducked his head and limped away as swiftly as he could, his feet almost tangling in her robes.

"Remember—you mustn't fall asleep." Mother Hesper smiled at Lenka, whose face was cracking into a huge yawn.

Lenka slammed her mouth closed and backed into her cell.

"See you in the morning," Mother Hesper said as she closed Toby's door on him. "And don't forget sunset prayers."

The sound of the bolt being drawn made him shudder and he put his hand into his pocket to touch the fork tine that he had broken off at dinner. It wasn't a screwdriver, but it was something.

Suddenly, a high-pitched note trembled in the still air of the passageway and his head jerked up.

The single voice was joined by others—the teens were singing. Arthur's deep voice cut through the sound, giving it layers, and Toby closed his eyes to listen. It was a hymn to the Sun. A farewell as it sank beneath the horizon and a plea for it to return the next day. Sunset prayers.

Slowly, the song died until only the single high note lingered in the air once more. Toby sat up with a start. He had slumped backward and his breathing had slowed right down.

"That was lovely," Ayla's voice snapped from next door. "A lullaby isn't exactly going to keep us awake tonight though, is it?"

Toby laughed.

"What should we sing then?" Arthur shouted.

"Oh for . . ." Toby could picture Ayla rolling her eyes. "If you have to sing, then sing something lively."

"Like what?" Summer squeaked.

Toby grinned. As the others debated, he took a deep breath. Then he walked to the cell door, put his face close to the airholes, and began.

"What do you do with a drunken sailor? What do you do with a drunken sailor? What do you do with a drunken sailor? Early in the morning?"

There was a long shocked silence, then a loud giggle from one of the girls.

"Hooray and up she rises, hooray and up she rises, hooray and up she rises, early in the morning."

Most of the group joined in. Toby strained his ears; he couldn't tell if Ayla's voice was among the cacophony.

"I do not know this one," Zahir complained.

"It's easy to pick up," Celeste called. "Just sing the chorus. *Hooray and up she rises.* It's about the Sun."

Toby had managed to retain an air of the devout, while singing about drunkenness.

"Only you," Ayla muttered.

"I can't remember the next verse." Toby stopped singing. "I know you know it, what's next?"

"I don't sing," Ayla snapped.

"Ayla . . ." Toby begged. Her name became a chant that filled the corridor. "Ayla, Ayla."

"Oh fine . . ." she said.

Toby stifled a laugh.

"Put him in the scuppers with the deck pump on him . . ." Although she tried not to sing, it was impossible not to fall into the rhythm of the words.

When the song was over, there was barely a pause before Uzuri shouted from her cell. "Now one from our country." And Zahir began to drum on his cell door.

Time slipped by. Toby had no idea how long he had been in the cell or how long it had been since the group had stopped singing.

The teens had fallen into low discussions about the Sun. There had been a lengthy argument over who was more devout: Lenka and Matus or Adele and Adrien, but generally the teens were simply talking to pass the time.

As the evening dipped into the depths of night, however, the cool temperature and the deep quiet began to seep into their bones and they dropped into silence.

"Summer, are you awake?" Arthur banged on his door.

"I'm here," Summer answered sleepily.

It was an exchange that was repeated among the pairs over and over again as the night dragged on.

"Lenka, are you there?"

"Uzuri, talk to me."

"Leila, Leila?" The American boy's voice was growing increasingly urgent. "Leila!"

Finally, he received an answer. "I'm up, Noah." But Leila's voice was low and sleepy and Toby knew she had been falling asleep when her partner had called her name.

Toby himself was beginning to worry. He had stayed away from the small camp bed at the back of his own cell, preferring to sit on the hard floor for the added discomfort, but now, even the cold earth was beginning to feel like an embrace. He had slipped down, stretching his legs out before him and leaning on his elbow.

When his chin jerked forward and he bit his tongue, he gasped. He grabbed the tine of his fork from his pocket and jabbed at his leg again, hissing with the pain.

"Ayla," he called. "Talk to me."

"What do you want me to say?" she responded immediately. Toby blew out a rush of air. She was awake.

"I don't know." He got to his feet, racking his brains. He couldn't ask her about life on the *Banshee*—they were meant to be sheep farmers from the Falklands. "What's your favorite food?" It was a dumb question, but better than nothing.

Ayla snorted. "My favorite food?"

"Yes, tell me what you like to eat."

"Depends on the time of day," she said in the end. "I like oatmeal for breakfast, if it's made properly, you know, with milk. I had syrup in it once. It was . . . unforgettable."

"Have you ever had chocolate?" Toby pressed his head on the wall between them, as if to get closer to her.

Ayla laughed. "Of course not. No one has."

"I have," Adele's voice chimed in. "Once."

"They have chocolate in France?" Ayla asked.

"In what's left of Belgium, actually," Adrien replied. "Our oldest brother is a trader. He brought it home—he said it was one of the very, very last pieces."

"It's all gone now," Adele added.

"What else do you like?" Toby pressed.

He could almost hear Ayla thinking. "I hate fish," she said in the end, and he snorted loudly.

"Seriously?"

"Yes. I'd almost rather eat anything else. Gull meat, sprouting potatoes . . ."

"But if you had a choice for your last meal ever?"

"Do you *have* to?" Arthur grumbled from his cell. "I didn't eat, remember?"

Toby's stomach was rumbling, too. "Sorry."

Ayla was quiet for a bit, then she spoke in a low voice. "Can you hear me, Toby?"

"Barely."

"Good," she spoke even quieter. "Curry," she said. "When we go to India . . ." She fell silent. "Well, that's what I'd have if it was my last meal."

Toby raised his eyebrows.

"What about you?"

He sighed. "I liked the stew we had at lunchtime. I wonder if Peel could make it, if he had the ingredients. What about your free time, what do you like to do?"

"I don't get free time, you know that."

"You must, at least sometimes."

"No." Her voice stayed low. "But I liked it when Nell taught me to read. She traded everything a couple of years ago, but for a while we had two real books."

"Which ones?" Toby had learned to read from stock manifests and Dee's atlas.

"Something called *Harry Potter and the Goblet of Fire.*" Ayla's voice held a smile. "And the other was *The Lord of the Rings.*"

Toby dropped his eyes. "I like to make stuff," he offered. "Engines—the others call them toys, but they're prototypes really."

A snore cut across their conversation.

"Who's that?" Toby jerked to his feet and heard Ayla leap to her door.

"I don't know."

He strained, but couldn't tell. "Who's awake? Call your names."

"Arthur."

"Summer."

"Zahir."

There was a pause, then, "Uzuri."

"Adele."

"Brody."

"Moira."

"Bianca."

"Cezar."

"Is it Lenka?" Ayla called. "Did she fall asleep?"

"I'm awake," Lenka replied sleepily. "You had better be, too, Matus."

"I'm up."

"That's not everyone." Toby hammered on his door. "Hey, come on! Name call."

Finally a husky voice from the end of the row. "Celeste. I'm awake."

"As am I. Aldo."

"Who does that leave? Who's missing?" Uzuri called.

"It's Adrien," Adele whispered. "He's the one snoring."

"I didnae hear the 'mericans, either."

"We're here, we're awake." It was the girl. "Aren't we, Noah?" There was silence. "Noah? Wake up."

"I'm awake."

"But that means we can go to sleep now, right?" It was Cezar. "Now we're not last, we can go to sleep"

"We've lost," Adele wailed.

"Not necessarily, Adele." Uzuri's deep voice was a comfort. "Adrien was first to sleep, which means you are losing *now*. But you remain awake. If you can stay that way until a pair both fall asleep, then *they* will be out and you will remain."

"You hear that, Cezar?" Bianca snapped. "You have to stay awake. If we both sleep before Adele . . ."

Arthur rumbled. "This is a trial to prove our worthiness to be the Sun and Moon. We all have to stay awake. Think of the Sun."

"The Sun. . . . Praise the Sun." The mantras rang out along the passageway and Toby leaned on his door. His whole body started to sag and he jerked back to his feet.

"This is no good." He rubbed his eyes again and stifled a yawn. "How long till dawn?"

"There's no way to know." Even Ayla sounded tired now. "My gut tells me we're a way off yet."

"Mine, too." Toby knew he had a decent internal clock. "I'm going to do some push-ups."

"Don't tire yourself out."

"I'm hoping it'll keep me awake."

But after the first ten, Toby's arms began to shake and he found himself face down on the floor, unwilling or unable to lift himself up again. He closed his eyes for a moment, just briefly, intending to remain awake.

"Toby!" Ayla's voice whipped him out of it. It was as if she could sense what he was doing.

"I'm fine." Disorientated, Toby staggered to his feet and began jogging on the spot.

Ayla lowered her voice again. "Think about a problem," she said. "That's what I'm doing. Work out how we can solve *our* problem."

"That's . . . a good idea."

Toby sat cross-legged in the middle of his cell. They had found the inverters, but they were inside the locked crypt, guarded, at least during the day, by two large uncles. Toby shuddered again as he pictured the empty-mouthed guard outside the Reliquary turning on him.

Could there be another entrance? He considered asking Ayla what she thought, but decided to save their conversation for a time when he was sure everyone else was asleep.

The wall in between the cathedral and their quarters backed on to the crypt. If there was a way to get through it, they wouldn't need to pass the guards at all. But how could they dig through a wall without being seen?

And there was the added problem that they were locked in their cells at night. Would they have to steal the inverters during the day?

Toby dug his nails into his palm. He'd had the *Phoenix*'s inverter in the palm of his hand and lost it.

If they managed to get the inverters, could they get out without resorting to Ayla's suicide pills? Toby went over their entrance. If they wanted to leave the way they had come, they would have to go back through their quarters and into the cathedral without being seen by attendant brothers and sisters or guardian uncles. Then they would have to get through the main door, which was magnetically locked, across the courtyard without being spotted, and through the massive double gates, which seemed to be operated from within. If they managed all of that, they would then have to make it to the northernmost point of the island without being stopped by any of the Gozitan islanders.

It seemed impossible. His mind raced, finding no way out of the maze. Frustrated, Toby dug his nails into his palms. The only other way out was through the rear courtyard and over the glass-topped wall, which Ayla thought would drop them over the jagged cliff edge and which was watched by more guardian uncles. The sanctuary of the Solar Order really was a fortress.

Still, if he could cling on to rigging in a storm, he should be able to manage a cliff climb. If they wanted to escape before the actual festival, they'd have to go over the wall. Would it be possible to arrange some kind of distraction?

As his mind hit one dead end after another, a scraping sound from the back of his cell made him spin around. A tiny hatch slid open and eyes glittered in the cavity. So that was how they were being watched.

Who was looking at him? Was it Mother Hesper?

Toby stared back; he refused to be the first to drop his gaze. Finally, the grate scraped closed and cold fingers slid up his spine. There was no way for him to know when someone was behind there, listening. Conversations with Ayla would have to wait.

TWELVE

The corridor slowly grew lighter, as dawn brought a warm glow to the plastic bottles.

Cries of relief from the teens welcomed the brightening and Adele led the group in a prayer for the rising of the Sun.

Adrien had slept only briefly, but Toby knew that he would have been seen. He wondered if anyone else had napped in the night, thinking they were protected by cover of darkness.

He stretched and yawned. His whole body felt heavy, his arms like weights, his legs numb. He rubbed his gritty eyes and stared, as a spider the size of his thumbnail scuttled across the back of his cell and began to spin a web between the legs of his bed.

"Everybody out."

Mother Hesper was marching down the corridor, robes flapping behind her like great wings.

"Is it breakfast time?" Summer asked as she staggered from her cell. Her eyes were bloodshot and red-rimmed. It wasn't too difficult to tell that Adrien had rested: he was the only one who didn't look as if his eyes had been washed in the salt. Adele glowered at her twin, who ducked guiltily away from her glare.

"Into the courtyard," Mother Hesper ordered.

"Can we use the bathroom?" It was the American, Leila. "I need to use the bathroom."

Mother Hesper hesitated. "Yes. You may use a toilet."

"I want to brush my teeth," Summer muttered. "I feel like I've been eating dust."

Toby ran his tongue over his fluffy teeth—his mouth was dry and tasted like sour stew.

"We have mint leaves you can chew." Mother Hesper pointed. "This way."

He turned as Ayla emerged and leaned on the door frame of her cell. She appeared nonchalant, bright even, but a closer look revealed eyes that were even redder than Summer's.

"Morning." He tried to sound cheerful, but his voice was a rasp, as though he hadn't used it in a week.

"That was fun." Ayla didn't move. "Only a few hours left now. Looks like the twins are going first after all."

"The bells chime just after midday," Arthur agreed. "We're nearly there." He turned to Summer. "Hear that?"

Summer nodded wearily.

The teens gathered in the courtyard. Although it was barely morning, the sun blazed down and Toby hid his eyes behind his forearm.

"What now?" he muttered.

Mother Hesper stood beside Father Dahon on the steps. She was smiling.

"I don't think we're going to like this," Ayla muttered.

"Each of you will have an attendant." Father Dahon nodded as a troop of sandaled brothers and sisters lined up next to the teens. Sunburst pendants swung from their necks and Toby flinched away from the daggers of light they thrust into his face.

"The brothers and sisters are here to make sure that you don't stop"—Father Dahon licked his lips—"because now you must run."

"Run?" Adele was horrified. "I thought we just had to stay awake!"

"If you love the Sun," Mother Hesper said. "You will push yourself and run."

Cezar gestured to his leg. Lack of rest had twisted it up beneath him. "I'm not sure I can . . ."

"You will do your best. That is all the Sun requires." Mother Hesper folded her hands.

Slowly, in fits and starts, the teens began to run. Arthur set into a solid lope, Noah and Leila not far behind. The others stretched out behind them.

"How many laps do you want?" Arthur called.

"Until we say you can stop," Father Dahon replied.

The brothers and sisters ran beside the teens, their robes flapping around their knees. Arthur grinned as the brother assigned to him struggled to keep up.

"How far do you think one circuit of the courtyard is?" Ayla whispered.

Toby narrowed his eyes. "A third of a nautical mile?"

"Ashes," Ayla swore and lurched into a jog.

Toby groaned and followed her.

By his second lap he had a terrible stitch. Toby thrust his fist into his side, gasping with pain. Beside him Ayla was keeping pace, but her breathing was labored. They were pirates, used to climbing rigging and navigating the confines of a ship, not running.

Most of the other teens were ahead of them, the only ones behind Toby and Ayla now were Bianca, red-faced and panting, and Cezar, who was limping far behind.

Those ahead were also staggering—exhaustion sending them careering from walls and spiny bushes.

Barely able to pick up his feet, Toby stubbed his toes yet again and yelped. "How long do we have to keep this up?"

"Just . . . keep . . . going," Ayla gasped.

The attendants beside them were quiet, only speaking when it looked like someone was going to stop.

"Oh, my Sun." Summer dropped back to jog beside Ayla; her face was bathed in sweat and her long blonde hair was hopelessly tangled, dropping into her eyes as she stumbled onward.

Arthur slowed to wait for them to catch up and grabbed Summer's arm. "Stay with me."

"Why are they making us do this?" Bianca panted from behind.

"They're trying to tire us out," Ayla said.

Summer giggled and then, suddenly they were laughing; stress and exhaustion bursting out in hilarity.

Cezar caught up with them as they slowed. "Look."

Ahead of them, Lenka tottered to one side on shaking legs, then collapsed. Toby could hear her labored breathing. Matus dropped to her side and pulled at her. "Get up."

The brother who was running alongside him grabbed Matus by the arm and shoved him onward. "You don't stop."

"What about Lenka?" he wailed.

"She's asleep." The sister attending Lenka seemed abruptly sympathetic. "You've got to stay awake now."

Adele looked back and her dull eyes lit up. "Why not give up, Matus?" she called. "Don't you want to rest with Lenka?"

Toby lurched past. "At least get her in the shade," he shouted.

He could barely keep his head up, so did not watch to see what happened to her, but the next time he passed the spot, Lenka was gone.

Six times around the courtyard and Toby's legs felt like jelly. There was no way they were going to be able to bear his weight for much longer. Cezar was struggling on, but his limp had become so pronounced that he was literally jerking sideways as he ran and his face was screwed up with the pain.

"They have to let him stop." He gestured to Cezar then grabbed the brother who was panting at his side. "You're killing him."

"No one's died from the run yet," the young man said, but refused to meet his eyes.

Suddenly, as one, Brody and Moira stopped. They leaned against one another and sagged to the ground. The brothers who had been watching them tried unsuccessfully to persuade them back to their feet.

"We're nae asleep," Brody murmured as Toby reeled past. "We just cannae run nae more." Exhaustion had thickened his accent.

"Up." The angry brother shoved at them, but Moira slipped sideways. "Up!" the bearded man shouted again.

Brody glowered up at him. "Make me."

Summer tottered to a halt just ahead of Toby, her eyes unfocused.

"Keep running," the sister beside her bawled. "Don't you believe in the power of the Sun?"

"The Sun," she mumbled and her knees collapsed. Arthur was there to catch her. With a loud exhalation of breath, he heaved her on to his shoulder.

"What are you doing?" Summer gasped.

"Running," Arthur muttered, and he did.

Summer clutched at him, awake, but barely.

"He's a machine." Ayla looked impressed. Toby just grunted.

After another circuit of the courtyard, Toby was no longer thinking. He was just watching his feet, willing them to keep moving.

"Stop." Ayla clutched his arm.

"Got to keep running." He shook her off.

"Not any more. We can stop." Ayla released him, unwilling to run after him if it meant taking another step.

Toby staggered two more steps, three. Then her words hit him and he turned. The other teens were lying on the ground. Only the rise and fall of their chests told him they were still alive.

"We can stop?" His head felt like a foreign object wobbling on his shoulders. He didn't dare sit. "The bells haven't rung."

Ayla shook her head. "We still have to stay awake—we just don't have to run any more."

He lifted his head. Mother Hesper and Father Dahon had not moved from their spot on the sanctuary steps. Mother Hesper nodded at him. Permission to halt. The brothers and sisters who had shadowed them were now standing in the shade by the wall, watching, but no longer exhorting them to run.

Toby started back toward Ayla. Her trousers were dark with sweat and her lips were chapped from the blazing sun. Her eyes closed in a blink and took a long time to open back up again.

"Not long now." He forced a smile but it felt more like he was baring his teeth. "Let's find some shade."

An hour curled in the shade of the sanctuary wall and Toby and Ayla had begun to pinch one another to stay awake. Brothers and sisters walked among them, bending close and checking over and over again. "Are you awake?"

Leila was the next to fall; she simply curled in on herself, exhaustion dragging her into unconsciousness.

Adele's eyes flicked from Matus to Noah, willing them to sleep with desperate eyes. Until one of them slept, she and Adrien were still losing.

Summer's breathing began to deepen, her cheeks flushed like a doll's, her eyes closed and her head dropped on to Arthur's shoulder. Arthur sat bolt upright, his eyes watering as he fought to keep them open.

Zahir was awake, but Toby wasn't sure about Uzuri—she was sitting upright, her legs crossed, but her eyes were closed and she hadn't moved for a long time.

Celeste and Aldo were still holding hands. They sat facing one another, their foreheads pressed together, murmuring in low voices.

Somehow, Brody and Moira also remained conscious, singing strange prayers that Toby couldn't make out.

With a final anguished groan, Noah curled up beside his sister and passed out.

Adele's eyes widened in triumph. "Look!" She staggered to an attendant, caught her arm and dragged her over to the sleeping couple. "You see that, don't you? A *couple* is sleeping."

Ayla clutched Toby's arm and pointed. He wrestled his gaze in the direction of her finger and his heart leaped. The sundial had reached the center of the square. It was midday.

"The bells will chime soon." Relief was in her voice. "That was harder than I thought it'd be."

"We did it though." Toby leaned his head backward on the warm stone.

"Don't sleep now." Ayla twisted the pale skin inside his elbow. Toby barely felt it. As he rolled his head to glare at her, it throbbed with the ringing of the bells.

The teens leaned on one another as they staggered into the sanctuary.

"They'll let us go to bed now." Summer raised her head from Arthur's arm.

Toby hardly saw the opulence around him. He paid no attention to the lines of sunblind brothers and sisters kneeling for their midday prayers. All he wanted was to lie in the darkness of his cell until his head stopped pounding.

"Kneel before the Sun." Father Dahon was standing at the altar waiting for them.

Toby fell to his knees and tugged an unresponsive Ayla to his side.

"Midday prayers." Father Dahon bowed his head and the teens began to pray. Exhaustion turned their voices to a drone. *"We believe in one Sun, the Father, the Almighty, Heater of heaven and earth, Revealer of all that is seen, and unseen . . ."*

When they had finished, Father Dahon raised his arms. The sunblind brothers and sisters stood and processed back to their quarters. Toby stared as Morris swept by him, unaware, so close that his robes brushed Toby's feet.

Finally, Father Dahon spoke. "The first test has been completed. There were many failures, but only one *couple* showed true disdain for the Orb."

Toby looked around, wondering where Mother Hesper was. To his right, Noah and Leila held hands, their heads hung in shame. Adele bit her lip and glared at her twin.

Mother Hesper appeared at Noah's back. She had been waiting in one of the old chapels. At her order, two attendant uncles appeared and lifted the couple to their feet.

"We're sorry. We just couldn't stay awake," Leila moaned. "We love the Sun, we're devout. We had been traveling all night."

Mother Hesper nodded and the attendants brought the couple to the altar.

"As the Sun and Moon are paired, you were being tested as a pair," she said, and her voice was sad. "Although you were not the first to fall asleep, Leila, you were the first couple to do so." Mother Hesper fixed a sharp gaze on the flushed Adele. "You were lucky."

"The Sun watched over us," Adele said proudly.

"Praise the Sun," Adrien chimed.

"This couple has been eliminated. They will not be our Sun and Moon in the festival." Leila sobbed and Noah squeezed her hand. "However, you all had your chance to leave. Noah and Leila are now committed to the Solar Order, so they will become silent attendants, they will have the honor of working with the sunblinded and in the lower levels among our deepest secrets."

Leila brightened and Noah raised his head. "Praise the Sun," he said.

"Yes, Praise the Sun." Mother Hesper gestured and the attendants lifted the pair onto the altar. "There is just the matter of your . . . initiation."

Toby's head snapped up. Before he could cry out a warning, Mother Hesper grabbed Leila's chin and forced her mouth open. Then, as the confused girl frowned up at her, she picked up what looked like a pair of pliers.

Toby lurched to his feet, but Ayla grabbed his arm. "There's nothing you can do." She pulled him back down.

"What's happening?" Summer wriggled.

"Cover her eyes," Toby cried.

"Ashes!" Arthur closed a palm over Summer's face.

He was just in time. In one smooth movement Mother Hesper gripped Leila's tongue and sliced it off.

Blood spurted over Noah. Leila made an odd choking noise and Noah screamed.

The others were shocked into silence. Celeste fainted and Adele started to cry.

Noah tried to run from the altar, but the two attendants held him down.

"Stop," Toby shouted. "Why are you doing this?"

He was given no answer. Before he knew it, Noah and Leila were kneeling on the altar, their hands in front of their faces, blood dripping between their fingers. Ayla's eyes were pinned on the channels that were now running crimson.

Mother Hesper dropped the pliers and they bounced on the marble floor with a clang.

The two tongues lay in a wooden bowl that Toby hadn't noticed before. Now he couldn't take his eyes from it.

"Those who fail the trials become *silent* attendants," Father Dahon said, his voice echoing up to the fake dome on the sanctuary ceiling.

"After blindness, silence is the most precious gift of the Sun." Mother Hesper raised her hands in a sun sign. "Only those who fail the trials may become silent attendants and look after the most secret of all our mysteries." Her shoulders relaxed. "There can be only one winning couple. The true Sun and Moon will be sunblinded and trained to be mothers and fathers. The rest is silence."

Toby dragged his gaze from the pliers and looked at Ayla. Fury burned in his eyes. "Did you know about this?"

"I didn't," Ayla lowered her voice.

"Because if you did—"

"Do you really think I'd have put myself in this position?"

"Yes." Toby ground his teeth. "You thought we'd win."

"We can *still* win."

"We don't know what the other tests will be." Toby's hands curled into fists. "There's no way out till the end."

"I didn't know, Toby." Ayla touched his arm.

"She couldn't have." It was Summer, her voice was barely above a whisper. She climbed unsteadily to her feet. "*I* didn't know. I researched every source I could get my hands on before we came. I spent hours with our minister. Even he didn't tell me."

"They'd have no candidates if they told us." Cezar murmured.

"We would still have come." Lenka's face was pale, but she stood resolutely. "Our lives will be dedicated to the Sun either way. It is an honor."

"An honor," Matus echoed weakly.

"You may now rest or eat, it is up to you." Mother Hesper turned her back on them. "The next trial will take place tomorrow."

THIRTEEN

Toby woke up, disorientated. How long had he slept? He had one arm slung over his face, so at some point the sunlight must have disturbed him. He swung his legs over the hard cot and looked at his cell door. It was locked. Night, then.

"Ayla, are you awake?"

There was no answer.

He moved to his door. "Wake up."

The quality of the silence seemed to change and Toby remembered how Ayla woke—she went from fast asleep to firing on all cylinders in an instant, like a boiler.

"Ayla?"

"I hear you."

He sighed, relieved.

Then she spoke. "You still don't believe I didn't know?"

Toby said nothing.

"I couldn't have known it would be like this."

He leaned his forehead against the door and imagined she was doing the same. "We knew we were going in without enough information and we made the decision to go ahead anyway." He swallowed. "It's worse than we expected, but . . . we can deal with it."

"They keep their secrets down here," Ayla muttered.

"They don't have a choice. Silent attendants, remember?" Toby shuddered.

"What do you want to do?" Ayla whispered.

Toby turned to look behind him, checking the hatch in his wall. It was closed, but that didn't mean no one was listening.

"We could leave," he murmured. "Over the wall and along the cliff."

"And give up the mission?" Ayla hissed. "Even if we can get over the glass without being seen, there's no way off the island—not yet."

Toby banged his forehead on the door. "You're right. *Wren* might not be here yet. We have to stick it out for at least another day."

"How bad can it be?" Ayla whispered. "We can out-fight and out-think every one of these landlubbers."

Toby thought of Arthur and Cezar. "Maybe not all."

"We just have to stay ahead of the competition for a bit longer, while we think of something."

"Right." Toby closed his eyes. "Are you still tired?"

"Not really. My clock's screwed up. I have no idea what time it is."

Bells chimed and Toby jumped, shocked. "You hear that?"

"Yes." Ayla cocked her head as sounds emerged from the other cells.

"They ring just after midday, don't they?" There was a frown in Ayla's voice. "How come it's still dark?"

A figure swept past the outside of Toby's cell, a darker patch of shadow sliding through the darkness.

"Only darkness can teach us to truly love the light," Mother Hesper's voice rang out. "You will remain in your cells until you ask to be released. The first to beg for freedom will lose the challenge for their pair."

"So we just have tae remain in our cells?" Brody called.

"That's right. In your cells . . . in the dark."

Mother Hesper had been gone for some time.

"I don't see how this is going to be a problem." Toby was lying on his camp bed with his eyes closed. "I like the daytime as much as the next person, but I'm planning to sleep this one through."

Ayla made no reply, but his ears caught voices from a couple of cells down. It was Summer. "Arthur . . . when are they going to feed us?"

Toby sat up, suddenly feeling sick at the mention of food. If the bells had rung he had already slept through at least two meals. And he had skipped a meal the night before.

"Ashes," he clutched the camp bed with shaking hands. This was more than just darkness . . . it was another endurance test; the couples were going to go hungry and thirsty.

Suddenly, all Toby could think about was water: the rain the *Phoenix* caught in barrels, freshwater from streams, even the poisonous salt. He rolled over and leaned against the wall.

"Ayla?"

"I heard, Toby. We've had hungry times."

Toby nodded to himself. Now he knew what the alternative was, he would go hungry for as long as it took.

He thought of Adele and Adrien. Two meals a day she had said. How would the French couple cope with hunger?

The Scots would have no problem. He sensed that they had lived harder lives than any of them. What about the others? Arthur and Summer seemed decently fed, as did Celeste and Aldo. Would they suffer the most through this test, or would their own reserves keep them going when Toby and Ayla could not.

He ground his teeth.

"Go to sleep, Toby, it's the best way to get through this."

But Toby's body told him he had slept long enough so he lay in the dark, staring blindly at the ceiling.

This time around there was no singing and the couples who spoke did so in whispers, afraid of helping out their competitors. Toby knew that Arthur was speaking to Summer from the low rumble of his voice, but he couldn't make out the individual words.

Toby licked his lips. Was there anywhere he could get a drink? He touched the walls of his cell. They were earth—no chance of moisture. He touched his door. Surely the cool night air might mean moisture developed on the hard plastic. He had only to wait a few more hours to find out.

When the hatch in the back of his cell opened, Toby sat with his back to the wall. He would not give his watcher the satisfaction of his attention. Assuming they could see him in the deep darkness that was.

The darkness . . . Toby's eyes started to play tricks on him. In the farthest recesses of his cell he was sure that he could see movement. The shadows seemed to be gathering. Colors danced in his peripheral vision, but each time he turned his head there was nothing, only more dark.

He closed his eyes tight, forcing bright colors to burst behind his eyelids. That way he could pretend for a moment that the gloom was his choice.

He lay down and rolled onto his front, covering his head with his arms, keeping his fantasy going, not allowing himself to look, but it was impossible for Toby not to go back in his memories to when darkness did cover the whole world—when day differed from night only in the quality of the gray overhead. Then it was cold all the time and the *Phoenix* had needed her ice-breaker for more than the junk that filled the seas. Icebergs had floated down out of the North Sea and into the Pacific; whole islands of ice that slowly dissipated into the poisonous water, raising sea levels and freezing wildlife.

It had been worse on land. Even with populations decimated following the recessions, the wars and disease outbreaks that followed the eruption, the food reserves ran out. Those who did not fight for every mouthful died and populations headed for the rivers and seas—there was no power to run water, no sewage plants; they had no choice.

Toby had been born into a twilight world. Day had never followed night. When he was young, the sun, moon and stars were nothing but stories. The captain had navigated by following birds, spotting landmarks, and noting the direction of the wind and the shape of swells. And, of course, he had the compass and sextant that never left his side. Some of Toby's earliest memories were of his father working with his charts and the sextant, staring at the slight alleviation in the darkness that told him roughly where the sun hung in the sky.

Toby desperately wanted to see the sun.

He rolled over and opened his eyes, almost believing that if he did so, light would shine in. It did not.

The hatch in the back of his cell opened once more. Toby curled his lip and ignored it. But when the hatch slid closed there was a slithering and skittering from the back of his cell. Alarmed, Toby rose to a kneeling position.

"Ayla . . . is there something in your cell?" he whispered.

Her answer was instantaneous. "Yes. For some time."

"What is it?"

"What do you think?"

Toby listened. The sounds grew louder, magnified by the darkness. Whatever it was seemed to be crawling up the walls.

"Insects," he groaned.

"Roaches." There was thump from Ayla's cell and the faint sound of crunching. At least she still had her boots—Toby's feet were bare.

"I hate roaches." Toby's skin felt as if it was trying to crawl around the back of his spine.

"At least it's something to eat."

"That's disgusting." Toby jumped as something touched his hand. Swiftly, he shook the insect off.

There was a loud shriek from Uzuri's cell. "What the Sun is this?"

Screams and shrieks began to fill the air.

"Fools!" Ayla muttered. "Roaches can't hurt them."

As desperate as Toby was not to lose the competition, he shuddered at the idea that two of the other teens would have their tongues pulled from their mouths. Who? Arthur and Summer, Cezar and Bianca?

"I want to go home," Summer wailed.

"Hold on," Arthur called. "They're creepy, but they won't hurt you."

Toby smiled grimly. Ayla had said the same thing of the blind brothers and sisters when they had arrived: creepy, but harmless.

Toby could feel movement on the blanket and his skin crawled. He was steeling himself to brush his bare hand across the material when his hatch opened once more. "What is it this time?" he asked, not expecting an answer.

But one came.

"Rats," a quiet voice said. "Good luck."

And the hatch slammed closed.

Toby hoped the rats were not as hungry as he was. On the other hand . . .

"Ayla, do rats eat roaches?" he called.

"R-rats?" Adele's screams turned to hysterical sobs.

"Hang on, Adele." But Adrien's voice was as shaky as his twin's. "Think of the Sun."

"I *am* thinking of the sun. I want to be out *in* the sun."

"Sing, Adele. Sing." Adrien started a hymn to the Sun, but Adele didn't join him. She only screamed louder.

Strangely, none of the others raised their voices, shocked to silence by the crazed sound of Adele's shrieks.

"Adele, for the love of all you consider holy, *shut the hell up*." It was Ayla. "You're acting like a baby."

For a second, the girl was shocked into silence. "There're rats!" she cried eventually.

"And roaches. So what?" Ayla snapped. "Have they hurt you? No."

"I-I don't like this." It was Summer.

"Well, you know what you'll like less?" Ayla growled. "Having your tongue cut out on that altar."

"She's right, Summer—be strong." It was Arthur.

Toby leaned against his cell door. "What happened to *it's a competition?*" he murmured.

"She was pissing me off."

He heard Ayla stamp across the cell, her boots crunching on roaches as she went. Then there was a loud squeak and a thud as Ayla booted a rat across the cell.

Ayla's scolding didn't keep Adele quiet for long. After only a few minutes, the girl began to sob once more, her cries getting louder and louder. Around his cot, Toby could hear the rats getting braver, closer. When one brushed against him he yelled as he thrust it away.

"Toby . . ." Ayla warned.

"Sorry. I'm all right." He sat back on his cot, drawing up his legs.

Then there was another kind of scream from across the passageway: Uzuri. This time it was a cry of surprise and pain, followed by a flood of words in her native language.

"What happened?" Toby leaped to his feet.

"One of them bit her." Zahir's voice was shocked.

"I guess the rats are hungry, too," Bianca called, her voice high-pitched and verging on hysterical.

"Stamp around," Cezar called to her. "They'll be more scared of you than you are of them."

"Nae rats," Brody said. "They're nae 'fraid of anythin' they can eat."

Adele's sobs rose again, louder and louder.

"She's driving me crazy," Moira shouted. "Adrien, shut yer sister up,"

There was no reply from Adrien.

"Adrien?" Toby pressed his hands against the door. "Are you all right?"

Still silence.

"The rat's have eaten him!" Celeste cried.

"Don't be stupid," Ayla groaned. "He's probably fallen asleep."

"Not likely." Toby kept his voice low. "Adrien, talk to me."

Adele carried on screaming.

"Adrien . . ."

"I-I-I can't!" Adrien's voice. *"Je ne peux pas."*

"Adrien . . ." Toby warned.

"He's breaking," Ayla breathed.

"Je veux sortir. Je veux rentrer . . . a la m-maison." Suddenly he was shouting. *"Je veux sortir! Laissez-moi sortir!"*

"What's he saying?" Arthur yelled, struggling to be heard over Adele's howling and Adrien's abrupt thumping.

"He's hammering on his door." Toby pressed his hands against his own. "Isn't it obvious?"

Adele's voice joined her twin's. *"Let us out!"*

When Mother Hesper came for the twins, she brought a torch. The guttering flame drew the couples to their doors like moths.

Even though he didn't want to see Adele and Adrien removed from their cells, Toby approached the heat and light. He stared at the flame and clutched his arms around himself. Would they all be forced to the altar and made to watch once more?

As Adele's door opened, she raced out of the cell and stopped before the blaze with a gasp of relief. Her whole body was shaking, she was pale and her sapphire eyes were bright red. She turned from the light only when Adrien flew from his own cell to wrap his arms around her. His hair was matted around his face, and Toby was horrified to see clumps of hair clinging to his fingers where he had been pulling it out.

Adele clung to her twin but then, as though struck, her knees collapsed.

Toby turned from the horror on her face.

"Let us go to the altar," Mother Hesper said.

"No!" Adele staggered to her feet then raced past Mother Hesper toward the stairs. The sister allowed her to go.

Adrien looked up into her skull-like face. Calm had descended on him. "There's nowhere to run?"

Mother Hesper shook her head and held out her arm. "Shall we?"

Adrien nodded as he looked after his twin. *"Louer le Soleil."*

Toby heard a scream from above—Adele had been caught.

FOURTEEN

Different areas of the courtyard had been annexed. Toby and Ayla sat in the shade of the far wall, facing off against Arthur and Summer, huddled under the limestone steps not far from Celeste and Aldo who were, as usual, holding hands with their foreheads pressed together.

Zahir and Uzuri had taken the right corner and Brody and Moira the left. Lenka and Matus and Bianca and Cezar were in the center. The couples whispered conspiratorially and occasionally glowered at their competitors. Around them brothers and sisters glided, quietly watching.

Ayla put her hands behind her head.

"How can you be so relaxed?" Toby felt the weight of a gaze on him and looked over at Arthur, who turned his head away.

Ayla shrugged. "None of this lot have anything on us. Didn't you hear all the crying earlier? Over a bloody insect or two." She shook her head. "We'll be fine."

"Yes, but what about the"—Toby lowered his voice—"things we came for? I've been thinking and thinking. I can't work out a way to get to them that doesn't get us caught by the guards."

Ayla dragged a hand through the short side of her hair then spoke under her breath. "We could fight our way in, but the problem is getting out again."

"Exactly."

"We can't get through the wall." Toby glanced up at the guard hut where a robed figure stood, scanning the courtyard.

"We're going to have to lie our way in," Ayla said. "We'll ask if we can visit the relics to pray."

"What if they say no?"

"Maybe we can get the others on our side." Ayla looked over her shoulder at Lenka and Matus. "They say they're so devout—we could persuade them to do the asking for us."

"You're not planning on telling them what we're doing?" Toby sat up straighter.

"Of course not." Ayla sneered. "We'll just make a big deal about how devout we are and that we want to go and pray at the relics. A day's rations say they'll demand it, too."

Toby licked his dry lips thoughtfully. "No bet. You're right."

Above them, the sun glittered on the glass shards that lined the wall, creating a barrier of light. Toby turned away, his vision blurring in the heat haze that rose from the dust. "I'm thirsty." He rose. "I'm going to get a drink."

Ayla stretched her long legs out in front of her. "I'm not ready to go in yet." She glanced over at the dim interior and Toby thought she gave a tiny shudder. Had she been more affected by the darkness than she claimed? Could he trust her if she wouldn't confide in him?

"I'll be back." He stood and walked away.

When Toby returned, Mother Hesper had arrived and the couples were standing in lines, ready to go back inside.

She looked at him as he slowed his steps. "Join your partner." Toby stood beside Ayla.

"In your cells, you will find buckets of wet clay," Mother Hesper said. "Strip yourselves, then cover your bodies, faces and hair. Let no part of you remain clean."

"Strip?" Leila frowned.

Mother Hesper inclined her head. "You may keep your underthings, but they too must be covered in clay. Once you all emerge, I will tell you what happens next. But act quickly—you must be back out here before the sun reaches the West Wall."

Toby stared at the bucket in the center of his cell. It was overflowing with what looked like sloppy gray mud. He put a hand in. The clay was cold and slippery between his fingers. He wiped some over his forearms and it crackled as the warmth of his skin began to dry it.

"We're going to have to move fast if we want to get back out there in time."

"We won't be quick enough if we work alone." Ayla leaned against his door frame. Her face, surrounded by her cloud of dark hair, seemed almost to float in the dim light. "You do me, then I'll do you."

Toby flushed. "Are you sure?"

"Let me know when you're ready." Ayla retreated into her cell.

The others had closed their cells and Toby knew they were stripping. He swallowed. He wasn't keen on Ayla seeing his bare body but he had no choice.

He tossed his shirt and pants on the bed, took a deep breath and left his cell. Ayla stood beside her own bucket of clay wearing nothing but a narrow breast band and a pair of shorts. Her long pale legs glowed in the low light.

Toby's eyes went to her chest and throat, which were already thickly coated with the clay slip. Pink scar tissue puckered at the edges of the clay. She hadn't wanted him touching her injuries.

"Ready?" She held her arms up at shoulder height.

Toby grabbed handfuls of the slick mud and pulled them free of the bucket with a sucking sound.

He hesitated then said, "Turn around."

Ayla turned her back to him and flicked her hair so that it dangled down her chest.

The mud was slippery and thick and underneath it, Ayla's skin. His fingers were hesitant as he smeared the mud across her shoulders and up to her ears.

Toby stepped nearer and slid his hands around her throat and under her chin. Her skin smelled sun-warm and his stomach knotted. This time, he had to put the mud on top of her breast band. Halfway down her spine, he ran out and had to return to the bucket.

Once he had filled his hands until they dripped, he returned and put his hands over her hips.

"Hurry," she murmured.

Outside, Toby could hear the others grunting in frustration as they tried to cover themselves, it wasn't long before he heard cell doors open and voices call out for help.

Businesslike as possible, he rubbed the mud into her hips. "I-I'll do your legs next," he said.

"Just get on with it." Ayla had dropped her arms. Her fingers dangled a hair's breadth from Toby's.

He closed his eyes, swallowed and rubbed his hands over her curves as fast as he could. Still, his heart beat faster.

Toby fetched more mud then kneeled to get to her feet, his face close to her thigh. He had to look away. Through her door his eyes met Zahir's. He was looking very serious as Uzuri covered him with meticulous care.

Toby rubbed his hands up and down Ayla's legs as quickly as he could, working his way from the back to the front. She turned for him and he found himself rubbing her shins.

He stood and loaded his hands again. Ayla was almost covered in the mud, only her face, arms and stomach left to do. Her hair stood out from her head where Toby had got mud in it and one eyebrow was raised.

"What are you waiting for?"

He cleared his throat. "I'll do your arms next. Can you lift them up?"

Ayla lifted her arms again and Toby began at her wrists.

Slowly he worked his way up to her right elbow then up to her shoulder. She writhed as he quickly did her armpit, a strangely intimate action.

"What about your left arm? I don't want to hurt you." Toby was thinking of the moment he had treated her burns on the *Phoenix.*

"Just be gentle." She offered the arm to him.

Using as light a touch as possible, Toby began at her recently broken wrist. Oddly, the more gently he touched her, the more aware of her he was; of the whorls in her skin and of the hairs that stood up in anticipation of the touch of cold mud. She had freckles on her forearms that made a pattern as decipherable as Hiko's tattoo. With great care, he daubed mud over the shirt that covered her burned shoulder and chest and spread his fingers over her chest.

"Your face?"

She nodded and, using only his fingertips, Toby pressed mud on to her wide forehead and down the smooth bridge of her nose, into the creases on either side and up to the delicate skin around her sea-green eyes.

When he'd finished he quickly turned and wiped the remaining clay on himself, coating the parts he didn't want Ayla to touch.

When he was finished she turned to him with a challenging grin. "Your turn. We'll have to go to your cell."

She walked past him and Toby let out his breath. In the corridor, he could see other couples. Lenka and Matus were already finished and were heading toward the stairs, mud drying in smears all over their bodies. Moira and Brody were close behind them, sloppily applied clay dropping off them in thick clumps. He glanced at Summer's door, but it was closed and there was no sign of Arthur.

He slipped into his cell.

Slap. Ayla wasn't gentle. Her palms moved quickly over his bare chest, brushing the hair and creating a tremor that ran to his toes.

"Turn around," she demanded.

Toby turned and tensed until her hands clapped on to his shoulder blades and moved inward, running down his spine and across his waist.

She grinned as she finished his arms and legs. "You look great."

She stepped close to do his face and her breath mingled with his as she smoothed slip over his cheeks. Toby closed his eyes, reminded of the night in his sleeping quarters when, for a brief moment, they had trusted each other.

Her fingers had stopped moving.

"Open your eyes, Toby," she whispered.

His eyes snapped open.

"That's better."

She stared into them, her thoughts unreadable.

Then she turned away.

Toby's throat bobbed. "We'd better go back to the courtyard," he said.

They were last out. The other couples were all covered in mud, looking like they had emerged from a swamp. Lenka's straw hair now stood up almost vertically, while Brody had decided to cover Moira's hair completely; her usual spikes were flattened as if they'd been waxed. Arthur had taken pains to leave Summer's hair mud free, but it still clung to her arms and back like seaweed. Arthur had coated her in mud so thick her body looked lumpen and still she kept her arms tightly around herself. Mother Hesper walked around the group, checking them. As the sun touched the West Wall, Toby clenched his fists—soon another two teens would be taken to the altar.

"Sit in a circle in the center of the courtyard." Mother Hesper pointed, as if they would be unable to work out where that was.

Toby sat with Ayla on one side of him and Summer on the other. Uzuri was directly across from him and his gaze settled on the flash of her dark brown eyes as she, too, checked around her.

"Sit comfortably." Mother Hesper swished forward. She stood so close to Toby that his skin crawled. Even over the mud that covered his nose, he could smell the must of her robes and something sour.

"In today's challenge, your dedication to the Orb will be tested. You must sit in the sun and not move. When you move, your mud coating will flake off, so we will know. You have until nightfall—the one with the least amount of mud remaining upon them will lose for their pair."

"All we have tae do is sit still," Brody said, moving his lips as little as possible. He gave a small smile and looked at Ayla. "Ye ever hidden from a Georgian patrol for three days?"

Ayla said nothing.

"We have." Moira was smug.

FIFTEEN

At first it was easy to remain still. Toby sat with his legs folded, his hands resting on his knees and his neck slightly bent. After a while he closed his eyes; the sunlight gleaming from the bronze sunburst on the sanctuary roof was reflecting from the metal sundial and making his vision blur.

Time passed.

Toby opened his eyes again, certain that he must have been sitting for an hour at least but the shadow of the sundial had barely moved. What did that mean? Had it really been only a few minutes?

He shifted his gaze upward without moving his neck. Uzuri and Zahir were utterly motionless, only the slight rise and fall of their chests told Toby that they were even breathing. There was no movement whatsoever to catch his attention and pull it one way or another. The teens all sat like statues, totally silent, streaked with silver where the mud had dried fastest.

Toby could tell where his own clay was drying because his skin had tightened underneath, pulled by the tiny hairs into the shell that was beginning to form around him. He glanced at his right forearm, fascinated by the process as the clay hardened, but underneath he began to itch.

He tried to turn his mind to something else.

Beside him he could hear Ayla breathing slowly, meditatively, in and out. He latched on to the sound, focusing on the measured inhalations.

But the more he thought about his inability to move, the more panicked his heartbeat became; it thudded against his ribs and forced his breath faster. He was sure the clay over his chest would soon shatter. Every muscle tensed. How was everyone else doing this?

"Toby." Ayla spoke out of the corner of her mouth. "Take . . . deep . . . breaths."

He tensed his arms even tighter, forcing himself to stay still and his breathing became shallow again.

"*Focus*," Ayla whispered, her lips barely moving.

On what? Toby pictured himself on the *Phoenix* with Hiko and D'von. Polly was on his shoulder and he was running, playing a game of catch with Hiko. The boys had rolled their sleeves up because of the sunshine and Hiko's tattoo flashed as he swung behind the mizzen mast and caught some rigging. Toby's stiff mouth tried to form a smile and he pressed his lips closer together.

In his mind, he and D'von swung after Hiko, whipping past the pirates on the deck below.

Then Toby thought of Dee, stuck on the cold rocks of Faroe Island. Had *Birdie* reached them yet? If so, she and Marcus would have already gone on to Reykjavik. Had they really tried to get on the *Banshee* with Ayla's note, or would they wait for a better ship?

A voice spoke to his right. "Keep . . . praying." He didn't dare look up to see which of the girls it was.

Someone else must be struggling with the challenge. Toby's heart rose slightly. He had seen no movement, but at least he wasn't alone in finding it difficult to sit still.

He closed his eyes once more. That's how they were doing it—praying.

Could he? Toby didn't believe what they did—that the Sun was listening, or that it was some all-powerful god capable of removing light on a whim.

But did he believe in anything else? There were a lot of different nationalities on board the *Phoenix*, each with slightly different beliefs. There were Catholics and Muslims, but also Methodists, Scientologists, and atheists. They'd even had a voodoo practitioner once.

He thought of his hands, moving on the *Phoenix*'s engines. Did they know that he, Toby, controlled them?

His mind spun around the question. Of course not, there was no mind in a machine. . . . But to a god, wouldn't Toby have as much agency?

This was impossible. Did he think that someone was listening in to his thoughts? No. But did he think it was worth reaching out and asking for strength from somewhere? Maybe the simple act of asking would be enough to access willpower that he didn't know he had.

His thoughts spiralled further and further inward. His breathing slowed and when Toby opened his eyes, time had passed.

Now he was thirsty. When he swallowed it felt as if there was a coil of thistle in his throat. He, at least, had drunk a cup of water before the challenge had started. Ayla had not. How was she feeling? He listened for her breathing again. It remained steady. She seemed fine.

Sudden claws dug into his leg. Cramp. Toby's eyes widened as he fought to remain still.

"What's the . . . matter?" Ayla murmured.

"C-cramp." Toby felt tiny flakes of clay crack and slide from his upper lip when he spoke. His breath came faster.

"Flex . . . your muscles . . . but . . . don't move."

"I *can't.*" Toby felt the pressure of tears against his eyes and groaned. Opposite, Uzuri turned her gaze on to him, anticipating his failure.

All he wanted to do was knead the cramp away.

"If you move . . . I'll kill you," Ayla rasped.

"I *know.*"

Every breath was a groan now and Toby knew the others were listening, circling around his failure like sharks.

Then, as quickly as it had arrived, the cramp vanished. The muscle in his thigh quivered, as if exhausted. The clay on his thigh had cracked, but not flaked, not yet.

As his chest subsided and his breathing slowed there was a sigh from his right shoulder, a huff of disappointment that terrified him.

Sweat began to trickle down his chest and sides, wetting the clay. The mud was protecting him from the sun's rays, but baking him alive. How long before nightfall?

There was a moan from his left, reminding him that he was not the only one struggling. He felt guilty relief.

This time when he took a deep breath, the clay on his chest

cracked. Toby watched in horror as fissures appeared and chunks of clay tumbled down his front like rocks from a mountain.

He held his breath, but then his fingers twitched without his volition; a tiny movement, which might not have been seen. Toby closed his eyes, now he was praying.

"It hurts," Summer whispered from Toby's right-hand side and he fought the impulse to turn and look at her.

The shadow of the sundial seemed to have skipped toward the wall. Night was approaching. How long had the group been sitting there? Toby had no idea, but he knew he could not keep it up for much longer. The tiny movement in his fingers had spread and muscle spasms periodically created fractures in his clay coating. He could feel the creaking of the shell on his back. Would it soon slide off in one great piece? When he swallowed, he could sense the armor over his throat lifting and falling. If that went, it would take out his lap as well.

"How're ye doin' there, Falklands?" Moira goaded. "Looks like yer Sun boy is struggling."

"Bite me." Ayla kept her reply short but Toby's heart thumped.

"None of you deserve this more than we do," Matus muttered. "Just move."

Was it Matus who had groaned earlier? Was he as desperate as Toby?

Then Toby heard quiet crying become louder sobs. He didn't dare turn to see who it was, but he knew it wasn't Uzuri, Summer, or Ayla. Moira had recently spoken and she sounded more pissed off than miserable. That left Bianca, Lenka, and Celeste. Was that why Matus sounded so desperate, because he knew his partner was dragging him to the altar?

"My leg." The words were whispered, but filled with pain and Toby knew who it was: Cezar.

"Pray, Cezar," Bianca said. So it was Lenka or Celeste crying. The noise was grating on his ears.

The sun dipped below the wall, shrinking from an orb, to a semicircle, to a thin line. Then it was gone, leaving streaks of red in the clouds.

A breath of cool air descended over the courtyard and Toby heard the squeak of bats.

Torches blazed suddenly as brothers and sisters proceeded down the cathedral steps. They circled the teens and Toby's neck prickled. The instinct to look up almost destroyed him.

Finally, Mother Hesper spoke. "Judge, Brothers and Sisters—which candidate has lost the most clay."

Toby found a new well of stillness inside him. As the heat of a torch burned on his back, he squeezed his eyes tightly closed. He did not trust himself not to look up at the attendant who examined him.

Footsteps crunched in the dust around him. He sensed the closeness of breath on his skin, then movement away.

"This one."

Toby jumped, the voice was overhead. He looked up, but the attendants were not pointing at him. It was the crier, her sobs so much louder now: Celeste.

Toby had barely spoken to the Italian couple. They were so

wrapped up in each other that they had no interest in anyone else, but their love had somehow lightened the atmosphere.

When Mother Hesper stalked behind them, Aldo simply reached across to Celeste's hand and squeezed it tightly. They helped one another to stand, staggering as their legs unkinked, then they pressed their foreheads together. Their whispered "I love you" fluttered through the air, then they stumbled, with quiet dignity, up the steps of the sanctuary. The door closed behind them with a hollow bang.

No screams sounded.

The attendants surrounding them bent down finally, with wet cloths. Toby thought the sister behind him was going to wash his face, but instead the woman held it to his lips. "Take this first, you need a drink."

It tasted musty, as if the cloth was old and unwashed, but the liquid slid down his throat and he closed his lips more tightly and sucked harder, getting every drop of moisture that he could.

Then the attendant took the flannel away and handed it back dripping once more. "Mother wants you to clean off the worst of it before you walk through the sanctuary to the baths." Sympathy lined her young face.

"Did you have to do trials like this?" Toby rasped.

The attendant shook her head. "I wasn't suitable for the festival." She turned to show him a twist of light brown hair. "You're lucky to take part . . ." She looked around swiftly and fell silent. Toby handed his cloth back to her. Under cover of darkness, she gave his hand a squeeze, then left with the others.

Toby tried to stand up, but his legs had completely seized. He rolled to his knees and saw Cezar clutching his leg with fingers that were bent into claws.

As they all struggled to rise, moans filled the air and bones cracked as they stretched.

Toby turned to Ayla; she was still covered in clay—hers had barely cracked.

"How did you stay so still?" he croaked, dust clogging his throat.

Ayla raised her arms above her head. "I pretended I was on watch." A loud crack and slabs of clay broke off her shoulders and shattered on the floor.

Moira sidled up behind him. "Ye only just made it through that test. How d'ye think ye'll do on the next one?"

Toby stepped closer to Ayla. "We'll do fine. Are you worried?"

Moira shook her head. "No' at all," she sneered.

Ayla placed a hand on his forearm. "Ignore her."

Toby nodded and turned his back on Moira, which put him in front of Lenka. She, too, smirked when she looked at him. "What's the matter, lost your tongue?" Her hair still stood up and in the firelight she looked like a demon. "Next time. Right, Matus?" Beside her Matus nodded, the torches flicking shadows onto his face.

Instinctively, Toby looked round. Arthur was watching him. It looked as if he wanted to say something, but then he headed toward the steps after Summer.

Toby and Ayla followed, separating only when they reached the bathrooms.

The tanks in the bathing house were heated by direct sunlight, meaning the water was never more than tepid, but Toby was grateful for the cool as he scrubbed the final streaks of dried mud into the graying tub.

He threw on his clothes. Zahir was in the next bath with his eyes closed; he looked like a jellyfish splayed in the water.

"Are you all right?" Toby touched his shoulder. Zahir didn't move, but he opened his pink eyes and looked at Toby.

"I am just thinking, Toby. What will they have us do tomorrow?" He closed his eyes again. "I believe in the Sun. I was meant for this." He sank lower in the water. "But . . . I am afraid."

Toby found Ayla in the courtyard.

"How're you doing?" He hesitated, then gave her hand a squeeze.

Ayla leaned close. "We need to move on this."

Toby nodded his agreement.

"Follow my lead," she whispered.

Mother Hesper was on the top step, watching Zahir as he emerged into the courtyard. He kept his eyes low as he passed.

The mother's own eyes were hooded by her low brow and her cheekbones sliced lines of shadow into her face.

Ayla marched up the steps toward her. "May Toby and I please pray inside the Reliquary?" She lowered her chin and made a sun sign. "I feel the need to be closer to the Sun than ever."

Mother Hesper frowned. "*Inside* the Reliquary?"

"Yes. Like the brother we saw."

"The Reliquary is only for those high enough in the Solar Order . . . brothers and sisters, mothers and fathers." Mother Hesper started to turn away.

"But the relics seem like proof that the Sun pays attention." Ayla hung her head and Toby saw the muscle in her jaw twitching. "I felt so close to the Sun in there and it's been so *hard* today. Hail the Sun." Ayla raised her hand higher, as if pressing the sister to agree.

"You are trying to seem more devout than us!" Furious, Lenka ran up the steps behind Ayla. "But you are not. *We* want to pray in the Reliquary, too." She nodded vigorously at Matus.

"That does sound like a good idea." Summer stepped forward. "We'd like to pray in the Reliquary as well."

"You would all like to do this?" Mother Hesper raised her eyebrows.

Bianca nodded. "A prayer before the relics *would* help me center myself . . . after . . ." Her eyes went to the door through which Aldo and Celeste had vanished.

Mother Hesper stared thoughfully at Bianca then finally she spoke. "You may have a few minutes in the Reliquary."

The guardian uncles were not happy about the visit, taking their time about moving aside and glowering at Mother Hesper as she unlocked the thick iron-wood door. The six couples filed past with their heads down. Only Ayla looked up, and Toby saw her taking note of the uncle's weapons, her face calculating. He caught her hand and drew her attention to give a small shake of his head.

She scowled and faced the door, but left her hand in his. Toby wrapped his fingers around hers as they entered the crypt.

Most of the couples went to the museum pieces. Bianca, Zahir and Uzuri dropped to their knees in front of the Egyptian statues, but the others remained standing, heads bowed.

Mother Hesper watched suspiciously as Ayla and Toby headed toward the inverters where they sat among the other strange devices, their Solaris symbols displayed.

"Don't you want to pray with the others?"

Ayla shook her head. "To me, *these* are the best relics—they caused the Sun to go out, so I know the Sun listens *here*." She stopped in front of them. "Praise the Sun," she said loudly.

Lenka's head flew up and she nudged Matus. "I want to pray there," she hissed.

"She's right." Moira turned. "Those relics're holier."

"Much." Toby nodded.

"Well, I wasn't distracted by the shiny things." Ayla gestured disparagingly at the jewels and museum pieces.

Arthur put a hand on Summer's arm as the girl jerked up, anger burnishing her cheeks.

Ayla leaned in close to Toby and pressed her lips to his ear. "Be ready," she mouthed.

Toby stepped closer to the relics. The inverters were near the front, piled together. A single grab would get him both, but only if no one was watching.

"You think you're so devout." Ayla looked at Bianca. "But there you are, praying in front of jewelery and other valuables like a banker with his money box."

Bianca abandoned the statuettes and leaped to her feet. Her long fingernails slashed the air and she faced Ayla, nose to nose.

"Girls . . ." Mother Hesper's voice held a warning tone but Ayla

put one hand on Bianca's hip and one on her shoulder. "Get out of my face," she hissed and she shoved hard. Bianca flew backward and thudded into the wall between the shelves.

As Mother Hesper cried out in alarm, Toby edged closer to the shelf on which the relics were displayed.

Lenka reached for Ayla's arms. "You think you're more devout than us?" she screeched. "You think *you'll* win the trials? There's no way you'll beat Matus and I."

Ayla spun around, as fast as Toby had seen her move; she knocked one of Lenka's grasping hands out of the way with her shoulder and as Lenka staggered sideways, she continued her turn, grabbed the girl by her neck and bent her over her knee, backward.

Lenka gasped, unable to cry out and with a yell Bianca jumped on to Ayla's back and yanked her hair. Ayla issued a sharp punch to Lenka's forehead, dropped the dazed girl and reached up. She put one hand on her own skull to prevent her hair being pulled any harder; then with the other, she grabbed Bianca, ducked and flung her over her shoulder.

The air flew from Lenka's lungs in a burst as Bianca crashed on top of her. Bianca screamed, rolling to clutch her spine.

Mother Hesper retreated from Bianca's thrashing limbs. "That's enough," she said loudly. "This is a holy place."

But now Moira and Brody were circling.

"You're nae better than us," Moira hissed.

Toby swallowed. It was as if all the tension that had wound inside them over the last few days had suddenly found an outlet. Could Ayla handle this?

Cezar hopped from foot to foot, looking from Toby to the others.

Toby knew he couldn't get the inverters while Cezar was watching him. Toby held up his hands in a gesture of surrender, making it clear he wouldn't get involved.

His back met the shelf. The items he so desperately wanted were right behind him and now a furious Mother Hesper was marching to the Reliquary door. Toby's heart thudded. "She's going for the uncles," he called.

Ayla nodded. Things had to get chaotic and fast. She surged toward Brody. It looked to Toby like she was punching wildly, but each fist landed with almost surgical precision, causing maximum damage without actually putting him out of the fight. When Moira threw herself into the fray, her own arms flailing, Toby realized the trio had drawn every eye, even Cezar's.

In one swift movement, he reached around and pulled his waistband open at the back. With his other hand he swept the two inverters off the shelf. When he felt them tumble inside he exhaled and took two long steps away from the shelf and the fight.

He bent down as if to rub away a cramp in his leg and pulled the inverters from the bottom of his pants. When he stood up, he slipped one into each pocket and returned his attention to Ayla.

Half of her attention was on him. When she saw him stand, she tried to pull back from the fight. Immediately, Moira took advantage of her loss of focus. Wrapping her arms around Ayla, she held her still, while Brody raised his fists.

Toby shouted, but he couldn't risk diving in to save Ayla and losing the inverters.

So he didn't move.

SIXTEEN

As Toby shouted, Bianca rolled back to her feet and grabbed Ayla's shirt. She yanked it sideways, ripping the material and Ayla struggled as the sputtering torchlight showed her scars to the group.

"*Ha!*" Bianca lifted one hand, her long nails flashing.

This had gone too far. Inverters almost forgotten, Toby dived forward to stop Bianca—and ran straight into an outstretched arm. Matus. He slammed into the floor, back first, gasping for breath. Immediately his hands went to his pockets—both inverters remained secure. But at Ayla's scream he looked up.

Her face was turned upward and her lips were twisted with agony.

Horror-struck, Toby watched Bianca dig her pointed nails deeper into Ayla's shoulder and drag downward. Ayla's scar tissue peeled like the skin of an orange. Four furrows filled with blood, which started to drip down her arm.

"Stop it!" Toby screamed.

Mother Hesper burst back into the room with two uncles at her back. Fury drew her features into thin lines and she shouted with rage until one of the big men dragged Bianca from Ayla's side.

For a second, Bianca fought, half-crazed. Then, she stopped

abruptly. She nodded to the uncle and, when he released her, she stepped backward, lifted her nails to her face and, slowly, licked them clean.

"You're sick," Toby choked.

Even Lenka slid her gaze sideways, unable to look at Ayla's injuries. When the second guard pulled Moira's arms from Ayla and pushed her away, Toby struggled to his feet, pushed Brody out of the way, and caught his partner as her knees folded.

"I'm going to *kill* her," Ayla seethed, shaking him free and reeling to her feet. She straightened and pulled her shirt closed, but not before Mother Hesper had seen her chest.

"Are those burns?" Mother Hesper stepped close and licked her lips.

"What of it?" Ayla threw her head back.

Mother Hesper exhaled. "Very holy. The heat of the Sun would burn us if we drew too close." She took hold of Ayla's collar with skeletal fingers and pulled it aside. She leaned in to examine the pink skin, turning her head one way and then the other, then her eyes went to the seeping wounds.

"Those could get infected." She dropped Ayla's shirt over the bloody marks. Immediately, the cloth began to redden. "We have an infirmary. I will take you there."

"I'm coming, too." Toby folded his arms.

"Your presence isn't necessary," Mother Hesper growled.

"I want him to come." Ayla's voice was shaking. Toby hoped she was putting on an act; otherwise, she was in even more pain than he had realized.

"Fine," Mother Hesper said eventually. "Both of you come to

the infirmary." She turned to the others. "Fighting like this is not acceptable. You will all be on half portions at mealtime. Now leave this place. The Reliquary is out of bounds to you until the festival."

Mother Hesper abandoned them outside the infirmary.

"In there. Your dinner will be waiting when you're finished."

Toby nodded and pushed open the patchwork metal door. Inside, flickering lamplight illuminated four beds—two were occupied.

"Celeste, Aldo!" Toby ran inside. The couple were unconscious in adjacent beds. Even in sleep, they held hands, their linked fingers bridging the gap between them.

They had been washed and dressed, but blood had dried on both sets of lips and Celeste's delicate features were drawn into a tight frown, as though she were dreaming badly.

As Toby skidded to a stop, a brother with very short black hair, wearing a white coat over his robes turned and glared. "Quiet."

"Hideaki!" Ayla stopped just in front of the man. "We thought you were dead."

Toby stepped closer. Now that he was looking for it, he could see the skull and crossbones tattoo that was almost completely covered by the man's growing hair.

Hideaki glanced quickly at the door. "Close it," he hissed. While Toby clicked the door shut, he checked that his patients really were asleep with a gentle nudge. Satisfied that they had privacy, he turned and embraced Ayla.

"Second—you came for me!"

"Not exactly." Ayla pushed him away. "We're here for the inverters."

"But you have a plan to get out?"

Ayla looked sideways at Toby, who flushed. They had a plan to get the two of them out. Hideaki did not fit into it.

"We'll find a way," Toby insisted.

"I know how to get to the inverters." Hideaki spread his hands. "It'll be easier with the three of us. I'll help you reach them, but only if I can leave with you."

Ayla cleared her throat. "Toby?"

"You trust him?" Toby glanced at the Japanese doctor. "What if he's gone native?"

"Gone native?" Hideaki spat and lowered his voice. "*Fuzakeru na!* Have you any idea what it's like in here?" He threw a bloody cloth into the sink. "I just had to stitch up six children who will never speak again." He closed his eyes.

"Being a silent attendant is meant to be a huge honor," Ayla mumbled. "They get to know the greatest mysteries."

"It's the sun, how damn mysterious can it be?" Hideaki snapped. "I'm no doctor but, as the most qualified here, I'm in charge of the infirmary. It's insane. You know some of them don't eat. They believe that they should be able to live on sunlight. Live on sunlight!" He shook his head. "I am constantly treating burns because they think it takes them closer to the Sun."

Ayla touched her throat, remembering Mother Hesper's words when she saw Ayla's own injuries: *Very holy.*

"Then there're the endless services and prayers to the Orb. I have to get out."

"I trust you." Ayla put a hand on his arm. "And I'll get us all out. As for the other—Toby?"

Toby put his hands in his pockets, but he didn't withdraw them. Had Ayla known where Hideaki was all along? Was that why she came up with a plan to get the inverters that meant she was sent to the infirmary? He was now facing two *Banshee* crew members. If they wanted to take both inverters and escape using the Tuinal, he couldn't stop them. Was the *Banshee*, at this moment, waiting offshore for its crew members, while the *Phoenix* anchored in Malta until the festival? Was this the double-cross Dee had warned him of? It made sense. Ayla had needed him to get the inverters, but she didn't need him any more.

"Toby?" Ayla frowned.

Toby retreated toward the door.

"Where're you going?" She looked at Hideaki and the doctor moved to block his exit.

"You trust him." Toby nodded toward Hideaki. "But how do I know you won't both betray *me*?"

Ayla went pale. "I thought we'd worked this out. I promised—"

Toby gave a bitter laugh. "What does a *promise* mean to a pirate from the *Banshee*?"

"You're being ridiculous." Ayla advanced, but she winced when her shirt brushed against her shoulder.

"All I have to do is yell." Toby clutched the inverters tightly.

"You wouldn't." Ayla shook her head. "Whatever happens to us, will happen to you. If they cut the tongues out of devotees, what'll they be willing to do to *us*?" She glanced at the door, then back at Toby. "We're in each other's hands. You can betray me to the Order, but I can do the same to you. You're as much in this as we are . . . and you have . . ." She pointed to his pockets.

Toby swallowed. "I keep one, you keep the other."

Ayla nodded. "Fine."

Toby took a deep breath and withdrew one of the inverters.

Hideaki gaped. "You . . . *How?*"

Ayla touched his shoulder. "You couldn't have done it alone."

"Aho!" Hideaki slapped his head, his face contorting as if he was holding back tears. "I've been here weeks and you . . ."

"Hideaki, don't beat yourself up—this wasn't a one-man job."

"It took both of us," Toby agreed. He was about to slip the inverter back in his pocket when Ayla held out her hand.

"I'll take that, thank you."

Toby hesitated.

"Toby!" Ayla's voice held a warning. "We had an agreement. Are you planning to betray *me*?"

"No!"

"Then hand it over."

Toby rubbed the Solaris logo with his thumb. Then he thrust the inverter at her in one quick movement. "Take it."

As Ayla closed her fingers around the inverter her shirt pulled at her shoulder again and she sucked air through her teeth.

Hideaki's eyes immediately lifted from her hand to the blood on her shirt. "Why did you come to the infirmary, Second?"

Ayla swallowed. "It's nothing." She dropped her hand to her side, clutching the inverter tightly.

Hideaki looked from Toby to Ayla, taking in his blond hair and her dark braids. He looked from Ayla to Celeste. "*Chikushō,* you are here for the festival, aren't you? I'll be stitching your tongue up next."

"No, you won't," Ayla snapped. "Don't you think I can win this? I'm the second-in-command—"

"She's injured," Toby interrupted angrily. "The cuts need washing out properly and she'll need antibiotics."

"I have none. Do you mind, Second?" Deferentially, Hideaki led Ayla to a bed and helped her to sit. It was a measure of the pain she was in that she allowed him to aid her.

Then he carefully peeled the shirt from her shoulder and Ayla inhaled sharply. His face tightened when he saw the injury. "Nail marks—this was done by some *busu*," he growled. "You were fighting?"

Ayla rolled her eyes. "It was part of the plan."

"You should have been friendlier with them from the start." Toby sighed. "Then they might not have hurt you so badly."

Ayla glowered at him. "This is a competition. We're not here to make friends. I've watched you sucking up to the others, it's—"

"It makes sense to have allies." Toby leaned in. "Why can't you get along with people?"

"I get along with my crew." Her sea-green stare darkened.

"But the other girls . . . If you just—"

"If I just *what*? How am I supposed to behave? I haven't met another girl since my sisters were killed." She clenched her fists. "Maybe if your mother hadn't . . ." She stopped and took a deep breath. "Now isn't the time for this."

Toby backed away until his legs bumped Celeste's cot. He held his breath as the girl stirred; then she tightened her hold on Aldo's hand and settled back into sleep. "You're right to remind me. I should go."

Ayla grabbed the sheet beneath her and twisted it awkwardly in her fingers. "Yes. You should leave while Hideaki treats me, anyway. I'll meet up with you in the dining room."

Toby's jaw tightened. "If that's what you want."

"It would be best." Hideaki narrowed his eyes. "I'll need to remove her shirt and clean the wound properly. I have disinfectant for the cuts. It will hurt." He addressed the last comment to Ayla.

Ayla nodded. "Go, Toby. I'll see you later."

As he walked out, Toby slid his right hand into his pocket and curled his fingers around the inverter there; his left felt dangerously empty.

SEVENTEEN

Toby was sitting next to Arthur at the dining table, but this time they weren't talking. Toby's gaze was fixed on the door as he waited for Ayla.

With every unappetizing mouthful, he felt the pressure of eyes lingering on him from across the room. He refused to acknowledge them: Uzuri, Lenka, Moira, Bianca, Summer.

"Is she all right?"

"Leave it, Cezar." Toby jabbed at a piece of chicken—it tasted like ash—in his mouth.

Mother Hesper sat at the head of the girls' table. Once more, she pushed the food around her plate without eating, her thin arms protruding from her robes like sticks. Father Dahon sat at the head of the boys' table. Each piece of meat reached his lips unerringly, yet he chewed messily, making loud slurping noises.

His thick black brows came together when the door slammed open.

Toby's attention snapped across the room to Ayla striding forward, not a hint of discomfort on her face.

She sat in the chair that had been left empty for her between

Uzuri and Lenka. Then she deliberately used her left arm to pull her plate toward her.

Arthur raised his head. "She's all right then." He seemed relieved. "I couldn't help . . . you understand?"

Toby nodded. "I get it."

"I couldn't leave Summer."

"Summer's not a baby." Zahir spoke up, his red-rimmed eyes blinking in the lamplight. "She's as determined to win as the rest of us."

"And she will . . . I'll make sure of it." Arthur speared his meat so viciously that his plate jumped on the table.

Father Dahon pushed his empty plate to one side, rose to his feet, nodded to the group, and walked out of the dining hall.

There was a brief silence then, gradually, conversation restarted.

Toby looked at Arthur. "If you lose, you forfeit your tongue; if you win, you lose your sight. You're okay with that?"

"Of course." Arthur frowned. "That's what we're here for."

The others nodded.

"Isn't it . . . ?" Arthur stared at Toby, his gaze sharpening.

Toby tensed. "Yes, of course. It's just now that it's happening . . . it's scarier than I expected."

"As long as Summer keeps her tongue." Arthur looked across the room. "She can't play the flute without it."

"We all want to keep our tongues," Matus snapped.

"You think it'll hurt—going blind?" Cezar whispered, and his Adam's apple bobbed.

"It doesn't take long." Arthur smiled at him. "Less than a minute if the Sun's out."

"And if it isn't?"

"Then it can take all afternoon," Matus sneered. "But we're in Gozo—the Sun's always out. Praise the Sun."

"Praise the Sun," Toby echoed. He stared at Cezar again. The boy was rubbing his eyes.

"Your family needs the money badly, huh?"

"We all do, don't we?" Brody had already cleaned his bowl and was peering hungrily at Toby's.

"To the elders, the money will be welcome," Zahir said.

"Sure," Matus muttered.

Toby sighed and, remembering his own words about getting along with people, pushed his bowl to Brody. "Here."

Brody looked stunned. "Th-thanks." He grabbed the food as if he was worried Toby would change his mind.

Toby turned back to Ayla, tuning the other boys out. She was eating slowly, taking her time, still using her left hand, determined to show that there was no issue. None of the girls were speaking.

"I'm not sure I can manage another trial," Cezar whispered. "I wish this was over."

Despite his memory of the darkness challenge, Toby welcomed the lightlessness of his cell.

He lay with his eyes on the ceiling, waiting for the familiar click of his door locking. As soon as the sister had completed her rounds, Toby reached under his thin mattress for the fork tine he had hidden there. He closed his fingers around the comforting sharpness of it. The fact that the tine was still there suggested to Toby that this might be a good enough hiding place for the inverter. Of course if the relic was discovered missing, the guards might well search the cells and, if they did, the first place they would look would be under the mattress.

Toby rolled to his knees and crawled under his bed. The dirt floor was hard, but he used the tine to scrape away at the floor nearest Ayla's wall.

The whole time he worked, he listened for a telltale sound of the hatch in his wall being opened. His shoulders tensed at every noise and sweat beaded his forehead.

After maybe an hour, Toby had managed to dig a small hole, but it wasn't nearly deep enough. With a sigh he got back to his feet. The ground was too hard. There was only one thing for it—he had to wet the hard-packed earth.

Pulling his bed as quietly as he could, Toby created a space between the wall and the bedframe. He quickly checked the hatch, worried that the noise might have called someone to check up on him, but it remained closed. Wishing he had drunk more at dinnertime, he wet the ground as swiftly as he could, then shoved the bed back into place. He paced for a few moments, waiting for the moisture to soak in, hoping he had hit the right place, then he crawled back underneath to dig once more.

Eventually, Toby was able to plant the inverter in the ground and pat mud back over it. It wouldn't hold up to a thorough search, but it was better than the alternatives.

He hopped back on to his bed, feeling jumpy, as if he felt the presence of someone behind his wall, but there was no movement. Toby closed his eyes, wiped his hands on his pants and tried to sleep, but he couldn't settle.

Unless there was something that needed to be done with the boiler, Toby usually slept in a room with almost fifty other pirates: those who weren't on watch or working night crew. He was used to sleeping in a crowd, but not to being watched while he did so. Now his shoulder blades itched and his whole body was tense. He couldn't fall asleep knowing that at any time someone could be peering in at him through the hatch in his wall, watching, listening.

He turned the fork tine over and over in his fingers, worrying at the metal like a comforter.

"Ayla, are you awake?" he called eventually.

There was a pause before she replied, but there was no hint of sleep in her voice. "Yes—but we can't talk here."

"I know." Toby fell silent.

Making up his mind, he rose and felt for the hatch. He found it despite the gloom and his fingers patted the splintered wood, feeling for the edge. He jammed the tine, so no one would be able to slide it open from the other side. Finally he would be able to fall asleep.

It still took what felt like hours.

"Is it morning already?" Matus staggered out of his cell, rubbing his eyes.

Toby slipped the fork tine into a hole he had created in the hem of his sleeve and joined the others gathering in the corridor. If anyone went to check his hatch they'd find nothing wrong.

Ayla smoothed her lopsided hair with her right hand. Toby noticed that she winced when she had to move her left.

"Did Hideaki give you anything for the pain?" he whispered.

Ayla shook her head. "Nothing to take away. It gives me an excuse to go and see him again later."

"Do you have your . . . ?"

"Shut up!" Ayla glanced at Mother Hesper, who had stopped trying to rouse Cezar and was watching them with narrowed eyes. She lowered her voice to almost nothing. "Hideaki has it."

Toby nodded as Cezar joined them. He looked tearful and his eyes were redder than Zahir's, as though he had been crying all night. Toby's heart clenched at the sight: Cezar was totally unprepared for the day ahead. Would he be next to go to the altar?

Bianca saw the same thing Toby had and grabbed Cezar's arm. "Didn't you get any rest?"

"I'll be fine." Cezar shook her off, but when Mother Hesper herded them toward the courtyard once more, Cezar's limp was more pronounced than ever.

As Ayla was in the cell nearest the door, she was first on to the sanctuary steps. Toby could not see past her, but as soon as the light hit her, Ayla froze and then backpedaled.

"What is it?" Alarmed, Toby caught her elbows before anyone else could see her retreat.

Ayla was shaking. "Do you think they had this planned already, or is it specially for me?"

"Get a move on," Bianca snapped. "We all want to see."

Ayla turned to Toby. "I-I don't think I can do this." Her usual composure had been shattered. Toby clutched her tighter as the others crowded into the doorway behind them.

"Get outta the way." Moira shoved and Toby stumbled.

"Walk with me." He pushed Ayla gently. She resisted and Toby had to wrestle her onto the top step and into the light.

At first, he was blinded by the morning glare, but finally Toby saw what had terrified his partner. "Ashes," he muttered.

He and Ayla stood motionless on the top step as the others shoved past and lined up in the dust. He jumped as Mother Hesper's hand landed on his shoulder.

"Is there a problem?"

"Of course not." Toby shook his head, but Ayla spun around in sudden fury.

"You did this on purpose, you skeletal witch."

Toby leaped between them and opened his arm. "Ayla, no!"

Mother Hesper merely raised her eyebrows. "If you don't want to take part in the challenge, I understand. Your decision will be honored."

Ayla's head snapped up, momentary relief clearing the cloud from her face. "You mean I don't have to do it?"

"Wait, what? How is that fair?" Lenka started back up the stairs.

"Of course it will be an instant forfeit, and you and your partner will go to the altar," Mother Hesper continued.

Ayla clamped her jaw tightly closed.

"Well?" Mother Hesper tilted her head. "What's your decision?"

Ayla remained silent, trembling against Toby's chest. He stiffened.

"Fine." Ayla stepped away from them both. "I'll do it. If you think you can break me with this, you don't know me." Her face was pale, but she marched down the stairs, past the waiting teens and right up to the mountain of dry kindling that was piled in the center of the courtyard.

Part of Toby was impressed. "Where did you get so much combustible?" he murmured.

Mother Hesper smirked. "Pilgrimages . . . offerings from the sea . . . our own plantations on Gozo. We have riches you've never dreamed of."

Toby began to follow her down the steps. "So this was already planned, you didn't set this up because you saw Ayla's injuries?"

Mother Hesper said nothing, simply swept past him and raised her arms. "A circle has been drawn around the bonfire."

Toby squinted at the ground. Sure enough, a line had been etched in the sand.

"Sit on the line," she continued. "The first one to move farther away will lose the challenge."

Toby jogged to Ayla's side. She stood by the line, trembling slightly. "Sit on my right. I'll shield your left side as much as I can."

Ayla curled her lip. "I'll be fine." Her spine was straight and the long half of her hair lay against her back. Toby looked at it with a sinking heart. She couldn't even pull her hair in front of her burns to protect the sensitive skin from the heat.

"Here." Toby pulled off his shirt. "Wrap that round your left shoulder on top of your own shirt, it'll give you added protection."

"What about you?" Ayla glanced at his exposed chest and handed it back.

"You know what the boiler room's like." Toby pressed the shirt back into her hand. "This kind of heat doesn't bother me." She hesitated, wavering. "Honestly, it's a hundred degrees in there. Take the shirt."

She sucked her bottom lip. "You'll be fine?"

"I'll get sunburn, but I can take it."

Ayla reached out a finger and touched Toby's nut-brown forearm, running her hand up to where the skin became pale on his shoulder.

"It'll hurt."

Toby caught her hand. "Not as much as having my tongue removed. The others are already sitting. Come on."

He held out his hand. Ayla blinked and then took it. He helped her sit and then sat himself, angling his right shoulder so that it provided some shade for Ayla's left. Neither of them looked at the others, but Toby sensed their relief. They were certain Ayla was going to hand them the victory.

Once they were ready, Father Dahon exited the sanctuary with a flaming torch. Ayla swallowed as Mother Hesper took it from him then, in one smooth movement, launched it over their heads and into the bonfire. It wedged in the side nearest Toby and Ayla.

Ayla had closed her eyes when the torch cartwheeled above her, but now she opened them, pinning her gaze on the licking flame.

"It's gone out," she whispered.

Toby's heart sank at the hope in her voice. "Just wait," he said, and he held her hand.

Ayla didn't pull away—instead she leaned closer, holding her breath. A glow grew brighter inside the pile of kindling as it began to smolder, a red bud that blossomed all of a sudden into a bright orange flower. Ayla's breath flew out of her as the flame went, in seconds, from a glow to a crackling blaze. Tendrils of flame wound between logs and slid from one combustible to the next, hissing as they grew between the cracks like vines. The color of the bonfire's heart deepened and darkened and the flames twisted higher into the sky, yellowing as they rose until they met the sun's rays in one single blaze.

Ayla covered her face as a gust of wind blasted smoke in her direction. Ash blew over Toby and settled into the hair on his chest.

He could feel his face reddening.

"There is water behind each of you. Use it only to drink." Father Dahon's sibilant rasp caused Toby to turn, carefully. He was terrified of accidentally moving from the line. Sure enough, a clay tankard of water now sat behind each of them.

"They're giving us water?" Ayla's surprise matched his own.

"The heat is going to be severe." Toby squeezed her hand again. "They don't want anyone passing out and winning by default."

"Makes sense," Ayla muttered. She took one more glance at the water, as if to reassure herself that it was real, then turned back to the fire.

Toby looked around. To his left, Zahir was already flinching and had covered his eyes with his hands. Tears were running between his fingers. Toby nudged Ayla. "The brightness bothers him," he whispered.

Lenka and Matus were coughing; the breeze had turned and was gusting thick smoke in their direction.

Ticklish sweat ran down Toby's neck and chest, drying before it reached his pants.

Uzuri was glaring at Ayla, silently willing her to break before Zahir. As the heat built, Ayla clutched Toby's hand more tightly. Her palm was wet in his and her hair was already sticking to her forehead. Her breath came in short rasps and her spine was ramrod straight. When she started to rub her broken wrist with her free hand, Toby knew she was thinking of the explosion.

The boiler fire was nothing like this. Toby rubbed sweat out of his eyes and ducked his head, no longer able to watch the flames. The bonfire had become an inferno. With a crack, a large log snapped in two and fell into the center of the blaze, forcing the smaller kindling to spread out, getting closer to Ayla's feet. She gasped and pulled in her toes. Toby held her to him.

"Don't run."

"I'm not going to," she growled, but she let him keep holding her.

The sound of the fire had developed into a roar. Summer had clapped her hands over her ears and Arthur was holding onto her long tresses, which were blowing in the direction of the flying sparks.

"I need my drink," Ayla moaned.

Toby could barely hear her. He nodded to show that he understood and she reached behind her for the tankard.

Before he could tell her not to, she had knocked the whole thing back. Rivulets of cool water dripped down her throat and soaked into her collar and Toby swallowed, suddenly desperate for his own water. He didn't dare drink. Ayla would need more.

All around them, the teens were reaching for their cups. Toby hung his head and tried to absorb the heat into his body, picturing the boiler room at its hottest.

He imagined that he could hear the sounds of the *Phoenix* around him, that the fire's snarl was the thunder of the engine running at full speed, that the hiss of the flames was the muffled sound of her paddles, and the crack and crackle of disintegrating logs was the crunch and crash of junk being smashed by her ice-breaker hull.

He pictured the captain's face when he handed him the inverter and leaned closer to Ayla, trying to shade her sensitive skin.

She was shaking now—her whole body a tense string that could break at any moment.

"It's okay to lean on me," Toby shouted.

"It's not okay! I don't lean on anyone." Ayla turned a glare on him, but her eyes were haunted. "I thought this would get easier the longer I sat here, but the heat is just . . ." She swallowed. "All I can think about is that explosion. I keep seeing it . . . feeling it slam into me . . . the smell of my own skin burning."

Toby put his lips close to her ear. He could feel the heat radiating from her face and the dampness of her sweat.

"Picture the sea," he murmured. He stroked her palm with his thumb. "Pretend you're on board the *Phoenix*. It's night, so it's cool, even below deck." He felt the slight easing of her shoulders. "You and I aren't sleepy, so we sneak past the others, snoring in their cots, we climb the ladder to the hatch, and we go outside." Ayla closed her eyes. "There's a cool breeze in the air and the salt is calm, junk is bobbing in the waves and the paddles are churning easily, moving us onward, toward the island. That's the noise you can hear, the roar of the *Phoenix* breaking the junk as she ploughs the salt." Ayla nodded. "We decide to climb to the crow's nest. As we get higher, the wind gets stronger and it soothes your skin." Her shoulders dropped a little more. "At the top we sit in front of the rail and look out. We could be the only people in the world. The salt is lifting us up and down and all you can hear is the creaking of the sails, the crunching of the junk and the muted roar of the paddles . . ." Toby stopped.

"We look up," Ayla rasped, "the stars are out."

"Yes," Toby smiled. "Cassiopeia is right above us, the plough is brushing the horizon, and Orion is low in the sky, his belt shining like diamonds."

"The seven sisters . . ." Ayla trailed off and Toby knew she had just thought of her own sisters, dead in the fire that had scarred her mother.

"The North Star," he said quickly. "We're sailing directly toward it: northwards, and growing cooler with every turn of the paddles."

"Then you put your arm around me . . ." Ayla whispered and she relaxed into his side.

"Yes," Toby cleared his throat. "I pull you close." He exhaled. "And I kiss you."

"You do?"

"Yes. I put my lips to yours and all the lights go out, so we really are the only people left under the stars."

The wind turned and Toby coughed as a cloud of smoke engulfed him and dragged him back to reality.

He blinked stinging ash from his eyes and checked on Ayla. She had flinched but seemed steadier. To his left, Zahir was shaking uncontrollably. His thick embroidered tunic was protecting him from the flames, but his throat was flushed scarlet from the heat. Toby knew the sun had burned his own shoulders and back, he could feel the prickle of tightening skin, but Zahir's neck and ears, where his high collar did not cover him, was already blistered and painful to look at. Zahir no longer tried to cover his eyes from the blaze—he simply sat with his chin on his chest, swaying. Beside him, Uzuri had taken off her linen robe and sat glistening in the firelight, her legs folded under her. The heat barely seemed to bother her at all.

Toby looked around more carefully. Lenka and Matus had

suffered from the smoke—their mugs were empty and their faces were pasted with sweat-soaked grime. They looked soot-grained like Toby did after a long stint in the boiler room.

Through the haze, he could just about make out Bianca and Cezar. Bianca was rubbing Cezar's leg for him, but neither looked like breaking any time soon.

How long could Ayla hold out?

As if the thought of her drew her attention, she clamped her fingers harder on his.

"Here, drink." Although his own throat was aching, Toby pushed his mug toward Ayla.

She frowned at him. "That's yours."

"Drink." Toby coughed again. "I don't need it."

"You're coughing." Ayla glowered.

"Fine." Toby sipped, twice. As the warmed water slid down his throat, soothing, it was all he could do to take the mug from his lips. "I'm done. You have the rest." He handed it across and Ayla's free hand clutched the mug so tightly that Toby knew she had been desperate for it.

He watched her drink. She gulped at the water as though putting out a fire inside her own body. He glanced up to see Arthur frowning at him.

Now the heat was unbearable. The leaping flames had turned the center of the bonfire into a white-hot furnace. Toby knew it would melt metal.

"I don't know how much longer I can face this," Ayla whispered.

Toby lowered his voice. "For as long as you need to. We can't lose.

Apart from anything else, we won't be able to get the *thing* out of my cell if we get taken to the altar—we've never seen a loser return."

Ayla swallowed and Toby forced a grin. "You're not going to show *weakness* are you? What would Nell say if I beat you at this?"

Ayla pulled her hand from Toby's. "You're right, I'm her bloody second. She'd kill me. This is just a dumb bonfire. It can't hurt me." She tossed her head. "And so what if it does. I've taken worse."

"That's right." Toby opened and closed his stiff fingers, half regretting what he had said to Ayla. But it had worked. She no longer looked as if she was in any danger of moving from the line.

Uzuri leveled a glare at him. She had been relying on Ayla to break before Zahir. Toby swallowed his guilt. This time Zahir would lose.

EIGHTEEN

The moment Zahir and Uzuri were led away, the teens rolled back from the fire as fast as they could.

It was only when Toby was gasping like a landed fish in the shade of the sanctuary wall, that he realized Ayla had not come with him. She remained ramrod straight and unmoving, the flame-light playing hypnotically over her face.

"Ayla." Toby crawled back to her and touched her back gently. "It's over."

Slowly, Ayla turned her head. She looked left and right, her eyes glazed. Then a slow smile lifted the corners of her lips.

"I beat them all."

Toby nodded.

"Even you, *Phoenix*."

"Yes." Toby tugged at her collar. "Move away from the heat."

Swaying, Ayla allowed Toby to pull her backward, her legs pedaling as she retreated from the fire. Then she faced the others. Summer was a limp rag in Arthur's arms, Bianca was vomiting on the sand, while Cezar rubbed her back. Brody and Moira leaned against one another in the shade of the high wall, breathing shallowly.

Ayla opened her mouth as though to say something, then she shook her head, shoved Toby to one side and ran.

Toby's legs were jelly and he figured Ayla's had to be worse, but he still couldn't catch her. From the wall above, the weight of an uncle's attention shifted toward them.

"Wait!"

"Go away!" Ayla barreled around a corner.

"We're not allowed beyond the rear courtyard. There's nowhere to go and you'll bring the uncles on us."

"I just want to be alone." She spun on her heel, beads clattering. "I can't believe I let everyone see me like that."

"They saw you win."

She shook her head. "They saw me *weak*." She dragged Toby's shirt from her shoulder and shoved it back into his hands.

"Are you kidding?" Gingerly, Toby eased the creased material on over his burned back. "Even when they were sure you were going to fail, you beat them." He moved toward her carefully. "Now they know they've got no chance against us."

"You don't understand."

"I do. Nell has made you so afraid of seeming weak, you can't tell when you're being brave any more."

She shook her head violently, then sagged. "Everything will be different soon. I'll be back with her—with Nell and . . . you'll be with Barnaby."

"That doesn't mean anything."

"It means *everything*." She wheeled around again and tried to lurch into a run. Toby caught her arm.

"You've forgiven me for betraying you, haven't you?" Ayla whispered finally when she turned back to him.

Toby nodded. He had forgiven her, but he hadn't forgotten.

"Why?"

Blindsided, Toby stammered his answer. "It was a complicated situation. I was wrong to pressure you to join our crew and we didn't leave you much choice—I see that now." He rubbed his elbow.

Ayla cleared her throat. "Would you forgive me again if I . . ."

"What are you saying?" Toby caught his breath.

"Nothing. It's just . . . are we strong enough to get past anything? I don't want to lose you."

Toby exhaled. "You won't." He pulled her close. "We're rock."

Her tangled black hair smelled of smoke and her cheek against his was sticky with soot and sweat. As he tightened his arms around her, Ayla's trembling slowed and eventually stopped.

She pushed him back and looked around swiftly—there was no one close by. "We have to get out of here. We're down to the strongest couples. If we lose a challenge, there won't be any chance to get those *things* out."

Toby held a finger to his lips. He felt itchy, as though they were being overheard.

They stood in the shade cast by the giant bronze circle on the sanctuary roof. The glass-topped wall sliced into the horizon on their left and to the right was a recently constructed part of the sanctuary, all concrete and metal. A window was open above their heads. Toby pointed and Ayla nodded and walked farther on.

Toby rubbed his stinging smoke-burned eyes. "You're right," he murmured.

Ayla shot a look at the wall.

"You're not thinking of climbing *that*?" Toby's mind raced—how would they get over the top without getting shredded?

Ayla snorted. "No. We get the *things* and"—she looked around again, lowering her voice until it was barely a whisper—"we take the pills *now*."

"Now?" Toby swallowed. "Rahul's waiting in *Wren* at the *north* side of the island. He won't see us being dumped into the sea here."

"It'll be fine." Ayla sounded confident. "No way your captain left you here without someone keeping an eye. Polly . . . or—"

"I haven't seen her." Toby pulled at a frayed edge on his pants. "What really worries me is that we don't know how they deal with their dead here. The original idea was to get the *things* out first, *then* ourselves. If we try and hide them in our pockets or something and *then* take the pills, who'll stop them from stripping us before we get thrown over the cliff? We'll be unconscious, helpless. If we do somehow manage to keep them hidden on our bodies, what if the rough salt knocks them out of our pockets and we lose them that way? It's too risky."

"It's too risky to stay," Ayla hissed. "We can tape them to us so they don't float free in the salt. Hideaki can do it. He'll be in charge of the dead."

"How do you know?" Toby shook his head. "Hideaki deals with the sick and injured, the dead might go somewhere else. They could have a mortician."

"Ashes." Ayla clenched her fists.

"And you promised Hideaki you'd get him out. What if he betrays us when he realizes we're leaving without him. Can you trust him not to do that?"

"Toby . . ." Ayla shook his elbows. "Stop thinking up problems. You and I should take our pills *tonight*, while we still can, while we have our tongues. It's the best way, the *only* way."

"It's *not*," Toby insisted. "You've already faced your worst fear. None of the other challenges will be a problem after this—what can they possibly do that would be worse than today?"

"I don't know," she murmured.

"Your plan is still good. We win the trials, we go to the festival, we hand the *things* to the captain, *then* we get out."

"I don't want to wait." Ayla's eyes pleaded.

Toby had never seen her like this. Everything in him rebelled against rejecting her plan. His own instinct was to get out of Gozo and here she was, asking him to go. But it wasn't safe. It wasn't the plan.

"We have to wait," he said sadly.

Ayla hung her head, then she shook him off and stepped backward. "I'm going to tell them I need some pain relief from the infirmary. I'm going to see Hideaki." She pushed her hair back over her shoulder. "I'm going to find out who deals with the dead."

Toby slipped despondently into his cell. He wanted to check under his bed, to see if the inverter remained safe, but he didn't dare. Nothing had been said, there had been no uproar. It hadn't been found.

He lay staring at the ceiling, clenching his fists.

Then Ayla stood in his doorway, her shoulders hunched low. "They have a mortuary well away from the infirmary," she said. "It leads directly out to the cliff edge. The silent attendants deal with the dead—it's one of their 'sacred mysteries.'" The breath burst out of her, as if she'd been punched. "They'll find the things on us. We have to wait . . . or go over the wall."

Toby sat and patted his mattress. He cut his eyes to the panel in his wall. Then, as Ayla collapsed beside him, he took his tine from his shirt sleeve and jammed it closed.

"What's that?"

"I don't want to risk anyone overhearing," Toby whispered.

"There's nothing more to say." Ayla groaned. "This was my plan, and now I've got to see it through—stop acting like a whiny baby. End of."

"What's that, your mother's voice?" Toby reached for her hand, but she didn't let him take it.

"You think I should cry about this? How does that help?"

Toby dropped his hand.

Awkward silence stretched between them until Ayla snapped it. "I know what the next challenge is."

Toby's eyes widened. "How?" Then he nodded. "Hideaki."

Ayla nodded. "He says it's a maze."

Toby quickly glanced down the corridor, even though he had already checked that everyone else was at lunch. "A test of intelligence then." He found his eyes pinned to Cezar's room. "Cezar will be our biggest problem."

Ayla agreed. "I can take him out of the game."

"Don't!" Toby sometimes forgot how ruthless Ayla could be. "We only have to beat one other couple—there are still three more. If Cezar comes first, it won't be a problem for us to come second."

"Hideaki gave me some pointers. He doesn't know the exact layout, but he said there are dangers. If we follow the sun sign with the short curved rays and avoid any route marked with barbed rays, we should avoid the most lethal traps."

"Lethal traps?" Toby frowned. "They wouldn't, would they?"

"What do you think?"

"I think these sun worshippers are sadists."

Ayla closed her eyes. "Apparently we've got a day off tomorrow."

"Thank the gods for that." Toby leaned against the wall just as a rattling sounded from the wooden panel in his cell.

"Someone's trying to listen!" Ayla hissed.

"Ashes."

As angry voices sounded, Toby jolted to his feet, bent and pulled the broken tine from the hatch. He hid it quickly back in his sleeve and hurled himself back on his cot. He grabbed Ayla as he went down and half pinned her beneath him.

"What are you doing?" she hissed.

"Shut up." He tangled his legs in hers, grabbed her hands and twined their fingers. Then he pinned her arms above her head and kissed her. Her lips were hot and cracked.

Toby's pulse pounded in his ears. Ayla bit his lip and now he tasted blood as well. She was going to hit him as soon as her hands were free. He pulled back, licked his lip and then, suddenly *she* was kissing *him*. This was nothing like the last embrace they had shared on the *Phoenix*. This was hungry and desperate and filled with yearning and fire.

Shaking, he touched his tongue against her lips and she opened her mouth. Their bodies pressed so closely together that he could feel her heart racing against his chest.

"What are you doing?" The light was blotted out of his doorway and Toby rested his forehead on Ayla's with a groan.

An older brother barged into his cell, strode to the wall, and tore open the panel. His shoulders jerked in surprise as the wood moved smoothly back into the wall. He spun around and glowered at Toby.

"What did you do?"

"Huh?" Toby looked up. "Isn't this allowed? No one said."

"What's going on?" Mother Hesper swept into the doorway.

"The brother here wanted to watch us steaming up the cell," Ayla snapped. "He got frustrated when the panel was stuck. It must've warped or stiffened in the heat."

"Well?" Mother Hesper tilted her head at the brother.

"It seems fine now." The brother bent and demonstrated. Mother Hesper pursed her lips.

"It's an offense to tamper with the workings of the sanctuary. The panel is here for your own protection. Should something happen, or should you become ill, this is how we know to get you help."

"Of course." Toby smiled innocently. "As I said, I never touched it. My hands have been busy *elsewhere*." Ayla rolled her eyes.

"Get out and join the others." Mother Hesper stood aside to let them pass. "Your behavior isn't appropriate."

"But it isn't forbidden, either?" Toby checked as they slid past, his hand still wrapped around Ayla's.

Mother Hesper glowered. "Consider it disallowed."

Toby bowed his head. "We'll join the others then."

The brother remained standing in Toby's cell as they left. He swallowed, thinking of the inverter buried under his bed, but he had no choice but to climb the stairs and leave. As they opened the door Toby looked back—Mother Hesper was entering his cell.

NINETEEN

Toby jerked to wakefulness. It had been a long restless, night and it felt as if he had only just managed to fall asleep. Now he lay, unmoving, pointlessly pretending sleep as two uncles burst through his door. When they laid their hands on him, he started to fight.

He opened his mouth to yell and a cloth was shoved between his teeth, muffling his cries.

"Toby?" Ayla must have heard the scuffle. He pounded on the wall, trying to warn her, but his arms were tangled in his light blanket, then grabbed by strong hands and he was lifted out of bed.

Ayla began to bang on her own door, shouting for him, and Toby heard stirring from other cells as her yelling drew attention.

He was carried, fighting all the way, into the corridor where Mother Hesper waited, beside Father Dahon.

She signalled to someone behind him and Hideaki stepped into view. "Sorry," he mouthed and Toby strained back, but could go nowhere. There was a sting in his neck and Toby felt as if he had been plunged underwater. His limbs were weighed down and his head grew too heavy for his neck. He tried to lift his chin, but it had been glued to his chest. His head lolled. Everything went dark.

"Toby, the paddles are slowing." The canopies outside the bridge shook with the volume of the captain's roar. "We're running out of power. Get down to the boiler room."

"Where's Harry? We swapped shifts." Using the mast like a fireman's pole, Toby slid from the crow's nest. His feet stung when they hit the deck—he had misjudged the final jump.

"You know Harry." The captain frowned. "I assume he's sloped off for a nap. You deal with the power, I'll deal with him."

Toby nodded and sped across the deck to the hatch. As he ran, he ducked under canopies that clattered in a sudden gust of wind. Poisonous spray hit his face. His cheeks burned, but he wiped them quickly, opened the hatch, and threw himself down the ladder. Again his feet hurt when they hit the ground and he frowned. He had been running around the *Phoenix* barefoot for years, he had calluses on his calluses—his feet never hurt. He wondered briefly if he should speak to Uma. Then he realized that the *Phoenix* was moving up and down more sharply than ever. Their forward momentum had almost halted.

"*Harry!*" he shouted and he hit the passageway to the boiler room at a dead sprint. "What's going on?"

Toby heard the paddle grind to a halt as he slammed through the door. Polly was waiting for him, hopping from foot to foot on her perch above the attemperator.

"Pretty Polly," she shrieked. She was frustrated as all get-out, but using parrot speak, so Harry had to be around somewhere.

"*Harry*, where are you?"

"*Toby*, thank the gods! *I'm up here.*"

Toby looked up. Harry was hanging from the ladder that led to the blowers. His teeth and the whites of his eyes were all that Toby could see. It was as if Harry had been dunked in soot. "I think there's a blockage."

And that was when Toby felt it: the whole boiler was shuddering.

"Harry, get down from there, she's going to blow!"

Harry's eyes widened and he tried to start down the ladder. "I'm stuck!" he yelled. "I can't get down."

"What're you stuck on?" Toby moved as if to run forward, but Polly flew into his face, forcing him back toward the door.

"My shirt's caught." Harry was struggling. The boiler started to make a high-pitched squealing noise.

"*Ashes*," Toby whispered. "Take it off, Harry, now."

Harry squirmed, trying to get out of his shirt and Polly screamed into Toby's face, no longer caring that Harry heard her. *"Get out, get out, get out!"* Her claws slashed at his forehead.

Pale with shock, Toby stumbled into the passageway, blood pouring into his eyes, trying to fend her off. "Polly, *stop*!"

But Polly didn't stop, not until he had reached the end of the passageway and gone through the buffer door.

"Harry . . ." Toby tried to go back and Polly flew at him once more, screeching.

"There isn't time," she squawked, her wings a flurry of color and dusty feathers.

There was a moment of breathless inhalation as the air seemed to be sucked into the passageway then a snapping of tension. The ship rattled like a can. There was a blast of heat, a roar louder than thunder, and Toby grunted as if he'd been hit in the solar plexus.

"The door's holding," he gasped, cold with shock. On the other side, half of the ship was missing. The heart of the *Phoenix* had been ripped out and he knew it was his fault. If he hadn't swapped watch with Harry . . .

"Harry," he whispered. If the explosion hadn't killed him instantly, his friend had already been dragged into the salt.

He looked down as his feet began to burn. The blast door was no longer holding back the corrosive sea and water was sloshing around his ankles. Banging on the other side told him that junk had flooded in. They were sinking.

The *Phoenix* was going down.

Toby ran for the ladder. The captain would know what had happened and emergency protocols would already be in motion, but some of the crew were sleeping off a night shift. He had to wake them.

The *Phoenix* creaked and the whole ship tilted sideways. Toby gripped the rungs just ahead and found himself hanging at a right angle to the ladder.

He had to get through the hatch. He used the ladder like monkey bars to drag himself to the handle, but the water was already at his waist. If he opened the hatch, would he flood the ship even faster?

Gripped with indecision, his survival instincts took over—if he didn't open the hatch, he was going to drown. His waist was tingling as the salt soaked through his clothes and began to burn. He hammered on the handle, but it didn't turn. The explosion had warped the opening enough to make the hatch stick. Hysterical laughter burst from his chest—he was going to drown inside a closed passageway of the *Phoenix*.

Screeching, Polly flew at the hatch, but there was nothing she could do. Toby was floating now in the orange water, his mouth pressed against the bubble of air trapped behind the closed hatch cover.

He gasped and tasted salt that seared his tongue and scalded his throat.

His eyes flew open.

Toby was floating. Literally. He had sagged on to his knees and the stinging salt had reached his waist. The burning of his cheeks told him that his face had just received a dunking.

He jerked upright and tried to wipe his skin clean, but his hands were trapped behind him. He shook his head, which felt as if he'd spent a whole night drinking Peel's hooch. He was dizzy and sick and felt his mind was filled with fog.

Where was he?

The important thing was to get out of the salt. It was difficult to get to his feet without using his hands or arms, but not impossible. When he was standing, the water only reached his knees. He tried to wade out of it and was jerked to a stop by the pressure of metal on his wrists.

They had found the inverter in his cell. It was the only explanation. And he had been chained out here to die. He cleared his throat—it was so dry that it felt thick and coated with felt. How long had he been imprisoned there, unconscious, while the tide crept up his feet, his ankles, his legs, his waist?

He shook his head. It didn't matter. What mattered was, how

high would the tide get? Would he drown or be eaten alive by the acid currents that swirled around his feet?

"Toby?" The voice was barely more than a whisper.

Toby turned, but for a moment he was so dizzy that he couldn't see. Then the fog left his vision. Yes, he was chained to a metal stake, but he was *not* alone.

Summer's hands were secured in front of her and she was gripping the post they were chained to as though the rising tide might tear her from it and drag her away.

The ends of her hair were wet. So she had woken before Toby and risen to her feet. On Toby's other side Moira, Cezar and Lenka remained sagged downward, chins resting on their chests. Cezar's breathing was coming in rasps but Lenka's face was closest to the salt, her fine blonde hair flying upward in the breeze from the sea, as if repelled by it.

Chains looped from each wrist to join a central rusting ring, long corroded by the salt air.

"We've got to wake them." Summer's face was pale and terrified. "They'll drown."

Toby blinked hard to clear the film from his eyes and nodded. He backed to the stake and stretched his arms behind him as far as he could. He could just reach Lenka with the tips of his fingers.

He looked at Summer. "Can you get to Cezar?"

She shook her head and her knuckles whitened as she tightened her grip.

"All right." Toby managed to scrabble a tenuous hold on Lenka's collar and pulled her closer to him. The salt sucked back, trying to haul her into the tide. "Lenka!" His shout was loud enough to rouse the gulls that sat on the nearby cliff.

They lifted into the air with raucous squawks and Toby's attention fell on an opening in the wall beneath their perch—a passageway that stretched back into the darkness.

He swallowed hard. "It's the maze."

"What?" Summer's gaze followed Toby's.

"The next challenge," Toby muttered. "It was meant to be a maze. I thought we'd be doing it together, but the others must be doing it alone. I guess they have to find us before it's too late."

"Too late?"

Toby tried to gesture at the sea, but his tied hands prevented him. He tilted his head instead.

Summer gulped and then her blue eyes narrowed. "How do you know it's a maze?"

"Ayla told me." Toby wanted to clear the salt from his stinging cheeks and eyes. He settled for rubbing his cheeks on his shoulders. His eyes still ached. "Lenka! Come on, wake up." He shook her collar and she groaned, her head lolling.

"Cezar!" Summer started to shout.

It was Moira who woke first, jerking on her chain like a fish on a line. Her spiky blonde mohawk flopped into her face and she went face first into the water, only to splash back up shocked, but instantly wakened.

"What the *Sun*?"

"Get out of the water," Toby snapped.

"Wha . . . ?" Moira struggled to her feet and stood swaying.

"Cezar's waking," Summer called, and Toby turned to see the other boy stirring.

"Come on, pal. On your feet." As Toby's attention turned, Lenka slipped sideways out of his grasp. She splashed into a wave and her flyaway hair was flattened to her head.

"Moira, you're nearest—get Lenka," he called.

"Do I have tae?" Moira sighed, but she was already kneeling back down and using her shoulders to boost Lenka's head out of the water and back toward Toby. Between them, they managed to get the girl leaned against the stake, where Summer was willing to hold her steady.

"Now, Cezar." Toby cocked his head and Moira nodded. Then, as Toby splashed to his knees to complete the same maneuver, she hesitated.

"This is a challenge, right?" She frowned.

"So?" Toby glared up at her.

"Why the Sun would I want tae help youse?"

"It's not me you're helping, it's Cezar, come on."

Cezar was moaning again and the tide was pulling his pants. His skin was already red where the salt had burned him.

"Still competition, ain't he?"

Toby blinked. She was right. What had he been thinking helping Lenka and Moira when he and Ayla needed to win?

"Toby says the challenge is a maze. We're not competing." Summer said suddenly. "We're the prize."

"She's right." Toby's jaw tightened. "It doesn't matter what we do, the *loser* will be the last one out of that tunnel." He glanced at the opening in the wall.

Moira turned to follow his gaze. "You're saying we just have tae sit here and wait?"

Toby frowned as he nodded. "Why *us*?"

"We're all blond," Summer answered him. "We're Suns. The Moon has to follow the Sun—that's scripture."

"So they have tae find us?" Moira sneered. "Shouldn't be hard. The streets of Glasgow're a bloody maze."

"*Now* will you help with Cezar?" Toby snapped.

Finally, Moira nodded and the two of them got the semi-conscious boy to the stake, where he managed to grip the weathered wood for himself.

Toby examined the metal post. The ring at the top where their chains were attached was corroded. The tide would reach all the way up to it. He exhaled shakily and looked out to sea. The tide was still rising.

Had the challenge started? Toby felt the skin on his feet begin to peel away. He would soon be bleeding.

"Come on, Ayla," he whispered.

The sun traced its path toward midday and glittered from the salt like diamonds. All five of them were now huddled as close to the shore as possible. A distant scream made them all jump.

"What's happening?" Summer whispered, but Toby simply shook his head.

"Look!" Cezar shouted. "Someone's coming."

"Who is it—can you see?" Summer squinted into the tunnel.

"It has to be Ayla." Toby leaned forward. She alone had the secret to getting through the maze. She had to be first out.

It wasn't Ayla.

The person stumbling down the tunnel, looking behind him as though lava were chasing him, was Arthur.

He paused when he saw the group then, when Summer cried his name, he raced forward.

"I'm coming!" He burst from the tunnel and didn't stop. He plunged into the salt as though it were freshwater and threw his arms around Summer. "They said there was a time limit and that you were in danger." He looked around. "I had no idea it would be this." He lifted her hands gently. "Your poor skin, how bad is it?"

"I'm all right. You?"

"It was bad." Arthur shook his head. "There're traps. Brody stepped on a stone that moved and it tipped him head first into a statue. I had to leave him behind."

Moira gasped.

Arthur pulled a thin chain from his shirt. On it hung a blackened key and a label with a rough picture of Summer drawn on it. "Let me get those chains off." He turned to Toby, Lenka, and Cezar. "We had to find the correct key and then the exit. I don't know where the others are. Maybe they stepped on traps, too." He unlocked Summer's chains and lifted her into his arms.

"Unchain us, too." Lenka raised her arms. "It won't change anything, whoever is last out is last out."

"It won't work." Arthur carried Summer toward the beach. "One key, one lock," he said over his shoulder.

"Try," Moira pleaded, but Arthur shook his head.

Moira cursed as Arthur headed for a pile of rocks near the tunnel entrance.

Lenka yelled and pointed, and Toby's gaze was drawn back to the tunnel. This time, the figure sprinting for the light was definitely female.

"Ayla," he shouted, but there was no reply.

"Bianca!" Cezar cried gratefully as she drew nearer.

Bianca unchained Cezar and then stepped away, offering her partner no support. Cezar staggered out of the sea and onto the sand, his broken leg trembling like a mast in a storm.

Bianca didn't follow him. Instead, she ran her nails over Toby's cheek. "They got her," she said in a voice like honey. "I was planning to do it myself, but I didn't need to. She was ahead—had your key and everything—then she stopped to direct Arthur to Summer's key and that's when they got her," she laughed.

Toby's knees almost collapsed. "You're lying. Ayla wouldn't have stopped."

Bianca backed out of the water, giving a little wave. "Guess she figured she only had to beat one of us. Don't worry," she directed her final words to Lenka and Moira. "Toby's the one losing today."

TWENTY

The sun ticked on and the sea continued to rise in bursts. Now the tide reached Toby's ribs, sucking at his shirt. It felt as if a million ants were biting. It was probably a good thing that his hands were stuck behind his back, or he wouldn't be able to resist scratching, opening his skin, and poisoning himself even more.

After what Bianca had said, the girls had backed away as far as they could go and left him to his misery. Even Moira had no words to taunt him.

"Where are they?" Lenka muttered eventually.

"It's a maze—they're lost." Toby's eyes were pinned to the tunnel, still hoping.

Bianca had said that *they* had *got* Ayla, but Bianca didn't know Ayla the way he did. She would never give up. If she was alive, they still had a chance. The longer the tunnel went empty, the more likely it was that Ayla would be the next one out of it.

But time beat on, measured by the thump of his heart and the pull and push of the tide, and she did not emerge.

The water rose over Toby's chest. He could no longer feel his legs at all. Numb was probably better than tingling . . . or did that mean permanent damage? He thought longingly of Uma's barrier cream.

"They willnae let us drown, will they?" For the first time since he had met her, Moira sounded frightened.

Toby tore his gaze from the tunnel. Moira's spiky Mohawk gave the impression of height but now, as the tide bubbled at her chin, he saw that she was much shorter than he was.

"*Ashes.*" He closed his eyes.

If the girls drowned, they would be out of the running for the festival, the challenge over. If Moira or Lenka succumbed, he and Ayla would surely win by default. He pictured Ayla lying injured somewhere. The sooner the girls drowned, the faster Ayla could get help.

He owed Moira nothing.

The *Phoenix* was the important thing—Toby and Ayla had to win the competition and get the inverters out to her.

He was a pirate. He had lost friends, enemies, *and* loved ones . . . Toby was no stranger to death.

"Blast it all to hells and *ash*," Toby couldn't let her die in front of him. He waded awkwardly through the water to Moira. Her eyes glittered with terror and she was tugging ineffectually at her chains.

"You'll dislocate your shoulder," Toby snapped. "Stop it."

"We're gonnae drown!" Her accent was getting even thicker and she twisted as she floated in the lifting tide.

"Shut up." Toby crouched as low as he could without submerging his own face. He could not use his arms for balance, so he spread his feet and dug them into the sucking sand.

"What're ye doin'?" Moira gasped.

"Get on," Toby snapped.

"Are ye serious?"

Lenka gaped as Moira struggled on to Toby's bent thighs and lifted her face out of reach of the salt. Toby wobbled dangerously.

"You're going to fall," Lenka said eventually. She, too, waded closer. She leaned against Toby's back, propping him up. Then her fingers found his and she gave them a squeeze.

Arthur was yelling. Toby looked toward the tunnel. Two shadowy figures limped toward them. He sagged, his heart sinking at the inevitability of it: Matus and Brody.

How badly would it hurt to have his tongue removed? And what would be worse: being forced to work in the sanctuary for the rest of his life or knowing he had let down the *Phoenix*? The captain would try and get him out, of course, but he didn't think there would be any escape.

He returned his attention to the tunnel to see who would be out first. At first, he thought he saw a trick of the sun—it looked as if Matus had a third limb. Then the limb moved sideways and Ayla was behind them. She was catching up.

He jerked to his feet, dunking Moira into the salt.

"*Ayla!*" he yelled.

Her head shot up and she moved faster.

All three of the runners were shambling, exhausted. Ayla dragged one leg behind her, her hands clamped around her thigh. Matus's right ankle was at the wrong angle and each time he put weight on it, his whole body twitched. Brody had to hold on to the tunnel wall, half shuffling, as blood dripped from his hairline into his eyes. Toby remembered Arthur saying that he had hit his head.

As Ayla drew level, Matus tried to shove her. She dodged and almost collapsed as her bad leg took her weight, then she loped forward. Again, Matus tried to push her backward, but this time she was ready.

Instead of dodging his arm, she released her thigh and grabbed his wrist and elbow.

Toby gasped as he saw the crimson sheen of blood on her leg.

With a practised twist, Ayla forced Matus to his knees and used her good knee to dislocate his shoulder. Toby flinched at the crack and Lenka screamed as loudly as Matus. Ayla released him and he rolled sideways.

"Matus, think of the *Sun*!" Lenka shouted.

As Ayla overtook him, Matus rolled to his knees and grabbed her ankle with his good arm. Toby grunted as she went down with a thud and a puff of dust.

As Matus crawled up Ayla's legs, Brody stopped walking. He swayed, unfocused.

It was Moira's turn to scream. She jumped as high as she could, thrusting her face from the water. *"Brody!"*

Brody saw her, frowned, and staggered onward.

Ayla howled as Matus reached her injured thigh and punched it as hard as he could. She twisted and kicked but couldn't shake him.

"Brody!" Moira choked as a wave pushed her under.

Ayla managed to clamp her own good leg around Matus's throat, while Brody stumbled for the exit.

Toby watched, heart in his throat, as Brody moved into the light and paused. Then, as Moira's screams were once again lost in the salt, he wobbled onto the beach. Finally, he splashed into the water and had enough presence of mind to lift Moira out of the salt.

"Where's th' key, Brody?" Moira panted.

"Key?" Brody frowned.

"For the chains."

"The key!" Brody tried to hold her with one arm while he patted his pockets. As he searched, clarity returned to his eyes and his face fell.

"I'm gonnae have tae put ye down." He pressed his forehead to his cousin's. Moira nodded and he dropped her.

His search became so frantic that Toby's attention was pulled from Ayla's fight with Matus.

"Is it round your neck?" Toby muttered. "That's where Arthur's was."

Brody nodded and pulled desperately at his collar. "Oh Sun, I cannae find it."

He lifted Moira, whose head was fully underwater. "Ah cannae find th' key. Ah must have lost it when the trap sprung . . ." He glanced back to the maze. "Ah'll go back."

"There's no time," Lenka whispered.

She was right. If Brody left her, Moira would have only moments left, and Ayla and Matus would be out of the maze before he could return. Toby could see the thoughts chasing themselves over their faces.

"Look again," Moira spluttered. "It has to be on ye."

"It's not." Brody exhaled shakily. "Ah failed."

A whoop of triumph drew Toby's attention and he watched Ayla shake free of Matus and begin to crawl, leaving him lying still behind her.

She dragged herself toward the tunnel exit. Beside him Brody sobbed quietly, his tears vanishing into the rising salt.

"Matus!" Lenka was pleading with her partner to get up.

"Come on, Ayla," Toby called.

"Shut your mouth." Lenka whipped around to face him, her expression vicious. "*Wake up*, Matus!"

He started to stir.

"Ayla, he's coming around!" Toby screamed.

Ayla took a moment to haul herself to her feet then kept moving. The tunnel seemed never ending.

Behind her, Matus started to crawl.

Then Ayla was at the tunnel edge and passing the line of shade cast by the sun.

Ayla curled her lip at Lenka as she reached Toby. "They tried to stop me." She grabbed Toby's shoulders.

"Scum!" Toby spat. Brody and Matus had considered Ayla enough of a threat to hurt her, yet they had still managed to underestimate her.

He glanced at Brody, who was trembling with the effort of holding Moira out of the water.

"The key?" Toby asked.

Ayla raised her arm—it was wrapped around her wrist.

"Get me out of these chains." Toby bent over to present his lock. The salt sucked at his clothes and chin, but Toby raised his arms as high as his shoulders would allow.

Ayla unwrapped the key chain just as Matus crossed out of the maze. With a smirk, she raised the key, put it in Toby's lock and tried to turn it.

Nothing happened.

"Ayla?" Toby's heart thumped.

"It's not moving," she spoke through gritted teeth.

Lenka stood up straighter. "Matus, quick—there's something wrong with their key."

Matus started to run; hobbling on his injured ankle.

"Ayla," Toby warned.

He could feel her behind him, frantically shaking the lock. "I can't turn it."

"It must be the wrong key."

Ayla shook her head. "There was one for each of us. That's how I knew where Arthur's was, I found his before I found mine."

"Then it's just stiff. Try harder." Toby leaned down, trying to lift his hands higher out of the salt. Seawater thrust past his lips making him choke, but he forced himself to remain low, so Ayla could see what she was doing.

He felt, rather than saw, Matus splash into the surf.

His chains shook as Ayla yanked and pulled at the lock. Her howl of frustration undulated over the water.

Then, suddenly, the chains slipped free, his arms snapped open and Toby burst from the waves. He grabbed Ayla's arm, put it over his shoulder and pulled her on to the beach.

When he heard a clang Toby looked back. Lenka's chains were swinging back to the post. She, too, was free. Brody stood helplessly, holding Moira up, and watched them go.

Toby thudded into the rocks next to Arthur and Summer and started to strip off his sodden clothes. Summer hadn't removed her baggy cream dress—was she really so modest that she preferred to sit in salt-soaked cloth than remove it?

Toby forgot about the girl as the skin of his legs peeled off along with his pants and he squealed.

"*Ashes*, Toby, how long did they have you in the salt?" Ayla started to help him, her fingers gentle as she pulled his shirt over his head.

"Too long," Cezar answered for him. "Moira would've died without you, Toby."

"She still will, if they don't get her out of there right now," Arthur muttered.

"Where are they?" Toby growled. "Where are the blasted attendants? They must be watching to see who loses."

Cezar pointed. "There're hatches all along the wall. This must've been real entertaining for them." His voice was sharp with bitterness.

"How's your leg?" Toby grabbed Ayla's thigh. "What did they stab you with?"

"A sharpened branch." Ayla pushed his hands off.

"You shouldn't have pulled it out." Toby said, just as Matus dumped Lenka next to Bianca. He threw himself at Matus, thudding into his chest with a noise like a sack of grain hitting a deck. "I'll kill you."

"Arthur, stop them," Summer squeaked.

Arthur made no move. "Matus deserves what he gets," he said, turning his face away.

Toby punched Matus, hearing the satisfying crack of bone under his fist. Matus put his hands over his head. "It's a competition," he shouted. "What did you expect?"

"Not *this*." Toby grabbed Matus's hair and forced his head around so that he was looking at Ayla's bleeding leg.

"I can't blame you for cheating," Ayla said. She reached out a hand, silently asking Cezar to help her stand. "Ask Toby—I've cheated *him*. But if you're going to cheat, make sure you *win*. The fact is, at this point, if you think the only way you *can* win is to cheat then you've already lost." She turned her back on him.

Toby shoved him away and spat in his face.

Matus wiped the spit off, his bruised face murderous, but he said nothing.

"That was too close." Suddenly shaking, Toby sat down next to Ayla. He turned his back on the junk-filled horizon and was faced with Cezar staring hungrily over the salt.

"I don't want to lose my tongue," the boy mumbled, squinting into the afternoon haze.

"You won't." Ayla pointed. "Moira and Brody are still out there." She glanced back at the walls where Cezar had shown them the hatches. "You hear that?" she yelled. "They're still there. It's over. Get them out."

There was no sound and no movement behind the wall.

"Do you think they're waiting for Moira to drown?" Summer whispered, her face pale.

Toby clenched his fists. "I don't know what they're waiting for."

"I can't do this any more." Cezar looked at Bianca. "We can't win. Look at me." He thumped his twisted leg. "We have more challenges to go—more torture. And then we'll lose our tongues."

"We'll win." Bianca stood. "I'll make sure of it."

"How?" Cezar snapped, then he gestured, taking in Arthur, Toby, and Matus. "We don't stand a chance. Even if we do . . ." He hung his head. "I-I don't want to go blind."

Bianca gasped. "You said you'd do this for me—for our families."

"We *can't win*, Bianca. Our families won't *get* the money and the colony will be two workers short—for *what*? We thought that if we didn't get the crowns, we'd be sent home. Win-win. Well, that's not what happens, is it? I'm needed back home, I can fix the broken equipment and there aren't enough of us left healthy to waste two."

Bianca began to tremble. Her nails curled into her palms. "You *promised*."

"I didn't have all the facts," he said quietly.

"We can't escape." Bianca shook her head. "There's no way out."

"No way out of the *sanctuary*." Cezar stared out to sea again. "But we're out here now and there's no one to stop us."

"We're on a pile of rock—there's nowhere to go." Summer stared at him.

Cezar pointed out to sea.

"You're insane." Bianca retreated.

"You want your tongue torn out, B?" Cezar tilted his head. "You want to face whatever tomorrow's challenge is?"

"Whatever it is, I'll win it for us," she pleaded.

"No, you won't," Ayla spoke up. "If it's you or me, I know who I'd place my money on."

"Shut up." Bianca's claws snicked out. "Anyway, you're injured now."

"But *I'm* not," Lenka said quietly.

"They're right. I'm swimming." Cezar slipped down the rocks.

"You can't!" Toby reached for him. "You were in the salt, Cezar, you know what it's like. That was at the shoreline—you only had a taste of what it'll do to you farther out—the currents are poison."

"And what about your leg?" Bianca swung her head. "You're not strong enough."

"We only have to make it around the headland." Cezar stood in the waves now; orange water simmered at his knees and tin cans banged against the rocks with hollow thuds. "There has to be somewhere we can hide until the festival. They'll assume we've drowned." He looked at the others. "That's what you'll say, isn't it?" He was walking backward, the orange salt rising up his thighs.

"Cezar, it isn't possible," Toby begged. "Come back in."

Cezar shook his head, tears in his eyes. "I'm not going back, Toby."

"Can you even swim?" Summer called.

"There's a lake by our village." Cezar continued to retreat.

"Cezar!" Bianca looked wildly from her partner to the cathedral and back again. The sun blazed from the great bronze disc on the roof and lit up her hair. "You know I can't let you go alone."

"I know. I'm sorry."

"You could stay." Summer grabbed Bianca's arm. "They'll take out your tongue, but you'll still be able to work in the sanctuary."

Sadly, Bianca shook her head. "I want to stay, this place was my dream, but he's right. If our village isn't going to get the money, it needs us more than I need this." She sniffed and suddenly she looked very young. "I should never have talked you into it, Cezar, but you were the only blond in our generation and I needed you. I got you into this . . . so I should get you out."

"You're going to *swim*?" Lenka said. "You'll die."

Bianca shook her head. "Please! I can do it. Without me, *he'll* die." She cocked her head toward her partner. Then she carefully navigated her way down the rock.

She hissed when her toes touched the water and her eyes met Toby's. "It does burn."

"It'll get worse." He held her gaze. "You don't stand a chance—either of you."

"Maybe she does," Ayla grunted. She slid awkwardly down to stand beside Bianca, her path leaving a bloodstain on the rock. As she splashed into the salt, she glanced up at Toby.

Cezar was still splashing backward, as though terrified someone would catch him and pull him back.

Ayla turned to Bianca. "I don't like you and you don't like me."

"Whatever," the girl sneered.

"But we're alike, so just you listen." Ayla leaned close until only Bianca and Toby could hear. "You're strong enough, so you might get him around the headland. Keep your faces out of the salt if you want to have any chance at all." She paused. "Head for the cliff on the north side—there should be a boat."

"A boat?" Bianca's head shot up, her eyes narrowed in suspicion.

"Keep your stupid voice down," Ayla hissed. "Toby's family will be there—they'd never go far."

"And you're telling me this, why?" Bianca glanced at Cezar.

"He deserves a chance." Ayla shaded her eyes. "If the boat *is* there, tell the sailors Toby sent you."

Bianca swallowed. "We're not strong swimmers."

"Then you'd better get stronger." Ayla held up her hand and Toby pulled her back onto the rock. "Good luck."

"This is a mistake," Toby said for the last time. "Don't do this."

Cezar shook his head, turned his face to the horizon, and began to swim, doggy style. He passed Brody and Moira who watched him with horrified faces. Toby's heart sank.

TWENTY-ONE

"What's going on?" Mother Hesper's voice shattered the tension. Bianca caught her breath. Frozen in a second of indecision, she stood in the salt, staring from Cezar to the furious mother.

Then, as a dozen robed attendants ran from the tunnel and Mother Hesper hurried toward her, Bianca gave a little hiccupping sob, turned, and flung herself after her partner.

"Keep your *face* out of the water," Ayla shouted.

Bianca did not acknowledge her, but struck out strongly toward Cezar. She quickly caught him up.

"Idiots," Mother Hesper sneered. "There's nowhere to go."

Toby looked at her. "They didn't want to do another one of your challenges. Cezar would rather drown than go through what you've got planned for us next."

Summer looked at Mother Hesper, her doll eyes wide. "We could've died today—I thought you . . . weren't you watching?"

"Of course we were watching. Someone is *always* watching—like the Sun above us." Mother Hesper's fingers twitched into a sun sign. "It doesn't matter. The guardian uncles will patrol the beaches in case they come ashore and, if they drown . . . Well, the survival rate for this challenge was higher than expected." She looked over her shoulder. "Father?"

Father Dahon was standing in the shadow of the tunnel's entrance.

Toby squinted after him. "You expected some of us to *die*?"

Summer clung to Arthur and even Lenka paled.

"Your lives belong to the Solar Order now." Mother Hesper lowered her brows. "And yes, every year some of the applicants die at this stage. It is a prize worth dying for, don't you think?"

"Y-yes." Lenka nodded, making a very shaky sun sign with one hand.

"You are going to release Moira though?" Arthur stood and balanced Summer on the rock behind him. "The challenge is over."

Toby had almost forgotten about Moira. She and Brody remained by the post. Brody was watching Cezar swim away, but his arms were tightly around Moira, holding her up. There was nothing visible of the blonde girl but her eyes, nose and mouth, which she had upturned. Her gasps for breath were audible even over the crashing of the salt into rock.

Mother Hesper did not move.

"Then we'll get her out of there ourselves," Toby snapped. He looked at Ayla. "Brody dropped her key. We just need to find it."

"You mean go back into the maze?" Matus shuddered.

Ayla clutched her thigh and looked away.

"Well, *I'm* going. It's not like we're helping the competition. They *already lost*." Toby leaped from the rock, on to the beach. "Arthur?"

Arthur glanced at Summer. When she nodded he climbed carefully after Toby.

The attendants lining the tunnel closed ranks.

"What are you doing?" Alarmed, Toby turned to Mother Hesper. "What's the point in letting Moira drown?"

Mother Hesper smiled. "You're right, of course." She raised a hand that had been buried inside her robe. In it she had a single key. She threw it to the brother who had met Toby and Ayla at the wharf. "Unchain her."

Toby watched him pick his way gingerly through the salt. Moira's face disappeared underwater before he could get there. Even Ayla stiffened.

"Hurry!" Arthur yelled.

Finally the brother released Moira and Brody carried her to shore.

Mother Hesper spread her hands. "You will be happy to know that there is only one more challenge left. Take some time—worship in the cathedral. Prepare yourselves for a true fight. On the day of the new moon, we will know which of you are our Sun and Moon."

"New moon?" Summer tilted her head, calculating. "That's three nights away."

Ayla nodded. "So we get a break."

Lenka frowned. "You said '*a fight*.' You mean we'll be fighting each other?"

Mother Hesper smiled. "Haven't you been fighting one another since the beginning?"

Toby rubbed his legs—the high sun was drying them and they looked like raw meat. His chest and shoulders weren't quite as bad, but the itching and peeling caused by the chemical burns of the polluted sea was agony. Was he in any condition for a fight? Were Lenka and Matus?

He tried not to think about the condition Cezar and Bianca would be in by the time they found Rahul . . . *If* they found Rahul.

Ayla glowered at Mother Hesper. "So—can we go to the infirmary?"

Hideaki pursed his lips when he saw the teens lined up outside his door. Despite his swollen ankle and dislocated shoulder, Matus had managed to hobble his way to the front of the line and Lenka needed salve on her skin just as much as Toby did.

But as Hideaki told Matus to come in, attendants rushed past with Brody and Moira.

Moira's skin was sloughing off and blood now coated her chin and chest. Beside her, Brody bobbed, a massive bruise shining on his bloodied head and the same blood making a bib on his front.

"Put them in the usual beds." Hideaki sighed. He glanced at the rest of the teens. "This is going to take some time—why don't you rest in your cells? I'll send a sister when it's your turn."

"Us first," Matus warned. He had his good arm around Lenka, whose fine hair had dried into its normal halo.

Hideaki caught Ayla's eye. She gave an imperceptible nod.

"Fine," he said. "You first."

The teens staggered back to their cells in near silence, the rasping of their pain-filled breathing was the only sound in the corridor, and still Toby felt the weight of eyes on his back. When he turned, there was no one there.

"They're watching again," he muttered.

"They're always watching," Ayla groaned as she wrapped both hands around her bleeding thigh.

Lenka was hardly keeping upright. Only Arthur and Summer had emerged from the challenge almost unscathed.

"Do you still think it's worth it?" Toby asked suddenly, staring at Arthur. "We were supposed to die today."

"Mother Hesper didn't mean that," Summer breathed, looking around, sharp-eyed. Toby frowned. Was Summer slyer than she seemed—playing a game for the watchers?

"She meant it." Ayla pressed her thigh. "You didn't see those traps. I missed getting a spike in my chest by a centimeter."

Matus nodded. "I could have been killed, too." He pointed at his ankle. "I hurt myself rolling from a blade that was aimed at my throat."

"But she said . . ." Summer fell silent.

"She's helping you, isn't she?" Toby frowned. "That's why your hands were tied in front of you, instead of behind your back."

Summer looked at Arthur, who flushed. "She likes Summer." He closed his fists. "We haven't had much advantage, just the occasional tip-off."

"Which you didn't share," Ayla sneered.

"Would *you*? It's a competition." Summer snapped. "Toby said you knew about the maze. Did you tell anyone else?"

Ayla glared.

"I-I don't think Moira's going to make it," Lenka muttered.

Arthur looked at Ayla. "*I* wouldn't have made it through without you. If the next trial really is a fight . . ."

"It's every woman for herself." Ayla folded her arms.

Arthur nodded. "Still . . ."

"Still *nothing*." Ayla refused to look at him. "I shouldn't have helped you. I almost lost because of it." She pressed her lips together. "I'm sorry, Toby. I shouldn't have stalled, I should've got straight out as fast as I could."

"It's all right."

Ayla stopped walking and shook her head. "It isn't. You could've died. If it had been the other way around, I'd have reamed you out. So yell at me."

"I'm not going to yell at you." Toby looked at the wall where a small hatch was sliding open. "You did the right thing. I won't yell at you for that."

"I betrayed you," Ayla growled. "That should bother you more!"

"How did you betray me? It's nothing more than I would have done."

"We agreed to win this thing." Her beads clattered with her frustration. "And I almost blew it."

Toby reached for her, but she ducked away. "Shout at me, Toby." Her shoulders slumped.

"*I'm* glad you helped us," Summer murmured. "And so is Arthur. I wouldn't have lasted long in that seawater. Not like you, Lenka."

Lenka touched her own peeling arm before walking into her cell and closing the door.

Hideaki's cream felt like ice. Immediately, Toby's skin stopped burning and his tendons loosened. "Gods, that's good." He collapsed on to the bed. "How bad are my legs . . . will they heal?"

"There'll be scarring." Hideaki continued to slather the salve on with gentle fingers. "But you'll have full use of your legs. Unlike the Scottish girl."

Toby looked away from the beds where Moira and Brody were sleeping. "You drugged them?"

Hideaki nodded. "The infirmary had everything I needed to patch you up. They've done this before."

Ayla was sitting on the bed next to Toby. A thick white bandage covered her left leg from her knee to the bottom of her tunic.

Hideaki lowered his voice. "You know the next trial is a fight, Second. You should have no problem with it—if you rest that leg properly."

Ayla grinned at Toby. "We can *win* this." She pumped her fist.

"What about Arthur?" Toby hissed.

"Size isn't everything," Ayla insisted triumphantly. "We sparred together, *we can fight.* We've *got* this."

"I know." Toby turned away from her.

"Then what's the problem?"

"What's the problem?" He clenched his fists and rolled back. "Seriously? You want to fight Summer? She's a child. Lenka is badly burned. Matus is injured."

"So am I . . ."

"That's not the point. It isn't like fighting in Tarifa. We'll actually have to *hurt* them." He opened his fists. "I-I'm not sure this is worth it."

"Are you kidding?" Ayla rose to her feet. "You want to give up *now*?"

"I don't know."

"I asked you to leave *days* ago. You wouldn't. Now we're committed. We can win this thing and we're going to. Have you forgotten why we're here?

"Of course not."

"Well then."

"What if we have to kill the others?"

Ayla hesitated, breathing hard. "All right, fine, we make a pact. No killing. We knock out—disable if necessary, but no killing."

"And what if Mother Hesper makes it a condition of winning? After today I don't trust her not to."

"They can't *make* you kill, Toby. If the others are down and have clearly lost, then they can't make you finish them off."

"What if they do, would you do it?"

Ayla glanced at Hideaki. "If I have to."

"You'd kill Summer?"

"If it's her or me." Ayla caught his hand, but he pulled it away. "You know who I am, Toby. You always have. But it won't be a problem—it won't be 'to the death.' They'll make us fight till there's a clear winner. That's right, isn't it, Hideaki?"

Hideaki nodded sadly. "I would like to think so."

Toby's legs were itching again. Ayla caught his hands as he began to rub them, aggravating the raw skin. "What if we win?" he said eventually. "Arthur and Summer lose their tongues."

"You don't care about Lenka and Matus?"

"Do you?"

Ayla sighed. "They signed up for this. Would you rather lose *your* tongue to save them from it?"

Toby shook his head. "I wish I was home," he murmured.

"We will be—as soon as the festival is over."

"And me?" Hideaki began to put his equipment away, speaking to the wall, rather than look at his second-in-command.

"And you," Ayla spoke softly. "You find a way to stay with our bodies and the boat will pick you up, too."

"We have some time off. What shall we do for two days?

Hideaki had wrapped bandages around Toby's legs and it was taking all of his effort not to pull them loose and scratch.

Ayla sighed. "We should get some practice in. You want to spar?"

Toby pointed at Summer, who was watching them from the other side of the courtyard. "You want to give away all your moves?"

Ayla narrowed her eyes. "Little spy."

"You need to rest your leg anyway." Toby looked at his own.

"So what—we pray, like Lenka and Matus?"

"We have to keep up appearances."

"For two whole days? I'm bored already. I'm not used to having nothing to do."

"Me, neither." Toby dug his nails into his palms. "I need something to take my mind off this itching."

"We need games—chess, checkers, poker, Perudo—anything."

Toby snorted. "Doubt they'll have any here."

"We could play checkers—we just have to find some colored stones."

"All right, checkers." Toby rolled to his feet. "Meet you back here."

Ayla nodded. "Bet I can find more stones than you."

There weren't many actual stones lying around the rear courtyard, but when Toby really looked he noticed a lot of flatter larger pieces of shell and grit compacted into the hard sand floor. He rejected any that were smaller than his thumbnail. Crawling around the dirt, focusing on his task, he didn't see Arthur come up behind him.

"What are you doing?" The boy crouched at his side.

"Looking for stones." Toby rolled another in his fingers and sorted it into his pile of paler colors.

"Weapons?" Arthur frowned.

Toby raised his eyebrows. "Checkers." He sat back on his heels. "You think we should be arming ourselves?"

Arthur shook his head. "They'll provide what we need."

"That's what I figure." Toby allowed a pebble to slide between his fingers. He cleared his throat. "I don't want to fight you . . . if there was any way out of this . . ."

"I know." Arthur sat and glanced over at Summer. "At least your partner *can* fight. I'm going to have to protect Summer."

Toby bit his lip. "You've got two days to teach her some moves."

"Not a lot of time—and with everyone watching."

"Right." Toby picked up a handful of pebbles and let them fall again. Puffs of dust rose where they landed. "This might not work but . . ." Again, Toby felt eyes on him and he looked up. A brother was watching them intently from the top of the stairs.

"I hate that someone always seems to be listening." Arthur picked up some of Toby's darker stones, flesh-pinks, blood-reds and mud-browns, and started to place them in a pattern around the pile.

"What if we ally?" Toby said eventually. "You, me, and Ayla. Just until Lenka and Matus are out—we can work together until it's just us left."

"I don't know," Arthur mused. "Don't get me wrong, but it's in my interest if Matus takes you down."

Toby nodded. "You're right. If only we could both win this thing."

"Only one winner." Arthur threw his remaining stones.

"If I could back out without losing my tongue—if I could just *leave*—I would. I'd let you have this." Toby rubbed his face.

"But you won't?"

"I want my tongue." Toby curled over his knees.

"Me, too—and Summer. So where does that leave us?" Arthur grimaced.

Toby plowed his nail through the stones, scattering them. "Can we at least agree to give each other the courtyard—two hours each, every day? That way you can train Summer, I can spar with Ayla, and Lenka and Matus can do whatever they need to do."

"You won't watch?" Arthur cocked his head.

"If you promise not to."

"We'll pray while you train."

"We'll do the same." Toby swept his stones into a close pile. "Agreed?"

"We'll need to let Lenka and Matus know."

"Lenka's still resting in her cell." Toby shoved his stones in his pocket and rose stiffly to his feet. "You have the yard now—Ayla and I will go around the side wall."

Ayla came around the corner, her hands cupped in front of her. "Got some."

"Me, too." Toby met her in the middle. "Let's go."

TWENTY-TWO

"Are you ready for this?" Ayla retied the bandage around her thigh, pulling it tight. They were both in Toby's cell and their doors were open.

"How can I be?" Toby touched his toes. "We're going to be fighting our friends."

"We weren't here to make friends, Toby. *I* didn't forget that," Ayla replied.

He groaned. She was right: this would be easier if he'd kept his distance. "Let me help you with that."

"No need." Ayla tightened the knot with her teeth.

"You did point Arthur to his key in the maze. I haven't forgotten."

"Only because I'd rather face Summer today than Moira." Ayla scowled.

"You didn't know about today back then."

Ayla pretended not to have heard him. Her boots jiggled on the ground. "When are they coming for us?"

"Now." Lenka was standing in their cell doorway. Her fists were wrapped much like Ayla's leg and she had tied her fine, flyaway hair off her face with a strip of bandage. "Can't you hear the bells? They'll be coming any minute."

"What do you want?" Ayla snapped.

Lenka shuffled from one foot to the other.

Ayla stood and put her hands on her hips. "You got some insult?"

Lenka shook her head. "Whatever happens today, it'll be over. One of us is losing their tongue. It might be me." She frowned. "So, I just wanted to say"—she leaned around the door to find Toby—"I won't forget what you did in the sea. You didn't have to wake me up and get me out of the water. You didn't have to help Moira." Lenka flexed her bound fists. "When we get out there, I won't hold back. So I just wanted you to know . . . I won't forget." She cleared her throat and looked at the stairs. "Mother Hesper's coming." She stepped away from the cell and her face hardened. "I won't say good luck." She turned and moved quickly back to her own cell.

Ayla suddenly looked around. "Toby, what if we don't come back here after . . ."

"*Ashes*—you're right." Toby's eyes widened. "I've got to get the . . ."

"Do it." Ayla marched into the doorway, blocking Mother Hesper's view of Toby's cell as she appeared at the bottom of the steps.

"Toby's not ready." Ayla pulled the cell door closed behind her. "He'll be out in a moment."

Mother Hesper narrowed her eyes. "He's got until you're all lined up outside your cells."

Arthur was first to emerge. He was shirtless and his skin looked like it had been oiled. With what, Ayla didn't know, but she knew that it would make it difficult to get a grip on him in the fight. As he stretched his muscles moved like those of a big cat. He was ready.

"Summer," he called.

Summer appeared in the passageway. Instead of hanging loose, her hair was wrapped tightly around her head in two thick plaits. She had pulled off her shapeless cream dress and now wore nothing more than a breast strap and shorts. Ayla blinked as she saw that the girl had the muscles of a fighter.

"By the Sun," Lenka whispered. "We've been played!"

Ayla reached behind her and began to knot the long side of her hair. There was nothing she could do about the short side—it would provide a handhold for anyone who got close enough.

"Matus," Summer called in a sing-song voice unlike the doll's squeak that she had been using. "Come out, come out, wherever you are."

Matus limped out of his cell. Two days had passed since the last challenge, but his ankle remained swollen and his shoulder was bruised with a green-yellow smear where it had been dislocated.

Ayla stared at him, then at Lenka. "What are you going to do?"

"Fight like blazes." Lenka stepped toward her partner. "Ready, Matus?" He nodded, his eyes grim.

Mother Hesper moved toward Toby's cell and Ayla sidestepped, blocking her.

"He won't be a minute."

"Out. Now," Mother Hesper growled.

"Toby," Ayla called.

The cell door opened and Toby stood in the doorway. Ayla's gaze flicked to his fingers; his nails were crusted with dirt. He nodded to her.

Then he caught sight of Summer and his face tightened.

The teens were marched through the sanctuary. Toby looked neither left nor right, but the golden glow of the decorations burned in his peripheral vision. Ayla's boots rang against the marble floor.

The inverter was a hard knot against his stomach. He had taken his bandages from his legs and used them to secure it, but he still worried that it could come out during the fight.

Toby push the inverter from his mind. He couldn't afford to be distracted.

The locks clicked and slowly the sanctuary door opened. There was a collective intake of breath.

The square in front of the cathedral was full. The sundial had been removed. Now in the center was a large ring, wider than the bridge of the *Phoenix* and twice the height of Arthur, created by sharp-edged junk-shards like gaping jaws. The sun glittered from the metal teeth and gaps between the junk allowed Toby to see inside to what seemed to be an empty arena.

Around the fighting ring there were tight circles of attendants on raised benches, more than two hundred brothers, sisters, and uncles; even the sunblind in their different-colored robes. The whole Order had come to witness the final trial.

"There're Noah and Leila." Ayla pointed and Toby shivered. Beside them, Toby saw Aldo and Celeste, chins lowered, unwilling to look up.

"Can you see the others?" Lenka whispered.

"Zahir and Uzuri." Summer nodded to the opposite side of the ring, where the African couple were almost invisible inside hooded robes. "I can't see Adele or Adrien."

"And Brody and Moira are still in the infirmary," Ayla murmured.

"The others seem all right." Arthur pushed in front of Toby. "Don't you think?"

"I doubt they've said a word of complaint," Matus said quietly, releasing some of the tension in the air.

"I might've liked you, Matus," Ayla murmered.

"Yeah? Well, now I'm going to kick your butt." Matus's words were defiant but his shoulders remained slumped and Lenka's hand slipped into his.

Toby turned and saw Father Dahon proceeding up the central aisle of the sanctuary toward them, his long robes brushing the pews, his face questing for sunlight.

"Move aside," Mother Hesper ordered.

Toby pulled Ayla closer to him and Father Dahon walked into the space, stopping on the very edge of the steps.

The watching crowd grew still.

"It's time," Mother Hesper said. She looked at Summer. "Make me proud."

Summer nodded and an attendant uncle opened a wrought-iron gate set into the arena. He gestured at Toby. He and Ayla were going to be first down the steps and through.

Once the wrought-iron gate had been locked behind the teens, they instinctively took up positions around the outside of the ring: Matus beside Lenka, Arthur next to Summer, and Toby with Ayla.

From inside, the wall seemed even taller, as oppressive as the junk dam the *Phoenix* had used to enter the Gozitan waters. Even though the area they had to fight in was perhaps ten feet square, the wall loomed, creaking as if it might collapse on them, and sharp spikes protruded, shrinking the arena even more.

Toby could see the attendants through gaps in the rusting junk, none big enough to let any of the fighters slip out, but wide enough to allow the audience to see what was going on.

The weight of two hundred rapt gazes fell on Toby and he bounced on his toes, feeling as if insects were crawling beneath his skin. On the surface, Ayla seemed calm, but Toby caught the twitch of her jaw that told him she was wound tight.

Toby knew Ayla could fight, but she had exposed weaknesses to the others—her burned and clawed shoulder, her injured thigh. Summer, by contrast, had no injuries and a lot more fighting experience than they had realized.

He shifted closer to Ayla. "Stay on my right," he murmured.

"If I can." She nodded at Arthur. "They're playing to win."

"From the beginning," Toby added.

Ayla blew a stray hair out of her eyes. "Do you think they really had no idea about the challenges?"

Toby didn't answer. It didn't really matter now.

Father Dahon appeared on a raised platform to the right of the arena.

He raised his arms. "You may have heard that this is a fight, but it is not a mere battle. It is a challenge." He signaled and two attendants lowered ropes, one on either side of the arena. They dangled almost six feet above Toby's head, far out of reach. From one rope hung a wooden staff, from the other a magnifying glass.

Then Toby heard the rasp of a panel opening. His eyes followed the sound to see a wooden hatch the size of a small box set into all the sharpened metal. It was open at the back so that he could see the crowd through it.

It too was out of reach.

Mother Hesper's face appeared in the opening. She held up a glittering diamond sun pendant, ensuring that everyone inside the ring and out could see it.

"Here is a single pendant," she called. "Diamond. The truest representation of the Sun that we have." The attendant crowd gasped in awe. Many of the brothers and sisters had never seen the Reliquary. "The winning couple will be the first to hold this pendant in their hands."

She placed the diamond inside the box and closed the hatch, cutting off Toby's view.

Father Dahon raised his own arms. "The Sun will aid his favored pair."

The crowd cheered and they all heard a bolt close.

Toby felt some of the tension slide from his shoulders. It was not, as he had feared, to be a fight 'to the death,' but instead a physical *and* mental challenge. How could he use a staff and a magnifying glass to open a bolted door?

Across from him, Arthur cracked his knuckles. He was frowning.

"Every few minutes a bell will ring," Father Dahon called. "When you hear it you must stop fighting, turn to the Sun and pray until the next bell—at which point the challenge will continue. Those who stand and pray will receive the Sun's aid. The ringing of all five bells will signify the end of the trial and the selection of the new Sun and Moon."

"We need to get the staff and the magnifying glass," Toby whispered.

"No. We take out the competition first," Ayla countered. "Worry about the puzzle when we're alone."

"All right."

A bell rang. The teens hesitated, looking at one another, then the brothers and sisters outside began to roar their support for the different couples.

Lenka swaggered toward the center, leaving Matus standing awkwardly at the edge of the arena. Summer nudged Arthur and he powered toward Matus with a burst of speed. As soon as Lenka realized what was happening she turned, but Arthur was already there.

Matus barely had time to lift his hands before Arthur raised a fist like a mallet and hammered him in the forehead, exactly where he had been injured in the maze.

There was a crack and Matus hit the ground.

Arthur shook out his fist and turned to Lenka, who skidded to a halt and backpedaled.

"I-I think he just killed Matus," Toby gasped.

"He put Matus out of the fight," Ayla hissed.

Toby ran to stand next to Lenka and raised his hands, palms out. "Arthur . . ."

Arthur powered forward like a juggernaut.

Toby took his foot in the thigh, where his skin had been badly burned by the salt. He turned from the force of the blow, instinctively crouching to take the weight on his other leg, then he shot out with his elbow, aiming for Arthur's ribs.

Arthur was pushing past to reach Lenka, but Toby's blow knocked him off balance.

Lenka took her chance and went at his face with her nails. Arthur pushed her away, his cheek bleeding and she retreated toward Ayla. Perhaps she thought that if Toby was trying to help her, then Ayla would, too.

Her mistake.

Ayla flew into a spinning kick at Lenka's chest and knocked her straight back into Arthur. He grabbed her in a sleeper hold and squeezed. Her fingers scrabbled on his forearms but her movements grew weaker with every passing moment.

Arthur was going to kill Lenka.

"There's no need for this." Toby hurled himself on to Arthur's back. His fingers slid from Arthur's oily skin and, unable to secure a grip, Toby slid back down.

"Ayla!" he yelled.

"It's a *competition*," Ayla snapped.

"He's going too far!"

With a final quiet exhalation Lenka went still and her head flopped forward, but Arthur kept the pressure on.

Toby ran for him again, this time launching into a kick that swept Arthur's back leg out from under him.

Arthur thudded to the ground and Lenka was thrown out of his grip like a rag. She lay unmoving and Toby's heart sank.

Arthur curled a lip and turned to Toby. "You shouldn't have interfered."

Toby started to retreat and then the bell rang.

"Stand and pray." The noise caught Toby by surprise. It was as if there had been nothing but the six of them. Now the world came crashing back in.

Toby was suddenly aware of the sun beating down, the swell and surge of the attendant's cries, and the scent of unwashed bodies and dust. Above, the staff and magnifying glass swayed on their ropes.

As Ayla moved to his side, Toby looked for Summer. She was watching Arthur with a small smile on her face.

Summer raised her arms. After a moment Arthur copied her. Toby looked at Ayla.

"We have to," she muttered and she too lifted her hands to the sky.

Toby grimaced and did the same. "Praise the Sun."

"Stand and pray," Father Dahon repeated.

Toby realized that he was talking to Lenka and Matus.

The crowd began to chant: "Stand and pray, stand and pray."

"Stop it," Toby yelled. "Can't you see them?" His arms began to ache.

No one came to remove Lenka and Matus and no help arrived for the four who were standing and praying as ordered. They had been promised help, but perhaps it was purely spiritual aid that Father Dahon had meant.

Then Ayla pointed. "Look."

The staff was lowering. Now the rope hung a good arm's length closer to Toby's head.

The second bell rang. It was time to fight.

"Stay with me." Ayla raised her fists.

Toby rotated his wrists and did the same, never taking his eyes from Arthur. The bigger boy was snake fast, he had already seen it.

This time, with a howl like the *Banshee,* Summer pounced on to Ayla's back and spun her. Toby turned to look and that was when Arthur hit him.

He ploughed into the earth. Knowing Arthur would be on him

immediately, Toby closed his hand around a handful of loosened earth. Aiming for Arthur's eyes, he flung the sand up, rolled sideways, and checked with one hand that the inverters were still wrapped tight against his stomach.

He scrambled up as Arthur cried out and began to circle towards Ayla.

Arthur followed. "Give up, Toby," he growled in a low voice. "I'll make it quick."

Toby shook his head. Arthur's curls were sticking to his forehead with sweat and he seemed to be growing larger and more powerful with each breath he took. How the hells could Toby have a chance against him?

A shriek of pain almost took his attention, but Toby didn't dare turn. If it was Ayla, there was nothing he could do to help, if it was Summer . . . well, good.

Frantically his mind took him through Callum's lessons in hand-to-hand combat. Eyes, ears, nose, throat, and groin: those were the weak points.

Toby had already targeted Arthur's eyes. The boy was happy to go sunblind anyway. Would that make it all right to gouge?

Toby opened his fist.

He would distract Arthur with a knife hand to the throat and then go for his eyes.

When Arthur charged, Toby was already moving. Arthur dodged backward to avoid Toby's hand at his throat but Toby shot upward with his fingers, aiming for the eyes. He missed with his index finger, but his middle one struck home.

Arthur screamed and knocked Toby away. The crowd noise built to a crescendo. As Arthur staggered, Toby took the opportunity to check on Ayla. She and Summer were on the floor. Summer was underneath, desperately trying to punch Ayla in the left shoulder, but Ayla was holding her down and leaning close. Toby remembered their own first meeting. Summer was about to get that same headbutt.

He turned back to Arthur. "Why don't *you* give up?"

Arthur kept one hand over his eye and began to pace toward Toby.

There was the sound of a smack and a cry from Summer. Both Toby and Arthur looked. Ayla was sitting back and Summer was groaning, her nose bleeding and her eyes unfocused. Ayla raised her fist just as the bell rang.

Ayla's fist came down.

"Stop." Mother Hesper's voice reverberated around the arena. "You must stand and pray."

"Stand and pray. Stand and pray," the crowd chanted.

"Cheater," Ayla roared. But she rolled off Summer.

Arthur ran and lifted Summer to her feet. Her plaits were coming loose and a red mark was blossoming between her eyes.

Toby took Ayla's hand and raised it into the air. "Praise the Sun," he yelled.

Above them the rope with the glass on it began to come down.

When the bell rang again, instead of attacking, Arthur boosted Summer on to his shoulders and she reached for the long staff.

"Stop them!" Ayla shouted.

Toby ran. Ayla was just behind him, limping now on her injured leg.

The staff was out of Summer's reach, but Arthur grabbed

Summer's feet and lifted her higher. She balanced on his hands and got hold of the staff.

Toby bowled into Arthur's legs, knocking him flying, but Summer was already somersaulting down, staff in hand.

Toby bit down on a curse as Summer stood, spinning the staff as professionally as Dee.

Ayla came to a halt. "You think that'll change things?" she said. "You think I can't take it from you?"

In one smooth movement, Arthur kicked Toby away and rolled to his feet. As Summer ran at her, Ayla used a crescent kick to knock the staff sideways with her boot. Then she stepped in close, so Summer couldn't use the staff against her and Toby relaxed: she had this.

Ayla turned so that her back was against Summer's chest and she gripped the hand holding the staff. As Toby watched, hands like steel bands wrapped around his biceps. He should never have taken his eyes off Arthur.

Toby struggled as Arthur began to run him backwards toward the jagged shards of metal that lined the arena wall. He tried headbutting, but could get nowhere near. His arms were pinned. He tried to raise his knee, but Arthur was moving too fast.

"*Toby!*" Ayla screamed.

The shadow of the wall fell on Arthur's face; cool shade bathing them in gray. Toby dropped his whole weight into the other boy's arms, aiming to throw Arthur off balance. It worked, and quickly Toby wrapped his legs around Arthur's knees to trip him. They rolled and came to a stop, inches from the junk-metal ring.

Arthur tried to force him nearer and Toby wriggled frantically.

Wham! Ayla landed on Arthur's back and punched down on his neck with both hands knotted together. His grip on Toby went slack.

As Toby squirmed out from under Arthur, Summer appeared as if from nowhere and slammed the staff down on Ayla's back. She cried out.

The bell rang.

The four teens pulled apart, panting raggedly.

Toby grabbed Ayla's arm and pulled her into the center of the arena, away from the baying crowd and the rusting metal spikes on the wall.

Arthur was bent over, his hands on his knees. Blood dripped from his damaged eye.

Summer clutched the staff tightly.

"We need a plan," Toby rasped.

Ayla nodded as she raised her hands. "Praise the Sun."

But there was no time. The magnifying glass began to lower and the bell rang once more.

This time, Summer and Arthur approached Toby and Ayla together, moving as one.

Ayla rubbed sweat out of her eyes. "How long did they practice?"

"A lifetime?"

Ayla was already moving. "Get Arthur," she cried. She ran straight at Summer. She was fast, but her limp had become much more pronounced. A small smile played on Summer's face and she adjusted her stance, aiming her weapon at Ayla's left leg.

Arthur circled Toby, his arms spread. Both of them were half watching their partners.

At the last second, Ayla switched her gait, threw all of her weight on to her left leg, and swept her right heel around. As she took

Summer's feet out from under her, the staff came down. Ayla hissed in pain as it struck her back, but she reached up and grabbed the weapon from Summer's fingers.

In one smooth move she snapped it on her knee and threw half to Toby.

"No!" Toby screamed. Had Ayla forgotten the puzzle? They needed that staff.

He caught the broken shard and faced Arthur.

"Your partner just ruined this for all of us," Arthur yelled.

Toby glanced at the splintered point of the broken staff in his hand.

Arthur started to back away from him and Toby drove him toward Lenka's crumpled body. Too late, Arthur saw her outflung arm. He tripped and fell. Instantly Toby leaped on his chest and held the pointed stick at his throat.

"It's over," he yelled.

The crowd howled their fury and frustration. Arthur and Summer were the clear favorites.

There was no bell; no sign that anyone had heard him.

"I could kill him," Toby shouted. "We've won." He looked for Ayla: she was lying on top of Summer, choking the girl with her own half staff.

What were the sun worshippers waiting for?

Summer's blue eyes drifted closed and the attendants surrounding the arena seemed almost ready to rush them and save her. Through the gaps in the wall, Toby could see them sway. His heart pounded and he touched the inverters.

Ayla stood and marched toward him.

"Finish it," she snapped.

Toby shook his head. "I can't—not without killing him."

Ayla glanced toward the cathedral steps. Father Dahon and Mother Hesper now stood side by side, watching. "They're not going to stop the fight. We haven't finished the trial."

Arthur began to struggle and Toby pressed the stick against his throat, hard enough to break skin.

"I'll deal with this," Ayla said. "Get out of the way."

Toby shook his head. "I won't let you kill for me."

"How long are you planning on sitting there then?" Ayla said. "I won't kill him."

Ayla gripped Arthur's chin, twisted his head to the side and raised her stick.

Her weapon came down so fast it was a blur. There was a thud as the blunt end of the staff connected with the soft spot behind Arthur's ear.

With surgical precision, Ayla had knocked him out.

Trembling, Toby sagged back on to his heels. The bell rang and he and Ayla stood up.

"Pray, pray," the attendants chanted.

After so much practice, the words came easily. *"We believe in one Sun, The Father, the Almighty, Heater of heaven and earth, Revealer of all that is seen, and unseen . . .*

Slowly, the magnifying glass was lowered until Toby could reach up and grab it. His hands closed around the metal circle surrounding the central glass. He pulled it from the rope and the attendants started to call out. Some shouting for Arthur to wake, others cheering Toby on.

He caught sight of Zahir, smiling painfully at him through one of the gaps and nodded.

On one side of the metal there was a hole, if the magnifying glass was stood upright, the hole would be hidden. Toby could fit his thumb inside. He touched the glass through it, then he compared the hole to his broken stick.

"What's the problem?" Ayla cocked her head.

Toby looked at the panel in the wall; it was well above his head and surrounded by metal spikes.

"We need the full length of the staff." He avoided her gaze.

"Is that all?" She knelt by Lenka and tugged the cloth binding from the girl's hair. Then she handed the linen strip to Toby. "Here, now you can fix it."

Toby fitted the ends of the staff together again. The cloth was long enough to wrap three times around the break, holding it tight.

Sounds of appreciation broke over the wall. Toby glanced at the sanctuary steps. Mother Hesper stood with her arms folded, glaring at him.

He turned back to Ayla. "Did you think of that before you—"

Ayla raised her eyebrows. "Of course I did." She laughed quietly. "You really thought I broke the staff without considering how to fix it afterward."

Toby flushed. "Sorry." He brightened as he slotted the staff into the hole in the side of the glass. "There."

"Now what do we do?" Ayla put her hands on her hips.

"Now we use the sun." Toby stepped over Summer as he made his way to the wall beneath the panel. "It doesn't just give out *light,* but *energy*. Think of the solar panels." He held the staff up above his head, angling it so that the light from the sun hit the magnifying glass and shone through on to the wooden plate.

The crowd began to cheer, Summer and Arthur forgotten.

Ayla grinned as the wood began to smolder. Finally, with a hiss and pop, a flame burst into life. He fed the flame with the sun's rays until a hole big enough for his hand was eaten into the panel.

Then he dropped the staff.

Together they stared up at the blackened wood. "It's still out of reach." Ayla rubbed her temples. "If I wrap your shirt around my hands I could climb—"

"No." Toby shook his head. "You'll be cut to shreds. Maybe they'll send us another bit of equipment at the next bell."

But no bell rang. The crowd grew restless, Toby felt disapproval radiating through the junk walls.

"How long are we going to stand here?" Ayla whispered. "Arthur and Summer will wake up soon."

"I know," Toby said. Then he slapped his forehead. "Remember how Arthur and Summer got the staff?"

Ayla nodded, already moving toward him.

"You think you can balance on your bad leg?" Toby bent so she could climb on to his back.

Ayla ignored his question. She leapfrogged on to him and landed sitting over his shoulders. Toby took her weight and straightened.

"I'm not high enough." Ayla put her hands on his head. "I'm going to have to stand."

"Let me get closer." Toby walked carefully toward the wall. If he tripped or lost balance, he would tip Ayla on to metal spikes. "I don't like this," he muttered.

"Compared to climbing the masts or standing watch in a high wind, this is nothing," Ayla whispered.

Toby relaxed. She was right. He stopped a small step away from the wall and planted his feet.

"Put your hands on your hips," Ayla said.

"You don't want me to hold your feet?"

"No, I need your shoulders wide and stable."

Ayla got her left foot on his shoulder and then her right. He held his breath as her injured leg trembled. Then she got her balance and began to stand.

Behind them, Arthur groaned and Toby caught his breath. "Hurry," he muttered.

"All right." Ayla extended one arm; her fingers brushed the splintered hole. "I can't quite reach . . ."

Toby slid one foot nearer to the spikes. His heart thudded as Ayla rocked but held her position. Then her fingers slid inside the hole. The burned wood left charcoal smears on her wrist as she pulled her hand out and held the pendant high.

The crowd roared.

"Do you think we get to keep this?" she said, admiring the glitter of sunlight from the diamond.

"The bell's not ringing." Toby turned to see Arthur trying to get to his feet. "They're waiting for him to take it from us."

"I don't think so!" Ayla leaped from Toby's shoulders, wrapped her fist around the pendant and punched Arthur in the jaw. He thumped back down and lay still.

The bell began to ring and the crowd shouted for them. "Sun and Moon . . . Sun and Moon."

Once more Toby touched the inverters hidden under his shirt. They had done it.

He didn't watch as the others were removed from the arena.

Ayla hunched at his side, her fist clenched around the pendant as though daring someone to take it from her.

Mother Hesper and Father Dahon appeared at the arena's exit and the attendant crowd hushed. Mother Hesper's lips were pursed and her eyes tracked Summer as she was dragged away. Then she turned back to Toby and Ayla.

"Our Sun and Moon," she said.

The air rippled with the crowd's ecstatic cries.

Then Father Dahon spoke. "The favored pair—your Sun and Moon—will now be prepared for the festival."

TWENTY-THREE

Toby's new room could not have been more different to the cell he had woken in that morning. He was now in an area of the sanctuary he had not seen before, away from both the cathedral and the rear courtyard, in a villa raised off the ground by stilts. Its sides were open to the sun, light curtains drifted in the sea breeze and the large bed was covered in pillows. In the center of the room a bath set into the floor was filled with steaming water that scented the air with rosemary and bergamot.

Clean yellow robes hung on the back wall. They were simple, dress-like and floor length, with a wide hood and gold link belt. He would look like Father Dahon.

"Ayla?"

"I hear you." Ayla's apartment was so close to his that their billowing curtains occasionally tangled. He heard a splash and then a sigh as she lowered herself into her bath. "Relax, Toby, we've got a week before the others arrive to meet us at the festival. Enjoy it."

"How can you, after what we've done?" Toby looked at his hands. His knuckles were scraped and his nails encrusted with dirt and blood. His throat and ears were blistered from the sun.

Slowly, he removed his shirt and dropped it on the floor. His chest was still an angry red from the salt and around his stomach the stained bandages were still tightly wrapped.

He looked around him. He seemed to be alone, but in this place, who knew? He undid the bandages and caught the inverter as it fell. Where could he hide it now? There was no burying it here.

Toby still had the fork tine stuck in the hem of his sleeve. He wriggled it out, used it to slit the side of a pillow, slid the inverter inside and pushed it under the pile at the back of the bed. It was the best he could do.

Then he pulled his pants over his protesting legs and dropped them on the floor. Bruised and aching, he stepped into the water.

Toby laid his head back on the edge of the bath and allowed his muscles to loosen. The water leached the dirt from his skin and grew dark.

Toby closed his eyes. Exhaustion wrapped around him and pressed him against the porcelain. He slept.

Toby's aches and pains had all but gone. He was dressed in yet another new yellow robe, his feet were bare and his hair had been oiled until it shone. The challenges that had led up to the day of the festival almost seemed a distant dream. But that morning, when he had carefully removed the inverter from his pillow and strapped it to his shoulder with the old bandages, he was well aware that the haze of the last few days had been nothing more than a brief escape from reality.

When they were not being ordered to pray, lectured on their future duties, or being offered fine meals and drinks, Toby and Ayla conversed in soft voices. They were unable to talk openly, due to their endlessly rotating entourage, but managed to speak in code about life on board their ships.

Toby learned that Ayla had collected the beads in her hair in every port she visited and realized that they formed a map of her life, right back to the very first time she stepped on board the *Banshee*. He learned that, sometimes, the *Banshee* was so silent that Ayla felt as if she was disappearing, so she would shake her head to hear the clattering and feel real again. He already knew that she loved to fight but he discovered that she saw each kick or strike as a step in a dance and that when she fought she heard a beat.

Toby wasn't stupid: he knew his feelings for her had grown too big for him to handle. Each time he thought of the day of the festival when they would return to their ships, his heart ached.

And now the day of the festival had arrived.

Toby stood outside his room, refusing to be herded by his entourage of brothers until Ayla emerged. Finally she came out. Her hair had been braided into a complex style and her precious beads shone.

Her long gray robe had silver threads that sparkled as she moved. Toby looked down at his own robe. His had gold woven through the yellow.

Ayla looked at him. "Very . . . shiny."

"Back at you." Toby stared at her boots poking out from under the robe. "You're wearing those?"

"We tried to tell her," a sister whispered. He received a knife-sharp glare in return.

Toby picked at a loose thread on his sleeve and heard a small gasp from a sister behind him. He dropped his hand.

"Are you ready for this?" he asked and Ayla nodded. When Hideaki had visited to tend her wounds, she had retrieved her inverter. Toby assumed it was now tucked into one of her incongruous steel-capped boots.

"We must go." A young sister stepped in front of Toby and gestured toward the corridor. "The festival gifts await your inspection."

"Praise the Sun," Toby murmured dutifully.

Ayla reached across and took his hand, squeezing his fingers before pulling away. Toby's breath caught at the unexpected gesture, then he realized that she had left something in his palm. He closed his hand around it and, as soon as the attendants had turned away from him, he opened his hand and looked at the tiny bluish pill.

This was how Toby would die.

Under the pretext of adjusting his robe, he managed to tuck it into the hole in his sleeve left by the loose thread.

They were guided away from their villas and into the rear courtyard. Toby raised his eyes as the shadow of the cathedral fell over his face. There in the center was a wagon piled high with pale yellow cloth. Each piece had a small embroidered sun in the center. Standing beside the wagon was Mother Hesper.

"I thought the sanctuary collected all depictions of the Sun," he muttered. "Now we're giving these away?"

"These have been purified," Mother Hesper said. "That's why

they're so special. Each pilgrim will be permitted a single depiction of the Sun to help focus their worship over the coming year."

"So we're to hand these out, one to each pilgrim?" Toby thought of the inverter. It wouldn't be too difficult to fold it into a piece of cloth.

"Toby." Ayla nudged him. Loading a final pile of cloth squares on to the wagon was a familiar figure.

Without thinking, Toby started toward her. "Leila!"

The girl looked up. She had lost weight and her brown eyes had sunk into her sockets.

Leila signaled for Toby to give her his hand.

At first he thought she wanted some kind of blessing, but instead, Leila took his hand and turned it palm up.

Then she started to form letters with her fingernail.

I . . . a-m . . . g-l-a-d . . . i-t . . . w-a-s . . . y-o-u.

Suddenly, Toby found it difficult to swallow. He nodded to show that he understood and Leila dropped his hand.

"Are you all right?" he whispered. "Are they feeding you?"

Leila gave him a tremulous smile, before the other attendants, at Mother Hesper's signal, hustled her off.

Ayla stared after her. "They'll be fine," she said eventually. "They're warm, fed, clothed . . . Some of them came from places where that wasn't the case."

Toby sighed. "It doesn't look like Leila's eating."

Mother Hesper loomed at his shoulder. "Many of the most holy choose not to eat. To live on sunlight is the purest form of worship." She was so close that he could smell her sour breath. "Regardless of her choice, my dear Sun, it does take some time to learn to eat without a tongue." She rolled back on her heels, pleased with the expression of horror on Toby's face. Then she pointed toward the steps. "Time to greet your pilgrims. You have until the sun reaches the apex of the sanctuary dome to give out all the gifts."

"Then what?" Toby didn't mean to whisper, but he did.

"Then it will be time for you to give a final gift to the Sun—your vision." Mother Hesper showed her teeth. "Make the most of the sights of today, they will be your last."

TWENTY-FOUR

The sanctuary doors opened and Toby was momentarily blinded by the glare. He had been instructed what to do in this moment and he raised his arms and face upward. Beside him, Ayla bowed her head and wrapped her arms around her chest. They were Sun and Moon.

He was hit by a barrage of sound. Mother Hesper caught his raised elbow and steadied him, sympathetic for the first time. "It takes some getting used to," she murmured.

There was no way to make out individual voices or words. Toby turned to Ayla—her hands were twitching with the urge to cover her ears.

"I've never . . . it's never . . ." Toby couldn't form a coherent thought. He blinked the light from his eyes and stared. The arena was gone—the whole front of the fortification had been turned into a giant open gate. In his whole life Toby had never seen so many people.

"Are there even this many people left living?" Ayla murmured. "Are they ghosts?"

Father Dahon, who had moved to stand behind them, spoke. "They're real. . . . I can't see them any more, but . . ." His blind eyes moved restlessly.

"You were the Moon once." Toby had considered Father Dahon old—his air of authority, his blindness, and his way of moving had contributed to a sense of great age. But now that he looked closely, Toby saw that Father Dahon was probably no more than twenty-five. This was what would happen to Toby if Ayla's pill didn't work.

Father Dahon nodded. "I was the first. I know what you are feeling right now." He pressed his hand on Toby's shoulder. "It's overwhelming, but you have the strength of the Sun. Don't let them see your fear."

He and Mother Hesper stepped back into the shadows of the sanctuary, leaving Toby and Ayla alone.

"Toby . . ." Ayla's voice shook.

"Can you see any of the crew?" Toby squinted over the waving crowd.

Ayla shook her head. "It's impossible. What if they don't make it to us before we run out of time?"

Toby shook his head. "They will."

Crowd was not the right word for the mass of people in front of them. The wharf where Marcus had been hanged had been crowded. Tarifa had been crowded. But there were spaces in a crowd, gaps between people so that they could move and jostle, shift and ebb. This was a solid press. No space for breath, let alone room for a band of pirates to elbow their way to the front.

"How did they all get here?" Toby breathed. "The sea must be packed with ships."

"Which means the *Phoenix* can't flee if we need to move fast."

Ayla fell silent as the wagon full of pilgrim gifts arrived. "Where do we go?"

Toby pointed. From a side door, two seats were being carried. Thrones. Toby's was gold with sun rays emerging from the top. Ayla's was identical, but silver.

"Oh my gods." Ayla's eyes widened. "The value."

Toby took a deep breath and started down the steps. "Let's get going."

Attendants placed the thrones at the cathedral steps and added padded cushions. He sat down and the ornate arms curled around him, hemming him in.

If he wanted to see Ayla, he had to lean to look for her, buried in the metallic wings of her seat.

As soon as Toby leaned back and set his elbows on the arm rests, the crowd fell silent.

But this didn't give Toby much relief; instead it intensified the worry worming through his brain.

Robed attendants began to pick out members of the crowd and funnel them toward Toby and Ayla.

Something was pressed into his hand. Toby glanced up and found an attendant at his shoulder. In his hand was a folded piece of material.

He knew what to do.

The first pilgrim fell to his bony knees in front of Toby, his bristled face suffused with joy. Toby shook the material out so that he could see the embroidery, then he shoved it toward the man, already looking for the next.

Then Toby realized that the kneeling man was not rising. His mind raced—what had he forgotten?

Beside him, Ayla was handing her own square of material to her own pilgrim. "Bless you," she said.

Toby swallowed: of course! "Bless you," he whispered.

The man sighed and closed his eyes; then an attendant hustled him off. Toby didn't see where he went; a second man, twitching with anticipation, was already kneeling in front of him.

The words Toby had to say seemed more and more divorced from meaning each time he repeated them, until they could have meant anything at all, or nothing.

A woman was kneeling in front of him now, but instead of lowering her stare, her slate-gray eyes bored into Toby's. He shivered, feeling a strange familiarity in the gaze. The woman's hair was blonde, beginning to gray. Years ago, Toby mused, she would have been a good Sun candidate herself. She was tall, and her muscles were like Ayla's, honed by hunger, sharp-edged under her clothes. Toby swallowed. Why had this woman caught his attention?

He took a piece of cloth from the attendant at his side and thrust it toward her. "Bless you," he muttered.

The woman didn't move and Toby thought for a second that she was not going to take his offering. Then she snatched the cloth and tucked it into the collar of her shirt.

"Thank you, Toby." She stood and walked away.

Only when she had gone did Toby realize that she had called him by name.

After what seemed like another hundred offerings, Toby had all but forgotten the stranger. He shifted on the cushion uncomfortably until a square-faced sister rested light fingers on his shoulder.

"These people have come to see the living embodiment of the Sun," the woman whispered. "Have dignity, it will be over soon."

Toby paled and looked at the sky. She was right—the sun had moved toward the dome. He glanced at Ayla, handing out cloth and blessing, over and over, seemingly unaffected by the heat, the stench of unwashed bodies and the ticking of time.

Toby barely saw the next person to kneel in front of him. He reached for the material and held it out.

Then the supplicant lurched forward as if falling and the attendant beside him gasped. Toby focused his attention.

As his gaze fell on the man, his fingers began to tremble. Toby took the cloth and, while the sister behind him glowered, he pulled both arms inside his sleeves and under cover of his voluminous robes, he wriggled the inverter from the bandage.

Inside his sleeve, he carefully wrapped the cloth around the precious cargo, then he returned his hands to view. To his left, Ayla was bending to her boot.

Simeon was kneeling in front of her. He looked tired and threads of sweat raced down his bare chest. Toby returned his attention to the pilgrim kneeling in front of him.

"It's all right," he said to the sister, as she shifted impatiently. "That's my father."

She nodded and allowed the captain to reach out a hand for his blessing gift.

Toby watched Barnaby and Simeon as they were hustled away from the thrones. It seemed to him that a fishing line stretched between them, more and more painful the farther away they moved.

Ayla reached across to touch his hand. "Ready?"

Toby nodded, keeping his father in sight.

The brother behind Ayla nudged her and she had to turn her gaze back to the front where a woman in a tattered gown kneeled. Where had all these people come from?

"Bless you," Ayla murmured. Then she pretended to cough and put her hand to her mouth before giving over the cloth.

Ayla was already slumping in her chair by the time Toby managed to free his pill from his hem.

There was a moment of horror, then the brother forced the shocked pilgrim to move on and Toby's sister slid in front of Ayla, sheltering her from the crowd.

Ayla was lying completely still. As he watched, the rise and fall of her chest slowed. The color drained from her face and her lips turned a bluish purple.

He couldn't stop his own gasp: "Ayla!"

Panicked attendants now formed a wall between them and the crowd shifted.

Quickly, Toby slid the pill on to his tongue. It tasted bitter and Toby wasn't sure if he was meant to swallow or chew it. He crunched it quickly, grimacing as the flavor flooded his mouth. He imagined that this was what death tasted like.

What if the pill turned out to be real poison? What if something went wrong with the plan after he was asleep? What if he never woke up? The gritty shards stuck in his throat as Toby shifted his gaze toward Ayla. As he did so, he spotted another familiar figure in the crowd.

"Nell's here?" he whispered.

She snaked in and out of the crowd, accompanied by a tattoo-headed *Banshee* pirate on either side. She was headed for his father.

Toby tried to surge to his feet, but his limbs were heavy and he fell to his knees.

There was no one to lift him to his feet—half of the attendants surrounded Ayla and others were running into the sanctuary or trying to control the panicking crowd.

From the floor, Toby couldn't see his father, Simeon, or Nell. He tried to get up, but his brain seemed to have no connection to his body.

He heard the sanctuary door crash open.

He fought to keep his eyes open as Ayla was lifted by four uncles and rushed up the steps with a furious Mother Hesper at her side. Why was he still awake?

Toby tried to call out again, but his lips were glued together, his throat unable to form sounds.

"The Sun, the Sun is on the ground." Someone from the crowd saw him and pointed.

A horrified sister ran to him, but it was too late—the crowd had turned to a mob, surging forward.

"Get the stand-ins," Mother Hesper shrieked. She abandoned Ayla, ran to Toby's side, and began to shake him.

He groaned, the only sound he could make.

"Get up!"

Toby tried to obey, but he was unable to move.

"Toby!" His father's roar cut through the noise. Toby spotted Simeon, Nell right behind him. They were coming to protect him from the mob. His head lolled slowly to the left and his eyes began to close.

"Don't you *dare*!" Mother Hesper slapped him, her bony hands stinging his cheek. He stirred.

"Get him to the infirmary—he'll be all right,"

Two brothers lifted him to his feet.

Toby wanted to scream. They were meant to think he was dead. Why hadn't his pill worked?

A line of uncles had appeared. They now lined up in front of the thrones, blocking the crowd from reaching them.

At Mother Hesper's shout, the captain's eyes had narrowed. If Toby's pill hadn't worked, their plan was ruined. He threw himself at the guardian uncles, Simeon at his side.

"Let me past. I have to get to my son!"

The captain drove a punch into the face of the nearest uncle but the others held him back.

Toby saw Arthur and Summer, as if in a dream, robed like he and Ayla, rushing down the cathedral steps toward the thrones.

"The new Sun and Moon," Mother Hesper yelled at the terrified pilgrims. "The *true* Sun and Moon. There is no problem here." She gestured to Toby. "These were struck down because of their unworthiness. You cannot fool the Sun. *Praise the Sun!*"

Gradually, the crowd stopped fighting. Only Barnaby and Simeon continued to wrestle, still desperately trying to get to Toby.

Summer stood and raised her arms, making a sun sign, as Arthur curled himself into a moon pose.

"Praise the Sun," Summer called.

Toby blinked. Arthur and Summer were tongueless—they had to be.

Again, he struggled weakly.

"Infirmary, *now*!" Mother Hesper snapped. "We cannot have two Suns out here." She pressed her index finger to Toby's forehead, forcing his head up. "I'm not sure what happened here. Perhaps you *were* rejected by the Sun for being unworthy." She tilted her head. "But don't worry, once you are sufficiently recovered, we will still be staking you out for the blinding."

She turned her back on him and Toby blinked tears from his eyes. How had everything gone so wrong?

As Toby stared, still frozen, his father and Simeon were hauled to their feet and dragged before Mother Hesper.

"True pilgrims don't attack members of the Solar Order. Take them to the cells," she said. Then she reached out and plucked the cloth from his father's pocket. "You don't deserve *this*." As she tugged it free, Toby could only watch in horror as the precious inverter tumbled out of the folded cloth. It bounced on the packed earth and rolled to a stop.

Mother Hesper's eyes flashed and she turned to stare at Toby. "Forget the infirmary. Take him straight to the cells."

TWENTY-FIVE

"He's sick. I'm the medic. Let me through."

Perhaps an hour had passed since Toby had been dumped on the floor of his old cell, unable to answer the shouts coming from his father down the corridor.

Finally his door was thrust open and Hideaki rushed in. "The silent attendants have placed Ayla on the beach to await the tide. She'll be fine, so long as your shipmates are waiting as they promised," he whispered. "When I last treated her, we arranged a meeting point—your boat should be waiting to pick me up outside the maze. I'll go there now and tell them to wait for you. There has to be a way to get you all there. I just need to *think*." His face fell. "What happened, did your pills not work?"

Toby shook his head.

Hideaki frowned. "Strange. But the symptoms should wear off soon." He lifted Toby's eyelids one by one and checked his pupils, then pressed his paired fingers against his wrist. Toby's pulse fluttered against the pressure.

Weakly Toby caught his hand. "You said *pills*," he rasped. "You mean *pill* right? Just one pill."

"No . . ." Hideaki said slowly. "Blue Death is a paired set: two pills. If you only took one . . ." He looked at Toby's useless limbs. "It looks like you had the paralytic, but no respiratory depressor."

Toby flopped backwards. Ayla had only given him a single pill . . . hadn't she? She *wouldn't* have betrayed him, not after all they had been through . . . would she? His heart began to calcify.

"My inverter," he said. "Did you see what happened to it?"

Hideaki nodded. "Mother Hesper returned it to the Reliquary."

Toby groaned. "Ayla's is locked away with Simeon, ours is gone. This was all for nothing."

Hideaki pressed a wet cloth against Toby's forehead. "They'll be coming for you as soon as I tell them you're sufficiently recovered. I'll hold off as long as possible, but you know they spy on these cells." He leaned closer. "So don't move if you can help it."

Toby caught Hideaki's sleeve. "If you can, get Simeon's inverter from him. You can take it to the *Phoenix* when you're picked up."

Hideaki nodded and Toby closed his eyes. He imagined Ayla being rescued from the beach by Theo and felt ripped in two—part of him wanted her safe despite her betrayal.

Why had she done it? They had stolen an inverter for each of them; the *Banshee* would have ended up with exactly what they needed. Why not stick to the original plan?

Hideaki moved Toby's arms and legs until they tingled. Life was returning to his body. He coughed and Hideaki held water to his lips. After a few sips, Toby felt up to raising his voice. "Captain?"

"Toby!" The reply was immediate. "Are you all right?"

"Save your voice," Hideaki snapped. "Do you want them to know you're better right now, or do you want a bit more time with your eyes?"

Toby clamped his lips together.

Hideaki gathered his things. "I'll try and find a way to get you out of here. Just hold tight."

The captain had given up shouting for Toby and the corridor was quiet apart from a monotonous thumping from Simeon's cell. Toby pictured him hurling himself against the thick plastic door, over and over again, trying to break it down.

How long did they have before Mother Hesper came for him? He knew she would come before sundown, and time was rolling on.

Suddenly, there was a thud against his cell door and it shuddered. Toby sat up.

"I'm getting you out."

"Hideaki?" Toby whispered.

There was something wrong with Hideaki's voice, it sounded thick and strained.

"Where're the uncles?" Toby stood on wobbly legs.

"Drugged." Hideaki pushed Toby's door open and turned his back before Toby could see his face. "I'm going for your captain."

Toby staggered to the doorjamb and leaned against it. The slanting light in the corridor told Toby it was afternoon—maybe three hours since midday.

Suddenly, his father rushed toward him and wrapped him in his thick arms.

Simeon followed.

"At least we have the chance to get one inverter out of here," Toby murmured. But the look on Simeon's face petrified him. "What?"

"I don't have an inverter." Simeon didn't meet his eye.

"Ayla gave it to you, I saw her."

Simeon nodded. "She gave it to me. I don't have it now."

The captain loosened his hold on Toby. "Did you drop it during the fight?"

Simeon shook his head. "It was secure in my pouch. But—"

"I *wasn't* dreaming." Toby breathed. "It was Nell. She was right behind you."

"Nell?" Barnaby asked.

Simeon hung his head. "She pickpocketed me . . ."

"Ayla set us up?" Even as he asked the question, Toby knew the answer.

"She used us all." Hideaki stepped into a beam of light. His face was pale and his eyes red. He had been crying, screaming perhaps. "I've been to the meeting place. There's no one there. She's left me behind."

Toby stared at the hem of his robe. "She promised on her sister's grave that she wouldn't betray me . . ." He tailed off.

"If the ship wasn't at your meeting point," Simeon said to Hideaki, "how are we going to get off this island?"

Toby looked at his father. "Where's the *Phoenix*? Can we swim?"

The captain frowned. "Certainly not. We have two fools on board who already tried that. They're half dead. Uma isn't sure she can save them."

"Cezar and Bianca," Toby whispered. "They made it!"

"If you can call it that." Simeon nodded. "Theo pulled them out of the bay. The girl was dragging the boy and they were going under when I spotted them. The last thing she said was your name, so we took them on board. They were both still out when we left this morning."

"At least let's get out of here," the captain said. "Someone will be trawling the coast on *Birdie*, looking for us."

"Unless Ayla told them you were dead," Hideaki grunted.

"You want to give up?" Toby asked. "I'm not waiting around to lose my sight. The rear courtyard's our best bet—we have to get over the wall and along the cliff."

Simeon nodded. "Let me go first." He strode past Toby to reach the bottom of the staircase.

"I knew you weren't working alone, thief," Mother Hesper announced as she stepped from the shadows. Uncles stood behind her. Simeon glanced at the captain, ready to fight, but the captain shook his head. There were too many of them and nowhere to go. "You tried to make a mockery of us. You tried to steal a holy relic. Worse, you seem willing to risk another cataclysm! I cannot imagine what you meant to achieve." She looked at Hideaki. "And you, of all people, should know that there is *always* someone listening."

Father Dahon moved into view at the top of the stairs, his pale eyes gleamed. "It's time," he said.

The captain stepped forward. "I won't let you blind my son."

Father Dahon blinked. "Your son was chosen above all others to be the Sun. He *will* be converted through blindness—as I was . . . and as you will be."

TWENTY-SIX

Toby was going blind.

He had long since lost edges. If Toby turned his head against the rope that held his forehead, he could see the blurred outline of the cathedral roof; nothing more than a smudge against a lighter background. Soon the sun would steal even that.

His vision would have been lost already, except that a cloud had built in the sky as they were being tied down, the first cloud he had seen on Gozo; maybe it was a sign. He wondered what it was a sign *of*.

Toby had no idea how much time had passed. They had removed his golden robe before tying him down and abandoning him to 'think on the Sun' and the prickle of sunburn that was re-emerging on his peeling chest and scarred legs was all he had to go by.

That irritation was nothing, however, compared to the itching of his eyes. He would have given anything to have been able to blink.

At first, they had shouted at the attendant uncles guarding the path; pleaded and begged, but they had received no answer. Perhaps they were silent attendants.

Beside him, Arthur and Summer lay in their own bonds, quietly murmuring prayers. They had started off with hymns, but their throats had dried out as quickly as their eyes.

The captain coughed, his throat full of dust. "How're you doing, son?"

Toby had to swallow before he could answer. "I'm okay." But all he could think was that Ayla had betrayed him and he was going to go blind.

"We're going to get out of this."

"Sure." Toby didn't even try to look at his father. He was staked out just the same as Toby and the others: his forehead tightly bound, his eyes taped open and his hands and feet stretched out to either side.

They weren't getting out of this.

The tape above Toby's left eye was peeling slightly. Among the pain of sunburn, cramping muscles, biting insects, grit, sand, and the agony of his vision being flayed from him, the peeling tape seemed the worst. He knew that if it would just loosen a little more, just a tiny bit, he'd be able to close his eye.

The skin on his cheeks was tight where his tears had dried. His ducts were empty now; not even the swimming of tears could protect his vision.

"Is Simeon still unconscious?" Toby strained against the ropes again and managed to gain a slight tilt to his chin. A trickle of blood wormed its way down his right temple.

"Must be," Hideaki croaked. "He's lucky. When he wakes up this'll all be over. It won't be long now, and if that cloud cover clears . . ."

"It'll be seconds, I know." Toby ground his teeth. After all he'd been through in the last few weeks, to end up like this. "Where do you think Ayla is?"

The captain didn't answer, but at the end of the path, where the silent attendants guarded them, there came the sounds of a struggle: grunts and thuds, but no shouts.

Toby strained for a second, but soon gave up. Whatever was going on, he could not see.

A cool shadow fell over Toby's face and he gasped, relief surging through him at the momentary respite from the glare. The shadow moved and he whimpered, as if he could get the darkness to remain.

Then the captain roared. "You! Leave us alone."

Simeon groaned his way to wakefulness and began to fight his bonds.

Toby managed to move his head just enough to see a blurry pair of legs. He frowned. Something about the outfit was familiar. He sagged back into position. "Who're you?"

When the figure bent over Toby, he recognized the woman from the festival, the one who had caught his attention with her intense slate-gray eyes. She put a cool hand over his eyes.

"Get away from him!" Toby heard the ropes around the captain creaking as he strained harder than ever, but all Toby could think was how wonderful her palm felt on his face.

Toby groaned as the woman shifted. "Don't go."

"I won't." There was a brief second of light as she replaced her hand with a strip of cloth.

"What are you doing?" Summer shouted suddenly. "Somebody help!"

Ignoring her, the woman carefully peeled the tape from Toby's eyelids and rolled the rope from his forehead.

The captain was still ranting, but the woman, whoever she was, had come to save them. What was the problem? Shouts from the end of the path told Toby that the uncles were on their way and he held his breath as the stranger sawed through the knots that held him. Finally, Toby's arms sprung loose and his hands slammed over his eyes.

"Free the captain," Toby choked. "I'll be all right."

"Can you walk?" The woman's voice was hard.

Toby nodded. "I will. Just get the captain and—"

He was pulled to his feet. "Then let's go."

"Wait." Toby had no plans to open his eyes; he stumbled as she caught his elbow and propeled him forward. The shouting was louder, Arthur and Summer's yells merged with those of the approaching guards.

"No time," the woman said. As Toby's feet faltered she adjusted her grip and started to drag him.

He struggled. "We can't leave without the others."

"You want to go back there?" The woman's voice was a growl now.

"Stop, in the name of the Sun!"

Abruptly the woman released him and Toby stumbled, still blind, but managed to keep his feet. He heard the hum in the air as she swung a blade.

Toby staggered away from the fight, but didn't dare go too far: they had been tied near the cliff edge and he had no idea how close he was. He tried to pry open his eyes, but his lashes were glued together and filled with grit.

"Wash your eyes out." It was the woman's voice again. A warm bottle was pressed into his hand then she vanished once more.

Toby tipped his head back. Somewhere in front of him, she was fighting.

Tepid water ran over his cheeks and Toby opened stinging eyes. He blinked until his lids no longer felt like sandpaper and tried to see. The world had narrowed; his peripheral vision was white and there were blurry spots dancing in front of him. Still, he could see the shape of the woman as she held off two guards. His father, Simeon, Hideaki, Summer, and Arthur remained tied on the ground. Simeon was roaring his frustration. Toby started to stagger toward them, but hesitated as he saw a dozen more uncles pounding down the path from the sanctuary.

"Run!" the captain yelled. "Don't wait for us. Get back to the *Phoenix*."

"No!" Arthur screamed. "Come back, you have a destiny."

"He's coming with me, Barnaby." The woman spun and slashed. There was a gurgle and the last of the guards she was fighting fell at her feet, blood pooling.

From beyond the cliff edge someone else called out, and Toby spun. "Dee?"

Marcus climbed over first and ran toward Toby. Dee was right behind him, silhouetted against the sky.

His rescuer took his arm and pulled him toward the beach path but Toby dug his heels in. "We have to save the captain."

"He'll be fine," the woman spat.

"Toby?" Marcus skidded to a stop as the woman raised her sword.

"Don't! He's on our side." Toby twisted, but her grip was like stone.

Dee glared. "*She* won't hurt him, Marcus."

"What—" Toby began.

"Are you blind yet?" It was Father Dahon. Toby squinted and saw the robed figure gliding down the path behind the uncles.

His skin prickled and he shuddered, unable to stop the thrill of fear that gripped his heart. "Did you see the Sun?" Father Dahon sang. "Spots in front of your eyes?"

Mother Hesper was at Father Dahon's side, screeching at them to come back.

Dee's mouth flattened into a line and she touched Marcus's arm. "If we don't get the captain right now, he'll be blinded or killed." Hatred flared in her eyes. "If you do anything to hurt Toby, Judy . . ."

"Judy?" Toby whispered.

Dee and Marcus turned and raced toward the captain.

"I'll hold them off while you cut the ropes," Dee shouted. "Cover their eyes."

"Come on!" The woman—Judy—dragged him on to the trail. Toby wanted to join Marcus, Dee and the captain, but confusion and shock had turned his limbs to wood and he couldn't make them obey. Could this woman really be his *mother*?

His legs were stiff from being pegged out and the dose of paralytic he had taken still coursed through his veins. Judy pulled him on, but he looked back. The captain was on his knees and Marcus was untying Simeon.

Barnaby lurched to his feet. "Judy!"

"Say goodbye," she yelled, "because you'll never see our son again."

"What?" Toby froze, but Judy shoved him forward.

The captain tried to follow, but a cry from Dee made him turn. The uncles had surrounded them. Dee swung her staff in wide arcs to hold them off.

"Ignore the pirates, get the false *Sun*!" Mother Hesper screamed.

"*Now* will you run?" Judy hissed.

Toby nodded. They had a head start, but Mother Hesper was catching up. Her face was a mask of grim determination.

"Judy . . ." Toby was horrified to hear the whimper in his own voice.

"Don't worry."

Sharp blades of dune grass sliced Toby's shins and stones skittered under his toes as he ran.

"There." Judy pointed.

A small gray skiff floated on the tide. Toby hurled himself into the sea and leaped on board.

Judy jumped down by his side. She grabbed a long string from the floor and shoved it into his hands. "Pull it."

"What?"

"Do it," she snapped.

With his eyes on Mother Hesper, Toby pulled. As he tugged he felt resistance, then smoke puffed and an engine sputtered and died.

His eye widened. "Gasoline? How did you—"

"Again!" Judy held her sword in front of her.

Toby pulled once more. The engine choked, then growled, then roared into life. Slowly, then with increasing speed, their little gray boat pulled away from the sand.

Mother Hesper and her guardian uncles had reached the shore. As they waded into the sea, their robes floated around them.

The uncles pulled poison-soaked robes from their chests and lurched back out of the salt. Mother Hesper raged at them, but they wouldn't return to the sea.

Toby stared as she splashed on alone.

"Stupid woman," Judy muttered.

"You're burning," Toby called. "Stop."

"Traitor!" Mother Hesper screamed. "Liar!" She waded forward, knocking aside plastic bottles and rusted cans, her mouth screwed up with agony.

"You can't go any farther." Toby pointed at the rising waves. "Give up."

Mother Hesper ignored him—the water was up to her shoulders now and her hair was lifting into the poisoned currents like seaweed.

Finally, Mother Hesper stopped. The water lapped at her chin. Then she started to wade forward once more. As she walked, she spoke. "My death curse upon you. May the Sun burn you all the days of your life. May the Moon never shine on your nights. May you suffer the loss of the thing you hold most dear. May you die in agony." She kept talking, getting louder and more crazed, until her words turned to bubbles. Soon, all that Toby could see were her eyes, then a wave covered her head and she was gone.

He sat down, staggered, and looked at Judy for an answer. "How could she do that?"

Judy shrugged. "Insanity? This religion takes people—blindness, starvation, death."

"Silence." Toby said quietly. Then he gasped as a dark shape

TWENTY-SEVEN

The boat smelled like the engine room on a bad day. Toby wrinkled his nose and, despite his interest in all things mechanical, he shifted farther from the billowing smoke.

He strained back toward the beach, trying to see the captain, but his sight remained blurred.

Tears filled his eyes, and he swiftly wiped them on his sleeve. Judy sat straight-backed, her eyes out to sea, one hand on the rudder as she guided them around the shallow rocks and headed for deeper waters. The breeze ruffled her blonde hair.

"So," Toby muttered eventually. "You're my mother."

Judy said nothing for a long moment. Then she gave a tight smile that didn't reach her eyes. "Don't you remember? I thought maybe when you saw me at the festival . . ."

Toby shook his head. "Sorry." He shuffled on the seat. "Will you take me back to my ship?"

"*Your* ship?" Judy raised her eyebrows.

"The *Phoenix*." Toby clenched his fists.

"You mean the ship your father stole. It rightfully belongs to General Hopewell."

"I don't know any General Hopewell. The *Phoenix* was always the captain's—he designed and made her."

Judy snorted.

Toby forced himself to take a long breath. If this woman wasn't going to take him back to the *Phoenix*, he had to get away. He glanced at the shore and tensed, poised to jump.

"I wouldn't do that if I were you." Judy touched his knee.

"Why not?"

"You know why not." She tilted her chin toward the salt. "And do you really want to go back to Gozo?"

Toby flinched. Could his mother's plan for him be worse than being recaptured by the Solar Order? As he stared back toward the island, racing through his options, he spotted someone on the rocks.

"Ashes." He leaned forward. Ayla was crouching on a rapidly shrinking island of rock, wrapped in a white sheet.

She saw their boat, rose to her toes, and waved frantically.

Why had no one picked her up?

As he watched, the rocks at her feet vanished and poisonous foam lapped at her ankles.

His mind raced and pieces of the puzzle started to fall into place. Dee and Marcus were on the island. He hadn't had time to think about why . . . Dee must never have truly abandoned the *Phoenix*. It had all been a set-up to take berth on the *Banshee* and find out what Nell was planning.

Dee would have made sure they were the ones selected to rescue Ayla and Toby, perhaps by claiming familiarity with Gozo, perhaps because they could not be easily identified as *Banshee* crew.

When Dee realized Toby wasn't with Ayla, they must have sailed right by.

He should leave her, just as Dee had intended. Judy was already turning the boat into the current that would take them out to sea.

"Wait." Toby could barely believe the words were coming out of his mouth.

Judy frowned. "You're coming with me. Accept it."

"I know." He took a deep breath. "I can make it very difficult for you to take me. Or . . ."

"Or?" Judy narrowed her eyes.

"If you pick up Ayla, I'll come without complaining."

"Ayla?" Judy sneered. "Your Moon. I don't know what you two were doing on Gozo—whatever it was, it didn't go the way you'd planned."

Toby swallowed and said nothing.

Judy drummed her nails on the rudder then drew her blade.

"I'd never hurt you, Toby—you're my son. But if you try me, I'll stab the girl in the throat."

Toby's vision faded in and out as he strained to see. The salt had risen to Ayla's knees by the time the boat banged against the rocks.

Judy handed the rudder to Toby. "Hold her steady." She leaned out over the side. "Take my hand," she ordered.

Ayla took a deep breath but she didn't move.

"Up to you." Judy began to withdraw her arm but Ayla leaped. She gave a small cry as the salt enveloped her and her fingers closed around Judy's.

Judy hauled her over the gunwale and Toby shifted his feet away from the trailing edges of her sheet.

Ayla crouched in the bottom of the boat, bedraggled and dripping. She looked up at Toby, eyes still hazy from the drugs. "How did you . . . ?"

"I should be blind, right? Or dead." Toby turned his face from her. "Just be grateful I'm not like you—*I* couldn't leave *you* to die."

"Toby . . ." Ayla started to speak, then she hung her head. "There aren't any excuses, but Nell insisted. I'm loyal to the *Banshee*, just like you are to the *Phoenix*. That's more important than our stupid *feelings*." She looked away from him, then back. "Anyway, *you* abandoned me to the St. George attack. We shouldn't trust each other. We're all out for ourselves. That's how it works."

"I could have died." Toby's mouth was dry. "They staked me out to take my sight. You left me to be blinded—after all we went through."

"I asked you to leave with me," Ayla said. "I *begged* you to go early, but you wouldn't, remember? Once the *Banshee* was at the island, I couldn't change the plan. Nell would've—"

"So it's my own fault you betrayed me?" Toby sneered.

"That's not what I meant." Ayla shrank back. "I don't expect you to forgive me . . ." She trailed off.

"I would never have done it to you," Toby said.

"You betrayed my son? He almost went blind because of you?" Judy growled and Toby flinched.

"*Your* son?" Ayla's eyes suddenly widened. "Toby, who is this?"

Toby paled. Suddenly, it didn't seem like such a good idea to have Judy and Ayla in the same boat. "Ayla—"

"You're *Judy Ford*." The name rasped from her throat, raw with hatred. "You murdering junk-dumper!" Ayla launched herself across the boat. Her hands curled into claws and she dropped the sheet that had been wrapped around her. It tangled in her ankles, but she still managed to land on Judy and knock her blade into the bottom of the boat. Toby grabbed the sword and threw it overboard.

When he turned back, Ayla had a hand curled around Judy's throat. She raised a fist, but Judy broke her hold and blocked the blow.

Ayla no longer seemed groggy, but Toby could see that her reactions were slow. He lurched forward to help her—if the two of them took Judy out, they could go back to the *Phoenix*—but before he could reach his mother, she hammered a fist into Ayla's temple and Ayla flopped down.

Judy rubbed her knuckles, sat up, and dumped Ayla to one side. "What the hell was that about?" She gave Ayla a kick, then bent and put her hands under her waist, preparing to roll her from the boat.

Toby caught her wrist. "Stop!"

Judy frowned. "You promised to go with me if I picked her up. I did. She attacked me. She's lucky I knocked her out first. She's going."

She heaved, but Toby clung to Ayla's shoulders.

"If she goes over the edge, so do I," he said.

Judy glared at him. "You wouldn't."

"I would." Toby forced resolution into his expression.

Judy sneered. "She betrayed you. Are you so weak?"

"If you say so." Toby shrugged.

Judy frowned. "Why not throw her overboard and be done?"

"She's my friend." Toby said quietly. "But then you'd know all about betraying friends, wouldn't you?"

Judy staggered back as though he'd hit her. Immediately, the rocking of the boat rolled Ayla back into the middle.

Toby carried on speaking. "Did you think we wouldn't find out what you did after we left? Ayla's the surviving child of Nell Wright. You had her sisters and father burned alive—and now you want to kill her, too!"

Judy's hand hovered at her throat and she took a breath, as if she was being suffocated. Toby curled his lip.

"It was Barnaby," she said eventually. As Toby bristled, she held up a hand, begging him to listen. "If he hadn't decided he was too 'principled' to make weapons for his own country and turned traitor to St. George, none of it would have happened. He took you from me and left. I couldn't stop him; he'd already gone when I got his message. He's a *kidnapper*." She spat the last words.

"There's no excuse for what you did," he muttered.

"I didn't know they'd set the fire . . ." She turned her face away. "I thought they'd go after Barnaby. I just wanted to get you back."

Toby's whole world slid to one side, his blurred vision adding to a sense of unreality. Suddenly, he saw Judy's point of view—her husband had turned traitor, taken her son and fled with him. She told the authorities and instead of helping her bring back her child, they burned down the house of the friend who had helped him escape.

"How did you know where I was?" Toby whispered.

"I've been following you for the last ten years. I went after every sighting of the *Phoenix*, but I was always too late or I couldn't get to you. Barnaby never let you leave the ship—did you never wonder why?"

"He was worried I'd be held for ransom."

"He was worried that *I'd* find you!" Judy shouted.

Ayla groaned and stirred, and Judy quieted her fury. "This is the first time the *Phoenix* has anchored for long enough for me to catch up. I was searching the festival for you, hoping you'd been let off the ship. Imagine my surprise when I found you on the throne."

"What if I'd wanted to stay?" Toby murmured. "For all you knew, I was there for my own reasons."

"I don't care." She clenched her fists. "A boy needs his mother."

Toby bit his lip, unable to answer, and she turned her gaze out to sea.

The engine chuffed as the boat sailed into the evening. Ayla continued to sleep. She twitched and groaned from time to time, and it was all Toby could do not to wake her—but he knew what would happen if he did.

Finally, the shape of a larger ship came into view. Toby squinted, but he could see only the silhouette against the evening sky, dappled with the glowing white spots that still filled his vision.

At first, he thought it was the *Phoenix:* a giant paddle at her side, but his smile faded as the silhouetted ship became clearer.

She was a long low vessel, bristling with hatches and painted a dark, unrelenting gray. He sat up, his heart suddenly pounding. At the front, half hidden by one of the floating spots in his eyes, a flag was flying.

"That's a St. George vessel," he yelled. "I don't think they've seen us. Quick, turn around."

"You're right, they haven't seen us." Judy stood up and waved. "Ho, the ship!"

"What're you doing?" Toby hissed. "Quiet!"

A voice rang over the waves, carried by the evening breeze. "Commander?"

"Send down the winches," Judy shouted. "I'm not alone."

TWENTY-EIGHT

Toby stared. "You're a Grayman! A commander!"

"You make it sound like a bad thing." Judy caught the first line that was thrown down and attached it to one end of their boat.

"It *is* a bad thing." Toby grabbed her arm. "The Graymen are evil, they've been after us for years."

"Because you're *pirates*, Toby. Attach the other line, will you? *We're* the good guys, you're the bad guys. *We're* the law."

"There *is* no law on the salt." Toby ignored the cable and Judy sighed as it splashed into the sea.

"There are laws, *our* laws—your father chooses to ignore them." She reached over him for the second line and started clipping it to the hook in the stern. When the winch was secure she gave the cable a tug. "Hold on." She sat and wrapped her fists around the rudder pole. Toby continued to stand, wobbling only slightly when the boat began to rise.

"St. George doesn't own the salt, no one does." Toby folded his arms. "We've seen the result of your Grayman *laws*. You can't take me up there."

Judy raised her eyebrows. "*You've* seen the result? You never leave the *Phoenix*."

"The crew has. You demand taxes people can't give, people who aren't even on the isle of St. George. You're nothing more than racketeers under the guise of a government."

"Do you believe every word you hear? The word of criminals, of people who are *fleeing* the law? If you've never seen for yourself, Toby, you can't judge."

The higher the boat rose up the side of the gray ship, the more panicked Toby became. Tension thrummed through him. He couldn't allow them to be taken on the Grayman vessel—they'd never get off again. "You're back at your ship, so why not let Ayla and me go in the boat?"

"Sorry, Toby, you won't be leaving until I can trust you to come back. I suspect that'll be a long time yet." She fixed him with her cold stare and Toby shuddered. "You're with me, now. You can see what it's like to be on the side of the law for a change."

"And Ayla?" As Toby said her name, she stirred and her eyes opened. She lay still for a long moment, then sat up.

"I shouldn't be surprised that you're still a Grayman," she said and gestured dismissively at the ship that bumped their starboard side. Her brave words belied the paleness of her cheeks. "What better job for a murderer than St. George Security?"

Judy ignored her and spoke to Toby. "The pirate you picked up will be going in the brig."

"You put Ayla in the brig and you'll have to put me in there, too," Toby said.

"Don't be such a child." Judy's eyes hardened. "I don't know what discipline is like on the *Phoenix*, but I can imagine: your father was always soft. On a St. George ship you obey your commander or you get thrown overboard, is that clear?"

"You've spent all this time looking for me, only to chuck me in the salt?" Toby glowered right back.

"You're correct." Judy rubbed her eyes with the back of a hand. "I won't have you thrown in the salt, but I will have you flogged."

Ayla guffawed and Toby spun to face her. "You think this is funny?"

She shook her head and leaned back. "Check out the new boss—same as the old one."

"What's that supposed to mean?" Judy narrowed her eyes.

"You know what it means, murderer. Life on that ship isn't going to be any different to life on the *Banshee.* At least my mother has a good reason to be a hard-faced maniac. What's yours?"

Judy scowled and looked up—their boat was almost at the top of the creaking winch. "My son was stolen and hidden from me," she murmured.

The boat rattled and rocked as it docked. Once it hung still, Judy stood up. Toby sank back into the seat, his eyes met Ayla's and he saw panic.

"What do we do now?" she mouthed.

Toby spread his hands. They were trapped.

A gray-coated man with a thin beard pushed a set of steps up to the side of the boat.

Judy took his hand and stepped down. "Out," she said over her shoulder.

Crewmen had gathered around their small boat.

Toby climbed down the steps. Despite the circumstances, the

movement of the deck was almost comforting compared to the stillness of Gozo.

Ayla landed beside him. She had wrapped the sheet tightly around her shoulders and she stood so close to Toby that the fingers of her dangling hand touched his.

"You found the boy!" An older woman squirmed through the gathered crew. She was hunched over, her long arms looping around her chest. She drew in close to Toby.

"I found my son." Judy's voice was drum-tight. "You'll want to report to General Hopewell."

"Oh, yes." The woman stared right into Toby's eyes until he shifted uncomfortably. "I see the resemblance." She wheeled back to Judy. "Now your son's off the *Phoenix,* the fleet can attack—as per your deal with the general. Get the coordinates off the boy. I'll be waiting in the telegraph room."

"What?" Toby jerked as if the salt had splashed him in the eyes. "You're going to attack the *Phoenix*?"

The woman turned around. "Didn't you know? The only reason the *Phoenix* hasn't been taken back to St. George all these years was that your mother struck a deal with the general. She demanded your safety in return for her silence about the Wrights' deaths. As long as you were on board, the *Phoenix* remained free. Now it's ours."

"You'll never find her," Toby laughed. "We have anchorages all over the place—safe ports, friends . . ."

"True." The woman smiled. "But now we have *you.* And you know all of them."

Toby sagged and Ayla's fingers dug into his forearm, forcing him to straighten. "Don't give them the satisfaction," she murmured.

Toby forced steel into his spine.

Judy turned to her son with a grimace. "I'd hoped to give you a little time . . ." She shook her head. "But as you've heard, we have none. Where is the *Phoenix* anchored?"

"I'll never say." He wanted to sound more confident than he did.

"Barnaby was on Gozo, so she can't be far. Where is she? Palermo? Catania? Monastir? Comino? Malta?"

Toby said nothing.

"Most likely Comino or Malta," Judy mused. "But again, which side—Valetta?"

Toby gave no sign that he heard her.

Judy sighed. "Toby, I *will* have you flogged."

"You have no idea what we've been through recently," Ayla scoffed. "That's no threat."

Judy rubbed her face. "I wanted our relationship to get off to a better start—I don't want to have to do this. Just tell me where the *Phoenix* is."

Toby set his chin. Ayla was right, what was a flogging compared to being chained in the salt?

"Toby, I'm your mother, I know what to do to make you talk."

Toby laughed. "You haven't seen me in ten years—you don't know me at all."

Judy shook her head. "But I know the man who raised you." She grabbed Ayla's arm and shoved her toward the waiting crowd of Graymen. "Whip the girl."

Toby surged forward but two Graymen grabbed him by the shoulders and forced him to his knees.

Ayla sneered. "Do you think I can't take a flogging? I'm Nell

Wright's daughter." She raised her voice. "Hear that, you cowardly dogs? I'm the daughter of the woman you burned. There's nothing you can dish out that I can't handle. Bring it on."

"Ayla, be quiet!" Toby twisted in the grip of Graymen, but they pressed him harder into the deck until his knees screamed and he dropped to his hands for support. He focused on Judy. "If you do this, I'll never forgive you."

"All you have to do is tell me where the *Phoenix* is." Judy crouched next to him, her faded blonde hair whipping in the breeze. A gap opened up between the Graymen, clearing his line of sight. For the first time he was grateful for the spots in front of his eyes. They had Ayla tied to a post with her hands over her head. The sheet pooled at her waist, only her breast band remained to protect the skin of her back.

"Don't tell them anything," she called. "I betrayed you—you owe me nothing."

"Please don't." He turned his eyes on his mother.

"Tell me where the *Phoenix* is."

He hung his head. "I can't say. Ayla, I'm sorry."

"Don't be," she shot back.

A big woman, muscled like a wrestler, started to remove her uniform jacket.

"I don't like to hit children." She cracked her knuckles.

"You should get your commander to do it." Ayla tossed her head. "She burns them alive."

The woman picked up a long thin piece of cable, wrapped with leather to make a handle. She swung it experimentally then looked at Judy.

Judy caught Toby's chin and forced him to face her. "Last chance, son. Tell me where the *Phoenix* is. It doesn't belong to your father—he stole it. It's time to return it to the rightful owners."

"I'm no son of yours." Toby tore away from her fingers.

Judy shook her head. "I'm sorry you're forcing me to do this."

"I'm not *forcing* you to do anything," Toby replied. "This is all you."

"You have to know I'd never willingly hurt you," Judy said. "But my deal with Hopewell protected you only as long as you were on board the *Phoenix*. If he comes for you . . . Well, my way is better."

He tried to turn, to beg, but the Graymen tightened their grip on his shoulders. "Just let us go—tell Hopewell you never found us."

"His agent already knows. Hopewell will sail from St. George on the next tide. He'll need the location of the *Phoenix* before his ship leaves the channel. Give it up, Toby."

Toby looked one more time at Ayla. She shook her head vehemently and he clenched his fists.

"Remember, this is your own fault." Judy nodded and the woman raised her whip.

Ayla set her jaw as the cable whistled through the hot air and cracked against her bare back. She twitched, but made no sound.

"Again," Judy called.

"Harder this time," Ayla shouted wildly. "Are you trying to tickle me to death?"

"Ayla . . ." Toby's voice cracked and the whip came down. This time Ayla flinched slightly, but still made no sound.

"Again."

"Stop," Toby begged.

"You'll tell me?" Judy asked softly.

Toby shook his head. "I can't. I just need you to stop."

Judy sighed again. "Tell me what I need to know and it'll all be over."

"Don't you bloody dare!" Ayla yelled. "Hit me again." She half-twisted towards the Grayman. "Come on, do it."

Judy nodded and the whip slammed down. The tip caught Ayla's chin and blood gleamed in the rays of the setting sun.

Toby groaned and closed his eyes.

"Look at her, son. Doesn't she at least deserve that you watch what you're doing to her?"

For a long moment, Toby kept his eyes closed; then he lifted his head and opened his eyes.

"Let me up." His voice was calm. "I won't go anywhere."

Judy gestured and the Graymen lifted him to his feet. Toby shoved them away and stood mast straight. His fixed his eyes on to Ayla's. "Again," he said. He looked briefly at his mother, before turning back to Ayla. "And don't call me *son*."

The whip cracked down again and again, but Toby refused to look away. Blood formed on Ayla's back as welts split and she sagged. Only the rope against her wrists held her upright. Still she made no sound, and the mad gleam grew in her eyes as she focused all of her attention on him. Toby kept his eyes on hers as though he could hold her upright with sheer will.

"What do you think," Toby said eventually, without removing his eyes from Ayla's. "Is this working?"

Judy growled. "Perhaps not yet." She waved at the woman to stop.

Ayla raised her head, breaking eye contact with Toby for the first time. "What's the matter," she whispered. "Your arm got tired?"

Tears gathered in the corner of Toby's eyes and he turned his face to the sky as he tried to force them back in. Then he frowned. His sight was still blurry, probably always would be, but he was certain that something flashed across the sky—something that reflected the evening sun as it flew.

Polly. She was circling high overhead, he was sure of it—despite his damaged vision.

"Untie the girl." Fury filled Judy's voice and Toby quickly looked back at her. "Put them in the brig together—let my son get a good look at her injuries. Once he's thought about what he's done, we'll have another talk."

The muscled woman pulled the ropes from Ayla's wrists.

She immediately collapsed and the woman lifted her up in her arms like a baby. "Idiot girl," she whispered, barely loud enough for Toby to hear.

Ayla smiled weakly.

The woman marched toward an open hatch that led into the depths of the gray ship. Left with no choice, Toby followed.

TWENTY-NINE

"I'm so sorry." All Toby could see were the bruises and clotting blood that covered Ayla's back. She lay on her belly, breathing shallowly.

"That wasn't much fun," Ayla whispered, "but you did the right thing. If the Graymen get Barnaby and the *Phoenix*, we'll all be screwed." She gasped as blood trickled down her side. "Think what he could invent for them."

"That doesn't make this right."

"It makes it necessary." Ayla lifted her head. "If it makes you feel better, I'll punch you in the face as soon as I can sit."

"Don't move." Toby said. "It looks like she was careful not to hit your left shoulder."

"Yeah, the woman's a peach." Ayla dropped her cheek to the cold deck. "If this gets infected . . ."

"It won't."

"It might." Ayla swallowed. "Do you think they've got an Uma on board?"

"Bound to." Toby forced brightness into his voice.

"Either way, I don't think they'll let me see a doctor," Ayla murmured.

Toby leaned down and pressed his lips to her ear. "I saw Polly."

Ayla's eyes flew open. "Are you sure?"

Toby nodded. "She can't fly far."

"If the *Phoenix* is near, this'll all be for nothing." Ayla grimaced.

"No, it means they're going to attack soon, before the fleet arrives. That's something Judy hasn't prepared for."

"Do you think . . ." Ayla started.

"What?"

"If Polly saw us both, if she told Barnaby . . . Do you think there's a chance he got a message to Nell?"

"I don't know. Maybe."

Ayla raised her chin again. "Let's hope so, because if Nell knows Judy Ford is in these waters, the *Banshee* won't stop till she's at the bottom of the ocean."

"In that case we've got to get out of here—we don't want to be locked in the brig of a sinking ship."

Ayla grimaced. "We should get out of here, anyway. I don't want to spend the rest of my life being tortured by Graymen."

Toby looked at the bars that trapped them inside. "I haven't got my tool belt, I can't jimmy the hinges."

"They think we're children." Ayla touched his hand. "They're going to underestimate us, so let them."

"What do you mean?"

"Tell Judy you want to talk. But demand medical attention for me first."

"Then what?"

"Then we see what tools they bring us."

Toby hammered on the bars and yelled for help. Behind him, Ayla curled up and sobbed piteously, all the time watching him out of one eye.

"She needs help," Toby shouted.

After a minute, Judy entered the passageway wearing a gray uniform with stripes on the shoulder and a sad smile. Her hair was pulled into a severe bun, making the hard lines of her face even harsher. "You know what my answer will be, Toby."

"I tell you where the *Phoenix* is, and you'll let Ayla see a doctor?"

Judy nodded.

"Fine. Just don't let her die."

Judy pulled out a book of recycled paper and a pen. "Tell me."

"Sort Ayla out first."

"Toby, I'm not stupid."

"And I'm not a liar." He pressed his face to the bars. "I can't think with her making that noise. There are a few places the *Phoenix* could be—if you want me to remember the coordinates correctly . . ."

Judy sucked air in through her teeth. "I bring the doctor in and you give me the coordinates?"

"Once I know she'll be all right."

"Fine." She wheeled on her heel and pressed a button on the wall. "Send the doctor down."

Then she leaned on the wall as Ayla writhed and wailed and Toby held his hands over his ears.

The doctor was the shortest man Toby had ever seen. His nose was flat and each breath whistled out of his nostrils. He held a black bag similar to Uma's and, although Toby knew that Ayla planned an ambush, he hoped she would allow the doctor to treat her first.

Toby stepped to one side as Judy opened and relocked the door. The doctor kneeled by Ayla. He shook his head as he looked at her wounds. "This is bad."

Toby held his breath. "Can you do anything?"

"I've seen worse." The doctor pulled a jar of cream from his bag and began to rub it on Ayla's back. Genuine relief softened her face and guilt stabbed him in the heart as he stepped in close and bent down to the doctor's bag. If he was like Uma, he would keep a set of scalpels and thread close by. Toby peered in and, sure enough, there it was—he lunged and grabbed the roll of material covering the blades. Swiftly he unrolled it, grabbed the largest, and held it to the Doctor's throat.

"What are you doing?" Judy shouted.

Ayla held out a hand and he passed her the rest of the roll.

"I figure you don't have a spare on board." Toby tilted his head at his mother.

"Put the knife down, Toby. You have no idea what you're doing." She gripped the bars.

"And you have no idea who you're dealing with," Toby retorted. "Let us out."

"Where are you going to go?" Judy sneered.

"Wherever we like," Ayla snapped. "Open the door." She stabbed her own blade into the doctor's leg and he screamed.

"Any closer and that would have been my artery!" He clamped his hand over the wound.

"You're not the only one with anatomy skills, doctor," Ayla said. She looked up. "Your son might have been raised by a 'soft' man, but I wasn't. You taught my family well, Judy—we don't know the meaning of mercy. And now I'm armed. Maybe Toby wouldn't kill the doc, but I won't lose a second of sleep over it."

"Commander . . ." the doctor begged.

Judy sighed and unlocked the door. Behind her, a trio of Graymen crowded into the passageway.

Toby helped Ayla to her feet, then he dragged the doctor to his. Ayla put the scalpel against his throat. "Tell them to get out of our way," she rasped.

Judy gestured and the men retreated. "I thought you said you weren't a liar." Judy glared at her son.

Suddenly, there was a wail—a high-pitched scream that shivered through Toby's bones like ice.

"What the . . . ?" Judy said.

"Your ship's still floating, so I know *you've* never heard the *Banshee*'s wail before." Ayla fixed her eyes on Judy as she spoke. "I guess my mother is excited to reunite with her old 'friend.'"

Judy's eyes widened. "How did they . . . ?"

"Commander." Another Grayman burst into the passageway. "The *Phoenix* just rounded the Maltese peninsula."

Relief broke over Toby. "If you want to know her exact coordinates, just let me know."

Judy straightened. "This ship is armed with weapons your father designed, Toby. One attacking ship or two, it doesn't matter, they don't stand a chance. Get back in your cell."

Toby laughed. "Hopewell's bringing a whole *fleet* to deal with the *Phoenix*! What do you think? Will he get here in time to pick the debris of your ship out of the salt?"

Judy pressed her lips together. "You've forgotten one thing."

"And what's that?" Ayla jeered.

"I've got you on board. Neither of your captains will attack as long as they think it puts their children at risk."

Suddenly there was a loud clang and the ship juddered. "What was that?" Judy shouted.

"That was my mother . . . not attacking." Ayla cocked her head to one side. "You underestimate how much she hates you. If she knows you're on this ship, she'll tear it apart to get to you, whether I'm on board or not."

Judy shouted. "All hands to battle stations!" She ran for the end of the passageway. "I don't have time to deal with you now. Go where you want—there's no escape."

Toby shoved the doctor away from them. He limped down the passageway, reproach in his eyes. "She's right, you know. You're trapped on a ship full of Graymen with nowhere to go."

Ayla laughed again. "That's where you're wrong, doc. Your Graymen are trapped on the ship with *us*. Oh, and before you go—hand me your jacket will you?"

Toby and Ayla watched the *Banshee* approach through portholes in the empty mess. The ship still screamed and Toby pressed his hands over his ears. It was as though Ayla barely heard it.

"There's Nell!" She had to shout over the wail. Toby followed her pointing finger. Ayla's mother looked almost exactly as he had first seen her—she had one leg on a pile of ammunition and her long coat whipped out behind her in the wind of their passage.

The *Phoenix* was turning behind the *Banshee*, drawing closer with every heartbeat. Her orange paintwork glowed in the sunset and the Jolly Roger snapped.

"They haven't fired again," he yelled. "They're going to try and board."

Ayla nodded, then the floor beneath them started to shake and a giant cannon slid into view.

"It's aimed at the *Banshee*." Toby curled his hand around Ayla's. "We can't just stand here while they sink your ship and steal mine! If I can get to the engine room, I should be able to do something."

"If we can *find* the engine room."

"If this ship was designed like the *Phoenix*, it'll be in the bowels."

Ayla nodded. "Then we go down."

The passageways of the gray ship were almost empty as they raced toward the ladders that led down into the gut of the ship.

The few Grayman they saw ignored them, more concerned with the coming battle. Finally they came to a sliding vault door. Toby touched a mechanism on the wall beside it.

"This is a failsafe—it shuts the corridor off. We're here."

Ahead of them the boiler room door was closed. A glass window in the metal was dense with condensation.

"There'll be Graymen in there," Ayla said as they tiptoed along the griddle. "And they *will* try and stop us."

Toby nodded. "There shouldn't be more than three."

"We've got surprise on our side, but there're only two of us . . . and I'm injured." She flinched as the doctor's jacket rubbed against her bleeding skin.

Toby stared. He'd never heard Ayla admit that she might not be able to handle a fight. "You're right—we won't be able to beat them in a fight." He paused, his mind racing. "And we can't fool them . . . but I do have an idea. Do you think you can maybe keep them off me for half a minute?"

"That's all the time you'll need?" Ayla sounded surprised.

"A boiler's a delicate beast." Toby grinned. "And I know where to stab it."

Ayla stood at the door and closed her eyes. The hand that held her scalpel was trembling.

Toby touched her wrist with light fingers. "We don't have to do this," he murmured.

"Thirty seconds, right?"

"That's all I need."

"I can fight for that long." Ayla exhaled. "Ready?"

"Ready."

She slammed the door open and burst in like a whirlwind. Toby was right behind her.

There was one engineer standing at the control panel, one relaying messages from the comms pipe, and a third cleaning out the constantly spitting blowers. They were all black with soot from their caps to their boots.

The Graymen stood frozen for precious seconds, giving Toby enough time to locate the delivery lines at the other side of the room. He shifted his grip on his blade, ducked and ran.

The engineer at the control panel turned. "Who're you?"

Ayla's foot slammed into his chin and he staggered. She spun as the second one ran toward her and her fist caught him in the throat. He choked and fell to his knees. The third, higher up, grabbed his broom as a weapon and leaped down. Fixated on Ayla, they had forgotten Toby.

The delivery lines snaked into the wall, just like on the *Phoenix*. Toby needed to identify the lines that were attached to the rudder, the paddles and the cannon.

"Ah, screw it!" He threw his arm over his face and started slashing.

Immediately, the chief engineer gave a shout of horror. "My god—what are you *doing*? Stop!"

Superheated steam lashed Toby as it powered from the sliced lines, shrieking so loudly that the *Banshee*'s wail was drowned out. Blinded, he screamed and staggered back. He felt a hand grip his wrist and tried to twist free.

"It's me," Ayla yelled. She dragged him toward the door as the engineers scrambled for something to repair the lines with.

The chief ripped his coat off. "Put out the fire," he yelled, "and stop the feed water."

"Can't, Chief!" The voice was filled with panic. "That's the valve we were repairing before the commander called battle stations."

As Ayla hauled him out of the door, Toby's face paled. "If feed water hits the empty drum there'll be an explosion that'll take out half the ship."

"Then run!" Ayla shoved him.

They sprinted to the ladder and climbed as if the explosion was already at their backs. "Can they repair the valve before it explodes?" Ayla shouted.

"With that much steam filling the engine room, they won't be able to see and the equipment will be scalding."

"One more ladder to deck," Ayla gasped. Her bare foot slipped on the rung, Toby caught her leg on his shoulder and shoved her upward.

They burst on deck and looked around wildly. Graymen glowered at them, but no one stopped them as they skidded toward the gunwale.

The wailing *Banshee* was already firing grappling hooks towards the Gray ship and Toby ducked as cannon fire pounded the deck house.

The *Phoenix* was also within range now and he could see his father aiming a blunderbuss.

"They can't come any closer," he said, his breath ragged. "If there's an explosion . . ."

"Don't worry about them, worry about *us*," Ayla yelled. "We're trapped. There's nowhere to go."

THIRTY

Suddenly, the *Banshee*'s wail cut off and Toby's ears rang with the sudden silence.

"Judy Ford, I'm coming for you." Nell's voice rang across the waves and her entire crew started to yell and jeer.

Toby turned toward the bridge, where his mother was surrounded by Graymen.

"I didn't know they would do it, Nell," she replied, her words amplified through a loudspeaker.

"Liar," Nell bawled. "Those men were under your command."

Toby jerked. His mother had told him the Graymen had gone against her wishes—that she thought the authorities would simply help get her son back. Who was telling the truth?

Ayla clutched his arm as a bronze-winged bird glided down and clattered on the deck at his feet.

"Polly!" Toby scooped her up.

"Your father's sending *Birdie*," she squawked. "Can you get off the ship while Nell distracts Judy?"

It was Ayla's turn to gasp. "You mean she really is holding off the attack until I'm safe?"

Polly's eyes whirred around to her. "Of course, what did you think? Now can you get off the ship or not?"

Toby looked at the winch above the boat they had arrived in. Graymen stood around it with drawn weapons. "I-I . . ."

"I know what to do." Ayla started toward the stern. "Stay low and follow me."

Toby lifted Polly onto the gunwale. "I have to send you back to the captain. Tell him I've slashed the delivery lines in the engine room and I think the boiler's going to explode. He and Nell have to stay back."

Polly threw herself off the ship and dropped toward the waves. At the last minute, her wings caught the wind and she began to glide in the direction of the *Banshee*. Toby's heart slowed its frantic beat and he turned to find Ayla. She was climbing on to a rail at the ship's stern.

"What are you doing?" Toby ducked and sprinted toward her.

"The hawespipe, remember?" Ayla gasped as the jacket pulled tight across her back. "I got on to the *Phoenix* by climbing the anchor chain—we can get off here the same way."

Toby threw a leg overboard just as Judy screamed his name.

"It's been great getting to know you," he yelled, "but I'm not staying."

Judy darted toward him. "*Stop him!*"

Three Graymen abandoned their posts and raced for Toby, but he spoke only to Judy. "I'm not your son any more. You have to let me go."

"Never!"

Toby shook his head and swung overboard. The anchor chain was directly below him, creaking with Ayla's weight. Theo and Marcus were frantically rowing *Birdie* into position below.

Toby looked up again as Judy slammed into the gunwale directly above him, chest first. "I'll shoot you down," she screamed.

Toby stared in horror as she pulled a gun from the belt of the Grayman next to her.

Desperately, he dropped and caught the anchor chain—it was thick and pitted with the poison from the salt, making it easy to grip. He started to slither down as fast as he could.

Judy aimed her weapon. "You're making me do this," she yelled.

The ship rocked with a massive explosion. Judy fell backward and Ayla and Toby screamed as the anchor chain lifted and then slammed back into the hull.

Toby grunted and his hands almost opened, but somehow he managed to keep his grip. He looked down. Ayla was swinging below him one-handed.

"Hold on," Marcus called. "You can make it."

"Of course we can make it," Ayla muttered, as she swung back to strengthen her grip.

Birdie bumped against the hull as a second, smaller explosion rattled Toby's bones and the whole ship tilted. "She's sinking, we've got to hurry!"

"Slide!" Ayla loosened her grip and dropped down the chain with a cry.

Toby winced as he did the same, the corroded metal stripping the skin from his hands. His feet slapped down into *Birdie* seconds behind Ayla and he staggered toward Theo, who steadied him. He shoved his hands under his armpits—he didn't dare look at them.

Theo sat him down and then he and Marcus grabbed the oars. They rowed as fast as they could from the sinking ship.

"We've got to get out of range, or it'll drag us down, too," Theo panted.

Toby looked back—the Gray ship sloped to one side, then slid into the salt and disappeared beneath the surface. For a moment, he thought he could see Judy clinging to the mizzen mast, but his blurry eyes failed him and when he looked again, there was no sign of her. Now, only debris bobbed on the surface. He could see no survivors.

Slowly, *Birdie* drew level with the *Phoenix*. As the winches were lowered, Toby stared vacantly, with his hands dangling between his knees. Ayla leaned against him, her palms tucked between her thighs.

"Do you think Uma will be willing to treat me again?" Her voice was faint.

"I'll order her to," Toby said. "I just can't believe this was all for nothing."

"For nothing?" Marcus frowned as he attacked the winch cable. "What do you mean?"

"We lost both inverters," Toby whispered, hardly able to say it out loud. "After everything we went through."

A tremor shuddered through Ayla's body and, with a shudder of his own, he realized that tears were running down her cheeks, leaving tracks in the soot that had daubed her in the boiler room.

Marcus cleared his throat. "You're wrong," he said. "You might have lost your inverter, but Ayla didn't lose hers. Nell took it at the festival."

"So the *Banshee* has operational solar panels." There was no triumph in Ayla's tone, she sagged even further.

"Wrong again!" Marcus spread his arms as *Birdie* started to rise. "Why do you think Dee and I were coming for you? Nell didn't keep the inverter any longer than you did. Dee and I stole it back."

"You mean the *Phoenix* has working panels?" Toby's eyes widened.

"Not yet," Theo rumbled. "The captain wanted to wait for you to come home."

As *Birdie* was lifted back on board, the whole crew was on deck waiting.

"Polly!" Toby's parrot glided to his shoulder and suddenly he felt balanced again.

"It hasn't been the same without you, boy." Arnav helped Toby from the skiff.

The moment his bare feet touched the warm deck, he felt something shift inside him. Tension fled from his shoulders.

"You're home!" D'von shoved through the cheering pirates and gripped his shoulder, making Polly squawk crossly. "I missed you."

"I missed you, too." A smile touched Toby's lips. "I'm *so* happy to be back."

Theo carried Ayla from *Birdie* and Marcus hopped out to land beside them.

"I suppose you need *me*, now." Uma grabbed his chin, turning his face this way and that.

Toby nodded. "Ayla first."

"Have you learned nothing?" she muttered, but then she saw

Ayla's bloodless face. "Get her to the mess hall, Theo. Hideaki's already down there treating Hiko, I'll follow right away."

"What's happened to Hiko?" Toby asked.

"Nothing serious," Uma soothed. "He cut his arm in the boiler room."

"Toby." The captain swept toward him with tears shining in his damaged eyes. "Judy's gone." He caught his shoulders. "Are you all right?"

Toby nodded, too exhausted to speak.

"I'm so sorry about your eyes." His father squinted at him. "I've spoken to Dee already. She says the sight-loss is likely permanent—we're lucky to have any vision left at all. But at least we have this." His father held up the inverter. "Marcus and Dee worked hard to get it." The captain nodded at Marcus. "We should all be grateful, but I thought *you* should get to do the honors." He looked at Toby's bleeding palms. "Are you up to it?"

Toby reached for it and the captain smiled. "The hook-up is exactly as you left it."

Toby closed his fingers around the inverter and turned to the rest of the crew. His eyes met Peel's, and the old chef nodded. "Finish it, Toby."

Polly spread her wings to retain her perch as Toby limped toward the bridge. To his right, the solar array was clear of the tarp that had hidden it from view. The last of the setting sun gleamed from the black glass panels.

Inside the bridge, he ran his fingers over the loose wires that lay almost exactly where he had left them, feeling like a stranger trying to slip back into his own skin. He had changed—would he ever be able to tell them what he had gone through?

Outside, they were waiting for the solar panels to power up. He looked up as the door banged.

"You know what to do?" the captain asked.

Toby picked up the wires that fitted into the inverter's sockets and clicked the components together.

For a moment, nothing happened, then a blinking red dot appeared and turned green as they watched. There was a shout from the deck.

The captain propelled his son out of the door. "Let's see."

The solar array seemed to be buzzing very gently.

"It's working," Toby said wonderingly.

Nisha shrieked. "Rahul—it's working!"

The pirates cheered, grabbing one another in celebration.

"Now, Toby," the captain said gently. "Go and find Uma."

Wearily Toby sloped toward the mess hall, allowing the blurriness of his vision to take over. He could picture the Gray ship vanishing under the waves. He had met his mother and now he had lost her.

Had she loved him, or had he just been a possession to win back, a way to punish his father for turning traitor to his country? He would never know.

He thought of her hard gray eyes. Life for Toby on the Gray ship would have been no better than life for Ayla on the *Banshee*. She had been as icy cold as Nell.

He paused outside the mess door and took a deep breath. His pulse raced at the thought of seeing Ayla.

He couldn't forget that she had betrayed him again, but she had taken a flogging for him, fought to help him sink the Gray ship, and got them to safety before it sank. He owed her. He pressed his fist to his forehead—he was fooling himself. It wasn't gratitude he felt toward his fellow pirate. He had been falling in love with her on Gozo and, despite everything, the seed that had taken root hadn't died.

Still, Ayla had made her own views clear—her loyalty to Nell was more important than '*stupid feelings*.' Once Uma had treated her, Ayla would go back to the *Banshee*. Toby would remain on the *Phoenix*. They had no future.

He opened the mess door and walked inside.

On his right, Ayla was sitting hunched over her knees while Uma's fingers patted lightly over her back. Her face was pinched and pale.

To his left was Hiko, his shirt pushed up to his shoulder. Hideaki was stitching a jagged wound. "Toby!" Hiko cried.

"Hiko, what happened?"

"Just a slip in the boiler room." His face was black with soot and the whites of his eyes shone through the dirt. "You did it! You got the inverter!"

"It's working." Toby grinned.

Ayla nodded, sighed, and looked back down.

"Sit still, Hiko." Hideaki sounded exasperated. He refused to look at Ayla.

Uma pointed to a chair beside Hiko. "Sit there, Toby. Hideaki's almost done with Hiko and then he can start looking at you."

Toby slumped into the chair, but his eyes kept sliding toward Ayla. She looked defeated.

"The Gray ship sunk," Toby said at last. "Your mother will be pleased about that."

Ayla jerked her head up. "Are you kidding? We stole her vengeance. She's got no inverter and no way to punish Judy Ford herself. We're only lucky she hasn't already attacked the *Phoenix*."

"She wouldn't," Toby said.

Ayla groaned as Uma tightened the bandage around her back.

Hideaki took a wet cloth and began to clean the blood from Hiko's arm.

"Thought so," he said with a smile. Hideaki held up Hiko's arm and grinned.

"Twenty thousand, one hundred and forty," he said. "I was always good at those. Why is that number inked on your arm?"

Hiko frowned. "What number?" He twisted his arm to look.

Hideaki pointed to Hiko's tattoo. "That one."

"That's not a number," Toby said. "It's lines. I've seen it."

Hideaki smiled. "It's Japanese—a multiplication problem. Fifty-three times three hundred and eighty."

"Twenty thousand, one hundred and forty." The captain strode into the mess hall, answering the problem as he crossed to stand in front of Hiko. "Why did you say you have that tattoo?"

"It matched my father's," Hiko said in a small voice.

Barnaby folded his arms and frowned. "Tell me about your father."

Hiko hunched. "He died when I was little."

"What else do you remember?"

Hiko clenched his fists, unwilling to speak.

"They were travelling when he died," Toby supplied. "Isn't that right?"

Hiko nodded, keeping his eyes lowered.

"Where were you going, Hiko?" Barnaby pressed.

"I don't know," Hiko wailed. "I was *little*. We were going somewhere *safe*. He'd been away, but he came back for us."

"Back from where?" Ayla asked, suddenly interested.

Hiko glared at her. "He was a fisherman—gone for ages at a time, that's all I remember."

"Hiko." Barnaby lifted the boy's arm in careful fingers, turning it one way and the other to look at the tattoo. "Is it possible that your father found the island?"

"That's where he was taking you!" Toby leaped to his feet. "The tattoo marks the coordinates."

"I'm going to fetch Dee." The captain ran from the room.

"We've found it," Ayla breathed.

"*If* they're coordinates," Dee said, turning Hiko's arm back and forth in the light of the lamp, "the island is nowhere close."

Toby was dying to know how she had stolen the inverter back from Nell, but the discovery of the meaning behind Hiko's tattoo had swept everything else away.

"Where is it?" the captain pressed.

"See here." She pointed to two small arrows in Hiko's tattoo. "I'm guessing these indicate direction so, assuming the coordinates are 20 degrees north and 140 east, it puts the island . . . here." She opened her atlas and pointed. "About 750 miles from the east coast of Japan."

Toby leaned in. Her finger rested on some writing. He nudged it aside. "The Dragon's Triangle," he read.

Arnav pushed through the gathered crew. "I've heard of that. We don't want to go there. Dragons live there—and devils."

Peel nodded agreement.

"Really, Peel, you're superstitious?" The captain frowned.

Dee turned to the back of the Atlas. "There's something here about it. It's been marked as a danger zone for shipping since 1950. There're undersea volcanoes."

"Which explains the dragon stories." The captain nodded.

"And might have caused the island to rise," Toby cried excitedly.

"It's not just volcanoes." She traced the words. "Magnetic anomalies, whirlpools, thick fog, sudden storms. It's practically unnavigable."

Toby's eye fell on the map, tucked into the back of the atlas next to Hiko's attempted translation. It seemed years ago that he had last seen it. He pulled it carefully from the book and turned it over.

"Avoid the fast mist and take three swift turns around the white doom spiral," he muttered.

"Let me see that," Peel snatched it from him.

"Careful," the captain warned. "It's meaningless, but that doesn't mean we're going to throw it out."

"It isn't meaningless," Toby said slowly. He saw Ayla, listening intently from the back of the mess hall. "Don't you see?"

The captain shook his head.

"The *white doom spiral,*" Toby pressed. "It's a whirlpool!"

"Ashes, he's right," Dee murmured. "And the fast mist—that's a sudden fog."

"So it means 'avoid the sudden fog or you'll be taken three times around the whirlpool.'" Dee jumped to her feet. "This isn't a map, it's *instructions*. There are a dozen haikus here. Taken in order, they're a guide through the Dragon's Triangle."

"Did your father have a map?" Toby whirled on Hiko.

Hiko shook his head. "I don't know. When the trader sold me at the slave market, he said he'd get a few pennies for all Father's things, too. He didn't leave me with anything." He ran his fingers over the tattoo.

"*That's* why the Tarifan port master had the map." Toby was almost jumping in his excitement. "He bought it from the trader when he bought you. It *was* your father's, Hiko. Your father knew where the island was and he was taking your family there."

"And now we have it." Dee added. "Permission to set a course, Captain?"

Ayla stood on the deck of the *Phoenix* and watched the *Banshee* approach. "Nell's coming," she said.

Toby touched her bandaged hand with his own wrapped fingers. "It'll be all right, the *Banshee*'s not wailing."

Ayla laughed bitterly. The wind shifted her hair around her face and she made no move to push it away. "I'll have to go back," she said eventually.

"I know." Toby leaned closer. "I wouldn't ask you to stay."

"Even though I know the coordinates?"

"Even though." Toby smiled wryly. "You might know where the island is, but you can't translate your copy of the map. Dee said the sea was unnavigable without it. We're not worried."

Ayla leaned on the railing. "We can just follow you."

Toby pulled Ayla around to face him. "You can try." A shout from the *Banshee* told Toby they were within hailing distance. "Part of me hopes you succeed. An island won't be fun without you."

Ayla's eyes widened as Toby took her face in his hands and kissed her.

The breeze caressed them and salt foam danced as the *Phoenix* dipped into a wave. Toby didn't care that they had an audience. Ayla's arms snaked around his neck and he deepened the kiss.

They were pirates. They had today. Tomorrow would take care of itself.

HOW TO READ HIKO'S TATTOO

Japanese multiplication works with lines. For example, if you want to work out 2 x 2 you draw two lines intersecting two lines and count the places they cross:

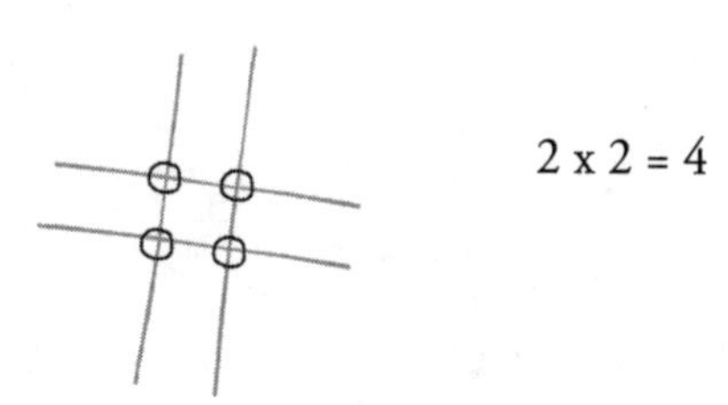

2 x 2 = 4

If you want to work out 23 x 2 you draw 23 as two lines, then a gap, then three lines. You then draw two lines the other way crossing them, as before. As you can see, we now have two sets of intersecting points, a group of 4 and a group of 6.

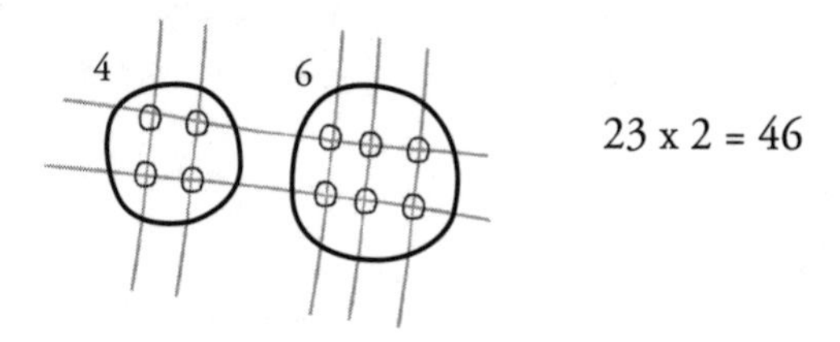

23 x 2 = 46

To work out a bigger number, such as 32 x 21, you will have even more intersecting groups. These need to be grouped together according to hundreds, tens and units as below:

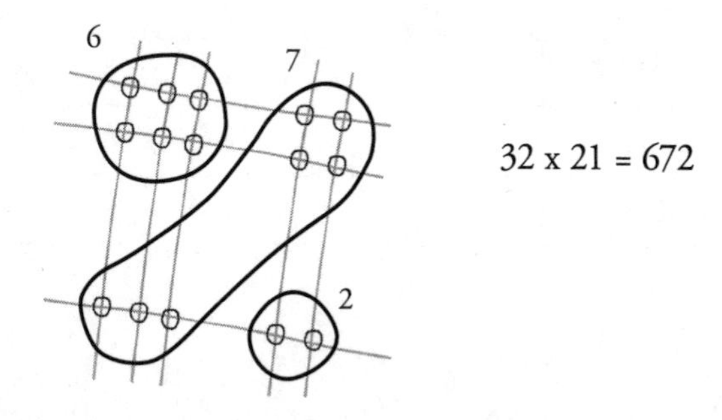

32 x 21 = 672

With even bigger numbers you have to start carrying units across when you add your groups. Here is 132 x 16: the answer is not 192,012! When the intersected lines move into double figures you need to start carrying figures across, working from right to left:

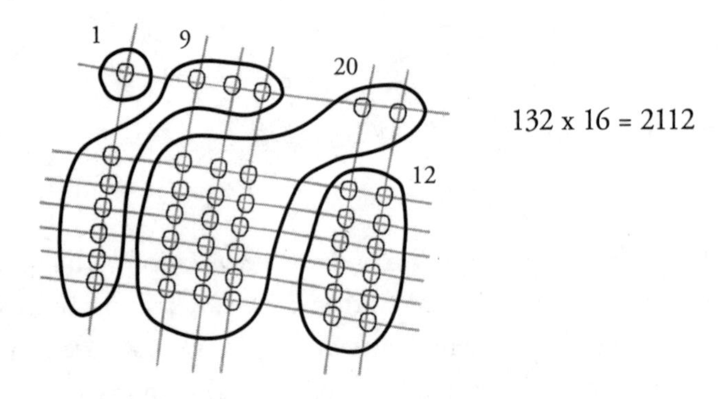

Here is a table to show the steps you need to take when you have answers in double figures. Don't forget to work from right to left!

1	9	20	①2
		20 + 1	2
		②1	
	9 + 2	1	
	①1		
1 + 1	1		
2			
2	**1**	**1**	**2**

This is what Hiko's tattoo looks like:

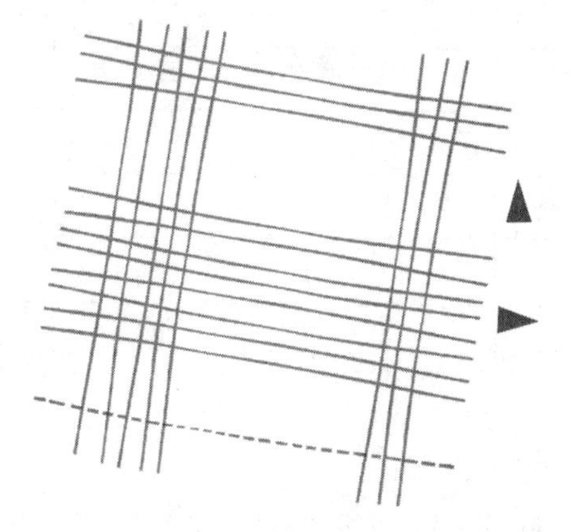

The pirates work out that the arrows signify compass points—north and east. The lines of Hiko's tattoo use the Japanese multiplication system to encode the coordinates for the island that Hiko's father found. Here is how you work out those coordinates from Hiko's tattoo. The dotted line is used to signify zero.

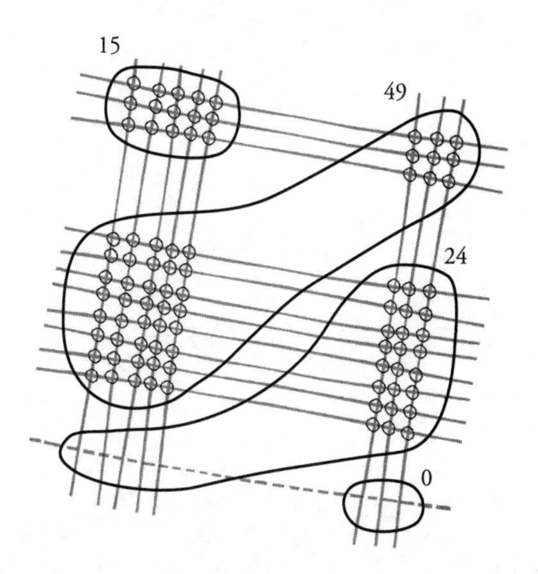

15	49	24	0
	49+2	4	
	51		
15+5	1		
20			
20	**1**	**4**	**0**

Once Hideaki has pointed out that Hiko's tattoo represents the number 20,140, the pirates puzzle over its significance. It is Toby who figures out that the number is in fact the coordinates 20 degrees north and 140 degrees east.

ACKNOWLEDGMENTS

This is the first time I've written a sequel and so massive thanks to Stripes and my editor, Ruth Bennett, for allowing me to stay in Toby's world a little longer. These characters feel like family now and I hope they get to their island.

Thanks to the wonderful writers Rhian Ivory, Sarwat Chadda, and Emma Pass who read and enjoyed *Phoenix Rising* enough to give me a quote for the cover.

And thanks to all the lovely YA writers who have offered support and company over the last few years—it's wonderful to feel like part of a community, even if we work alone.

Thanks to Jane Christophers, who has kept me plied with drink, taken the children when I'm at my wits' end, and is a true friend.

And thanks to all of my other friends and family, whose enthusiasm and support make writing such a fun task. You know who you are.

Special thanks to Andy, my husband, who has endless patience, and Maisie and Riley, my children, who do not have endless patience, but are endlessly inspiring and for whom I write, always.

And a final huge thank you to you, the reader, for sticking with Toby's story as long as I have.

Keep on reading, keep on thinking and keep on changing our world.

ABOUT THE AUTHOR

Bryony Pearce has always loved to write. She studied English Literature at Cambridge University and after working in London for a few years she dedicated her time to writing. Her debut novel, *Angel's Fury,* was longlisted for the Branford Boase Award and won both the Leeds Book Award and the Cheshire Schools Book Award. *Phoenix Rising* has also been shortlisted for several awards.

Bryony now lives in a village in the Forest of Dean with her husband, Andy, and two children, Maisie and Riley. She can usually be found reading, writing, ferrying children from place to place, and avoiding housework.

For more information about Bryony and her work, visit www.bryonypearce.co.uk or follow her on Twitter @BryonyPearce.